## When She Flew

"A taut, beautifully rendered novel about an injured war veteran, his bright young daughter, and a street-smart police officer who has lost almost more than she can bear. When their lives become entangled, what results has all the urgency of a thriller and offers a moving exploration of parental love and the lengths to which one person will go to take care of another."
> —Marisa de los Santos, *New York Times* bestselling author of *Love Walked In* and *Belong to Me*

"Jennie Shortridge has done it again. Her novels are delightful and compelling stories of real-world characters in mildly dysfunctional lives struggling for wisdom. This one, the story of a courageous and independent woman cop and a remarkably insightful feral girl, will grab you from the start and warm your heart with its originality and honesty. You'll want to share this story with your friends."
> —Selden Edwards, author of *The Little Book*

"A novel with real heart that takes the big issues of returning war veterans and child custody, the hard social choices that make us human, and explores them on an intimate scale. The voice of thirteen-year-old Lindy, interspersed throughout the story, is a welcome addition to the world of child narrators."
> —Erica Bauermeister, author of *The School of Essential Ingredients*

"A mesmerizing tale of love, damage, and resurrection, propelled by a girl whose gifts are a marvel of the human spirit."
> —Randy Sue Coburn, author of *A Better View of Paradise*

*continued . . .*

---

Written by today's freshest new talents and selected by New American Library, NAL Accent novels touch on subjects close to a woman's heart, from friendship to family to finding our place in the world. The Conversation Guides included in each book are intended to enrich the individual reading experience, as well as encourage us to explore these topics together—because books, and life, are meant for sharing.

Visit us online at www.penguin.com.

"Jennie Shortridge's heartfelt new novel takes the reader on a journey into the wilderness of the human spirit and the meaning of home. Against an evocative Northwest landscape, her beloved characters struggle with the ties that bind, ultimately finding the answer to what sets us free."          —Heather Barbieri, author of *The Lace Makers of Glenmara*

## Love and Biology
### at the Center of the Universe

"Jennie Shortridge invokes the spirit of the Fremont District with a charming new novel."                              —*The Seattle Times*

"Midlife crises are a bitch. Jennie Shortridge's book *Love and Biology at the Center of the Universe* makes that very clear. Set in the fictional town of Pacifica, Oregon, Mira Serafino finds out her husband, whom she's dated since high school, is two-timing. Instead of melting into a puddle of menopause and hot flashes, Serafino, a high-strung perfectionist, leaves her world behind and heads northward to Seattle, where she tries to bring out the bad girl that has been hibernating within."
                              —*Willamette Week* (Portland, OR)

"Smart, funny, and endearing, *Love and Biology at the Center of the Universe* is also deceptively wise....Deeply drawn characters with their seams and raw edges exposed, clever dialogue, and a snappy pace make this one terrific read!"          —Garth Stein, author of *The Art of Racing in the Rain*

"Like a Northwest Fannie Flagg, Jennie Shortridge gives us a wry and funny portrait of Mrs. Perfect, Mira Serafino. We all know where perfection can lead and in *Love and Biology at the Center of the Universe,* life becomes anything but *Family* freaking *Circle.* Steam a tall batch of half-caf mocha lattes for the club, throw on your slutty elf shoes, and discuss this delicious, sexy adventure of a mother at midlife."
                              —Diana Loevy, author of *The Book Club Companion*

"An honest and endearing look into the imperfect life . . . a middle-aged woman of unpredictable hormones and a heart as warm and rich as the espresso shots she delivers to her coffee house customers. Bruised but not beaten, the indomitable Mira escapes her not so perfect life in search of a new beginning and instead rediscovers the woman she was always meant to be. The true-to-life characters, rain-saturated Seattle setting, and flawless storytelling make this a book to remember."

—Karen White, author of *The Girl on Legare Street*

## Eating Heaven

"A remarkably affecting book."

—*The Denver Post*

"*Eating Heaven* is exactly the kind of book I most love to read—rich, funny, sad, sensual, and hopeful. . . . Jennie Shortridge is a wise woman and her books are a tonic to the heart."

—Barbara Samuel, author of *Lady Luck's Map of Vegas*

"Funny, sweet and, most importantly, original."

—*Seattle Magazine*

"A tasty novel."

—*The Oregonian*

"An immensely wise and readable book that will provoke amusement, tears, and thoughtful reflection."

—*Rocky Mountain News*

"Smooth writing, a cast of nicely developed characters, and a winning portrait of Portland, Oregon, add up to one good read."

—Nancy Pearl, author of *Book Lust*

## Riding with the Queen

"Shortridge does a fine job of molding her heroine into a sympathetic, even admirable character . . . hits all the right notes."

—*The Miami Herald*

"An absorbing novel of a family with hard edges but an unbreakable bond. . . . Shortridge's finely crafted sentences often use a single telling detail to suggest the larger picture. It's a notable debut."

—*Rocky Mountain News*

"Funny, sexy, smart. . . . Shortridge has done something few writers accomplish."

—*Statesman Journal*

"Jennie Shortridge writes with an easy grace and a backbeat of the blues that lends a quiet authority to this novel."

—Summer Wood, author of *Arroyo*

OTHER NOVELS BY JENNIE SHORTRIDGE

*Riding with the Queen*

*Eating Heaven*

*Love and Biology at the Center of the Universe*

# WHEN
# SHE
# FLEW

JENNIE SHORTRIDGE

NAL Accent
Published by New American Library, a division of
Penguin Group (USA) Inc., 375 Hudson Street,
New York, New York 10014, USA
Penguin Group (Canada), 90 Eglinton Avenue East, Suite 700, Toronto,
Ontario M4P 2Y3, Canada (a division of Pearson Penguin Canada Inc.)
Penguin Books Ltd., 80 Strand, London WC2R 0RL, England
Penguin Ireland, 25 St. Stephen's Green, Dublin 2,
Ireland (a division of Penguin Books Ltd.)
Penguin Group (Australia), 250 Camberwell Road, Camberwell, Victoria 3124,
Australia (a division of Pearson Australia Group Pty. Ltd.)
Penguin Books India Pvt. Ltd., 11 Community Centre, Panchsheel Park,
New Delhi - 110 017, India
Penguin Group (NZ), 67 Apollo Drive, Rosedale, North Shore 0632,
New Zealand (a division of Pearson New Zealand Ltd.)
Penguin Books (South Africa) (Pty.) Ltd., 24 Sturdee Avenue,
Rosebank, Johannesburg 2196, South Africa

Penguin Books Ltd., Registered Offices:
80 Strand, London WC2R 0RL, England

First published by NAL Accent, an imprint of New American Library,
a division of Penguin Group (USA) Inc.

First Printing, November 2009
10   9   8   7   6   5   4   3   2   1

Copyright © Jennie Shortridge, 2009
Conversation Guide copyright © Penguin Group (USA) Inc., 2009

 REGISTERED TRADEMARK—MARCA REGISTRADA

LIBRARY OF CONGRESS CATALOGING-IN-PUBLICATION DATA:

Shortridge, Jennie.
    When she flew/Jennie Shortridge.
        p.  cm.
    ISBN 978-0-451-22798-0
    1. Policewomen—Fiction.   2. Middle-aged women—Fiction.   3. Self-actualization (Psychology)
in women—Fiction.   I. Title.
    PS3619.H676W47 2009
    813'.6—dc22          2009022838

Set in Bembo
Designed by Ginger Legato

Printed in the United States of America

*For the good-hearted people of the Pacific Northwest.*

# ACKNOWLEDGMENTS

My utmost respect and appreciation to Sergeant Michael Barkley of the Portland Police Bureau for his time, his thoughtful responses to my many, many questions, and for his respect for the lives and privacy of those he serves in the community. Thanks also to Portland detectives Travis Fields and Heidi Housley, and Officer Dorie Scott of the Seattle Police Department. And without Miss Carol Frischmann, Lindy would not have had her birds. Thank you, Carol, for the hike and the owl and the magic of your world. Many thanks to my early readers who helped guide the craft and kept me going: Sherry Brown, Jeri Pushkin, Cindy Grainger, Stan Matthews, Carol Hickman, Heidi Yorkshire, Alison Galinsky, and Sandra Fischer. (Thanks also to Sandra for all her help with . . . everything.) Big grateful hugs and a toast to my writers' group, as amazing a writers' group as anyone could have: Stephanie Kallos, Randy Sue Coburn, Heather Barbieri, and Erica Bauermeister, who read and advised, as well as Garth Stein, Kit Bakke, and Mary Guterson. Thanks to our wonderful booksellers, whose support and friendship mean so much to writers, and even more to readers. (Patronize them, please, dear reader, as much as you can.) A big hug to Howard Wall at Penguin Group for taking me under his wing (sorry, I couldn't resist), and to all of the wonderful people at NAL and Penguin, whose hearts and souls make great books happen, from copyediting to cover design to introducing them to booksellers. Thanks to my editor, Claire Zion, who makes me a better writer and seems to feel as passionately as I do about every aspect of the book. Thanks to my agent, Jody Rein, for believing in my writing from the start, and to her capable assistant, Johnna Hietala, for making everything run smoothly. And most especially, always, thanks to my family for their love and fierce loyalty, and to my husband, Matt Gani, who reads, suggests, listens, loves, and comforts me, all while doing his own good and intense work in the world.

"For a long time, she flew only when she thought
no one else was watching."

—BRIAN ANDREAS

# AUTHOR'S NOTE

# WHEN
# SHE
# FLEW

# A Report on the Common Barn Owl
### by Melinda Faith Wiggs

The common barn owl inhabits almost every place on this Earth. They are the most widespread of all owls, and I think the most beautiful with their heart-shaped faces and deep black eyes. They are mysterious and pale and long-winged, and unique among other owls. Their ears are placed unevenly on their heads, which gives them superior hearing, and they never make that hooting sound you think of when you think of owls. They hiss, and their screech is so frightening that I used to think there were monsters in these woods, but that was back when I was young and new to the forest.

I know so much about barn owls because of Sweetie-pie. Pater rescued her from a fox when she was just a baby, and we nursed her back to health and fed her until she could fend for herself. She got used to us, I guess. She hangs out in our camp and sleeps where we sleep. Barn owls love to nest in man-made enclosures. That's why they are called "barn" owls.

Classified as birds of prey, they are foragers and carnivores. They hunt all night and sleep all day to digest the voles and shrews they catch. Like white ghosts, they fly low to the ground, as quiet as a night breeze on their fringed wing feathers, and steal animals away from their burrows and families. With those oddly placed ears, they hear the little animals even underground, so it's no use for them to hide. The owls' black talons are so strong they kill their prey instantly, snapping their necks as soon as they snatch them up, and eating them head first. Pater says at least the hunted don't suffer.

Sometimes I hate this about owls, but Pater says they're predators and that's just Nature's way. He says we're all God's creatures, all the species on this Earth, only some of us have to be more careful than others and mind our own business, blend in to our surroundings so we don't call attention to ourselves. That is the balance of things: some of us are predators, screeching and hunting and tracking down prey, and some of us must live quietly among the trees, just trying to survive.

# I

The baby clothes drew Jess first, even though her grandson was now turning three. She couldn't walk past the tiny flannel buntings, the three-snap onesies in pastel shades, without wanting to touch them. And the shoes! Target always had such cute baby shoes. Just small pieces of leather and cloth and rubber, yet they held so much promise: soon little Mateo would be toddling in baby Nikes, then wearing them to school. Then who knew? Kicking soccer balls, hiking the Cascades. Maybe becoming a cop, like she was, and like the boy's great-grandfather—her dad—had been. One moment they were babies, the next they were out in the world on their own. It all went by so fast.

*Too damn fast*, Jess thought. Nina, her daughter and Mateo's mother, would be officially out of her teens at the end of the year, Jess was staring down the road at forty. Her dark hair had been sprouting dull streaks she would soon have to admit were gray; laugh lines remained on her face even when she wasn't smiling. Jess would have loathed being a grandmother except that her grandson was the happiest, most beautiful baby she'd ever seen. Nina had been pretty and exquisitely formed from birth, with tiny shell ears and slim hands and feet, but she'd been quiet and reserved, reticent almost, even in infancy. Not bursting with energy and exuberance, like her son.

What size would Teo be now? Jess ran her hands along racks of little boys' jeans and corduroys. Fall clothes, and Columbia was stuck in a heat wave. She hadn't seen Teo since Nina brought him a couple months before for their June visit. He'd always been small for his age, but kids had growth spurts. Should she call Nina at work and ask, or would that only annoy her?

A table full of brightly colored boys' T-shirts lay dead ahead. T-shirts were forgiving. She could get him a size three for his birthday and he could wear it even if it was too big. Jess wheeled her cart over, even happier to find Transformer characters centered squarely on the front of each shirt. Teo loved the Transformers movie—she knew that much. As she sorted through the shirts, though, she sighed. There were at least ten different half-human, half-machine creatures. He had a favorite, but which one?

She pulled her phone from her purse and hit speed dial.

"You've reached Nina Villareal." Voice mail. It always shocked Jess that her nineteen-year-old daughter could sound so businesslike.

After the beep, Jess said, "Hi, honey. Listen, sorry to bother you at work, but I can't remember. Which Transformer is it that Teo likes? The one that turns into the truck, or is it the Hummer? I'm at the store right now, so if you get a sec, call me. I'm not on duty until three. Thanks!" She tried to sound bright.

Within seconds her phone rang.

"Neither," Nina said when Jess answered, not "Hello," not "Hi, Mom. How are you?"

"It's Bumblebee," Nina said. "He only talks about it all the time."

"Bumblebee, Bumblebee." Jess ruffled through the shirts and ignored the dig. "What does it turn into?"

Something across the aisle—a sudden shadow, an unspecific darkening—caught Jess's attention. A thin, middle-aged white man, a little too clean-looking, fingered the girls' clearance tank tops with a wary expression, eyes scanning, scanning. It was midmorning on a Wednesday. The lights were bright, the store busy with beleaguered moms, sugared-up kids, and prancing teens back-to-school shopping, and there he was, peering around like a spooked but hungry cat.

"Goddamn it," Jess whispered. It didn't matter where she was. She saw it everywhere, like some kind of cop curse—the city's dark side, the bottom of a rock turned over, teeming with peculiar life-forms creeping and crawling through dirt and rot. The dirt dwellers she dealt with were like subterranean worms and bugs: drug dealers and pimps, abusive parents, gangsters and thieves. She had tried for years not to notice them when off duty, but she couldn't help it. This guy didn't match the description of the suspect in recent sex-assault cases across western Oregon, but Jess wanted to get a better look. He was definitely up to something.

"Did you hear me?" Nina sounded annoyed. "I said it turns into a yellow car. Mom?"

"Mm-hmm," Jess said, maneuvering past the table to the other side of the aisle. "Okay, then, thanks. I, uh . . . I gotta go, okay? Bye now." She clicked the phone off and shoved it into her purse. She knew better than to say anything to Nina about what she was doing. It was exactly the kind of thing she'd always gotten in trouble for: paying too much attention to the bad guys and not enough to Nina. Now her daughter would say Jess was doing the same thing to her grandson: instead of focusing on his birthday present, all she could see was this almost-certain sexual predator. It was what made Jess a good police officer, but she sometimes wondered if Nina was right, if it had kept her from being a good mother. Wherever she went she noticed these things and acted on them. And not just at work.

When Nina was growing up, Jess had checked out every sleepover she had with friends. Was there an older brother, an uncle, a stepfather? All soccer and volleyball coaches were suspect until Jess got to know them. She'd had no problem letting teachers, neighbors, and sons of neighbors know that she wouldn't have a problem arresting anyone's sorry ass whoever tried to hurt a kid, and not just hers.

Early in Nina's life, they'd stopped going to church, and with all the revelations about priests in recent years, Jess felt more vindicated than ever about that one. Jess's mother didn't believe the stories about the priests, and insisted that her beloved Virgin of Guadalupe kept a special eye on young girls of Mexican descent. Jess had wondered as a child with an Anglo dad if that meant she only got special protection sometimes. At least Nina had a Latino father to up her chances.

Leaving her cart behind, Jess traversed the shiny floors

through bright fluorescence to the girls' clearance racks, where she feigned interest in a crocheted cardigan stretched out of shape by countless hopeful girls trying it on. She pulled it off the rack and held it up to inspect it. The man moved into the juniors' section, where two young girls, no more than thirteen, ogled flimsy dresses far too sexy for their age. Jess sighed, picturing Nina back in seventh grade, emerging from a dressing room in just such a dress and looking like a thirteen-year-old streetwalker. Jess had put the kibosh on all slutty wardrobe choices, but she suspected that her daughter wore whatever she wanted to as soon as she was out of the house.

Reaching into her purse for her badge, Jess slipped across the wide aisle to stand on the other side of the dresses. Through the gaps between them, Jess saw the tops of the girls' heads, hair shiny and probably smelling of strawberry or watermelon shampoo. They chirruped like little birds, giggles punctuating every other breathy sentence. Jess swallowed against an old ache. She missed that sound, along with the pop-diva music through the bedroom door, even the arguing. Just the dailyness of having a daughter, of having someone at home to cook and care for, and worry about, although Jess still did plenty of that.

"Excuse me." The man's voice, hesitant, halting. "Could you, uh, young ladies help me? I'm, I'm trying to pick out a dress for my daughter, and she's about, well . . . she's about your size, I think. Are you going to try those on? Could you try this one, too?"

Jess froze, waiting.

"Um, we gotta go," the taller girl said, and the two hurried across the store to the exit, then stood and clapped their hands dramatically over their mouths before laughing and loping off, escaping into the wilds of the mall.

Jess watched with a mixture of relief and disappointment. They were safe, but now she couldn't charge him with anything. He definitely was not the six-foot, two-hundred-pound suspect the sexual-assault victims had described, but she could still put the fear of god into him. She stepped around the rack and flashed her badge, shaking her head at the bulge in his dark trousers.

"Officer Villareal, Columbia Police. There are cameras everywhere, asshole," she said. "It's not like you won't get caught."

"I didn't do anything," he said, mildly defiant, but he shrank inside himself when Jess dropped her eyes to his crotch. "I was just shopping for my—"

"ID, please."

"But I—"

"Now."

The man's gummy face turned white. He fumbled in his back pocket, pulled out a wallet, and extracted his driver's license. Jess took it and studied it.

"Well, Mr. Leander, shall I call in for priors? Do you have a record?"

"No, I swear, this isn't what you think. I'm just shopping for"—he fumbled again in the wallet, pulled out a school photo of an adolescent girl with a forced smile—"my daughter."

"That so does not make me feel better." She pulled out her cell phone and hit speed dial for the station house, then relayed his information.

After thirty or so seconds, during which the man looked as

guilty as anyone ever had in Jess's presence, the officer at the other end of the line replied, "He's clean."

"Great." She snapped the phone shut. "Okay, Mr. Leander. I'm letting you go, but I will remember your name and this, uh, incident."

"But—"

"What I meant to say was, get the fuck out of here before I change my mind and arrest you." The obscenities, the threats— they were just part of the job.

The blood rushed back into his face all at once, the sudden red ugly, like something festering, and he squeezed his way through racks of clothes and out into the stream of people who flooded the mall to escape the late August heat. Jess felt sick knowing he'd try again, maybe even today, in another store, another mall, another neighborhood.

She returned the badge and phone to her purse and walked back to retrieve her cart. There'd be hell to pay with Nina the next time she talked to her on the phone, but there usually was. Jess found a size three Bumblebee T-shirt and decided to find a toy to match.

Teo's third birthday was a bittersweet occasion, both a cele-bration and a reminder of how long her daughter had been gone and how little Jess had been in the boy's life. Nina still insisted that she'd had no choice but to go live with her dad when she got pregnant at sixteen. It was so much more complicated than that, but it had left a cold white scar between them where they'd ripped apart—an ache Jess still felt deep in her abdomen, espe-cially when she heard teenage girls chattering, or saw moms and daughters shopping together, talking and laughing.

It wasn't that Nina was heartless. She wanted her son to have a grandmother. She brought Teo from Tacoma for twice-annual visits and allowed weekly phone calls, but phone conversations were not the ideal way to maintain a relationship with a small boy. The problem was more that Nina had no desire to have a relationship with Jess, and no recollection of the good things—of the love between them—before it all had gone bad.

On a whim, Jess headed toward the jewelry department. Her daughter loved big swingy earrings that shone against her dark hair, bubble bath, sweet-scented lotion—all things she couldn't afford to buy for herself. Jess could send them along with Mateo's present. Maybe she would wrap Nina's gifts, too, even though her birthday wasn't until December.

Jess stopped, then turned back toward the toys. Her daughter would see it only as manipulation, and perhaps it was. She couldn't imagine her daughter didn't still love her at some level, even if she wasn't willing to acknowledge it. At least now Nina had found a way to move into her own apartment, away from Jess's ex-husband, who drank more than Jess had ever felt comfortable with, especially for one charged with taking care of a young daughter and grandson. Without his constant influence, Jess thought, there might be a chance for her to be the kind of mom and grandmother she longed to be. She had to believe that.

If Nina would just listen to her, Jess would tell her daughter how proud she was of her for raising her son on her own—Jess had made the mistake of staying with Rick for ten long years, mostly for economic reasons. But if she said it, her daughter would think it was a dig at her father. "You always make him out to be the bad guy," Nina would say, so Jess had stopped talking about almost everything she would have liked to with her daughter.

Earlier in the summer, Nina and Teo's visit had gone the way they often did—somewhere between frustrating and nuclear winter. Nina had wanted to take Mateo to Wonderland Park to ride the carousel and feed the pygmy goats, and to the U-Pick-It strawberry fields, and to South Columbia Public Pool. She had an agenda in mind that meant Jess got no real time with either of them, baking cookies as she'd planned, or taking a walk along the greenbelt that ran behind her house to look for bird nests, which Teo dearly loved, or to pick a bouquet of dandelions. All of the simple, normal things she yearned to do with Teo, and Nina wanted to cart him all over the city.

"He's only two," Jess had said, sipping tepid coffee at the breakfast table. "He'll never even remember picking strawberries. Kids this young don't remember stuff like that. Wait till he's five. Can't we just have a nice day together here?"

Teo banged a spoon on the table while cramming Cheerios into his mouth. Jess put her hand over his to stop the racket, then took the spoon and placed it in her lap so he'd forget about it and concentrate on breakfast.

"I remember things from when I was two," Nina said, sliding her own spoon over to the boy.

Jess tightened her jaw, determined not to react.

"Fank oo," Teo said, grinning, half-eaten Cheerios falling from his mouth. He resumed banging the table. Nina smiled at him, the kind of smile Jess had given Nina when she was so small and happy and charming.

Her smile faded as she turned back to Jess. "I remember

when I was two and Dad took me to ride the ponies at that place with the big totem pole and the fake fishing pond."

"You were three and a half. And I was there, too, Nina. Whose idea do you think that was? Your father would have rather been . . . I don't know." She'd been about to say he would have rather been having brewskies with his buddies.

"But he was the one *with* me. He walked with me the whole time I was on the pony, because I was scared it was going to bite me."

"Yes, he did. All the way around that little circle." Jess shook her head and stood to clear the breakfast dishes.

"Do you have to do that?" Nina's voice wobbled, and Jess turned to look at her, surprised.

"What's the matter? I was just saying you never remem—"

"Do you have to ruin every happy memory I have?" Nina stood and held her arms out to Teo. "Come on, baby," she said. "Let's get ready for the day."

Jess felt guilty, of course, and followed her to her room. Once again, she'd done the wrong thing.

"Nina, come on," Jess said from the open doorway. "I didn't mean it like that."

Nina kept her eyes averted as she pulled off the boy's pajamas, saying, "Just forget it," and Jess wished more than anything that they could forget everything that had ever come between them, but Nina never would.

Later in the day, Jess stood outside the fence enclosing the old carousel, watching Nina hold Teo on top of a gilded horse. They laughed like drunken chimps as they circled around. They were both petite, with soft honey gold skin, and Nina's dark hair drifted behind her. Jess's heart filled at their beauty.

All the activities Nina had proposed for the day were things Jess had loved doing with her when she was small, but it was as though her daughter had wiped Jess from every happy childhood memory. Jess turned her back on the rickety wooden fence, even though an excited Teo called, "Grammy! Grammy! Look at me!" each time she came into his view.

She reached into her purse for a tissue, blew her nose, wiped her eyes, and turned around to wave.

"Hi, hi, hi!" she called. "Hi, sweet boy! Hold on tight!"

# 2

The great blue heron stands three to four and a half feet tall and has a wingspan of up to eighty inches wide, wider than I am tall by eighteen inches. I would like to lie in the wings of a great blue heron, in its downy under feathers, and listen to its heartbeat.

It has been my dream to see one up close, ever since I first read about them in the *Sibley Field Guide to Birds of Western North America* at the library. I like to draw herons and other birds, and write poems and stories about them. Birds are such happy things, and so free to flit and glide wherever they want, yet they always return to their nests. Maybe that's what makes them happy. Great blue herons hardly seem in the category of birds, though. To me they seem more like enchanted creatures waiting for someone to break the spell so they can change back into the princes and princesses they once were.

Great blue herons inhabit much of North America, but they

live in wetlands, not forests, staying near lakes and streams so they can fish. They have been known to eat voles, which is really just a fancy word for mice, but probably only when they can't eat fish. There are no wetlands in the Joseph Woods, but back when we had our car and we still thought Pater would have a job, we took a drive out to the river one Sunday and roasted hot dogs for lunch. We saw three great blue herons fly over us that day, like magic, like a sign that we were meant to be in Oregon.

Last year a baby orca and its mother wandered too far up-river from the ocean; we saw the story in *The Oregonian*. They didn't know how to get back home. Pater said all the fuss from people and boaters and news helicopters was probably confusing them more. He didn't say he thought they'd never find their way back, but I know that was what he was thinking. In my mind, I like to think they submerged so no one could see them under all that deep blue, popping up again when they were safely out to sea.

Last year, for my twelfth birthday, Pater found a book at the Joseph Woods Wildlife Sanctuary about our forest and its flora and fauna. He doesn't usually buy books, because we can borrow them for free from the library, and we sometimes find good ones in the free box at Goodwill. But he said I was getting older and needed some books of my own, so he bought me *The Wilds of Joseph Woods State Park*, by Carol Frischmann. I can't believe someone would write about where we live, and I would like to find Miss Frischmann one day and thank her, because in her book she says that the great blue heron has been sighted here, in my forest, on very rare occasions. That gave me hope.

I often walked along our creek looking for morels, stopping every once in a while to sketch a kestrel posing on a limb, or a clump of Johnny-jump-ups. The day everything changed, I was thinking about herons, so I almost wasn't surprised when I saw the tall swoop of gray-blue farther down the creek. I knew it could be a trick of my eyes, but my heart began to beat as rapidly as a hummingbird's. Could it really be a heron? Or was it just me wanting it that made it look like one? It could have been a piece of newspaper caught in a tree, a scrap of a hiker's coat or a camper's tarp. They leave behind the oddest things, like one shoe, or a camera bag. Things you'd think they would need and be more careful about. If I lost one shoe, or my coat, I'd hate even to tell Pater. He says the VA's four hundred dollars a month doesn't go very far, even without rent and paying for the energy that Nature makes for free. You still have to eat some store-bought food (even though we grow most of our own vegetables, and forage berries, herbs, and mushrooms). You still need basic necessities (his polite way of saying menstrual supplies and toilet paper, as I just can't make myself use leaves like he does). You still have to have presentable clothes for church, he says, and to save for the future.

The tall gray shape moved, and I crept slowly toward it, dropping the paper and pencil on top of the mushrooms in my pocket. I worried I would startle whatever it was because I wore my sparkly silver foraging dress over my jeans and T-shirt. The dress was Crystal's. I took it from her closet the night we left to remember her by. I wear it to collect mushrooms because it has a big pocket on the right side so I don't need to carry a bag. I took soft, quiet steps in the underbrush, slipping behind a hemlock when I was as close as I dared go. I leaned my head to the left of the tree, ignoring the tiny ants marching up a woody ridge, and slowly, slowly, I could see the creek, then in the middle of it, a bird: a big, beautiful blue heron. My breath came as fast as if I'd been running, and it was almost like I could cry. I was so overwhelmed by what I'd been allowed by Nature to see.

The heron didn't seem to notice me as I watched it dip its head down into the water, neck snaking in a long, graceful S curve. I was almost sure it was a male, even though there are no discernible differences between male and female great blue herons. I just felt that I knew this, and Pater says when you think you know something, you ought to listen to your instincts. The heron made a quick stabbing motion and lifted his head back up, pointing his beak toward the treetops, and gulped down the fish he had caught. One thing I can tell you: the great blue heron is the most elegant fisher of any waterfowl I've seen.

He kept wading downstream, looking for more fish, stopping here and there to poke his beak between rocks, then moving on. I crept behind him from hemlock to fir. I don't know how long I followed my heron. I've never been in a trance, but it felt as if I were in one that day, the rest of the forest and chattering birds fading away into the green afternoon light, and I could only focus on the heron's shaggy back feathers and the black of the flight feathers on his wings kept tucked at his side like closed fans.

When he turned his head toward me, I saw the black stripe behind his eyes. He looked right at me and didn't flinch, so I came out from behind the trees, still keeping my distance as I followed him into a clearing.

And then I woke from my trance and realized I was too near

the trail. I could hear people talking, and so could my heron. His head swiveled toward the sound, and then a wide woman with short gray hair appeared from behind a stand of alders across the clearing, binoculars pinned to her eyes, and she said in a loud whisper, "Hey, everybody, look! What's that creature doing in the woods?"

A crowd of other people gathered around her, slinging binoculars to their faces, and I heard a flapping, whooshing sound. I looked back at the heron and he'd already lifted from the ground, his long twig legs and feet trailing behind him as he flew up to roost in the treetops.

"Oh, no, we scared it," the woman said. As I turned to run, I heard her say, "Oh, my land, look over there! What is that girl doing here all alone? Where are her parents? Hey, you, little girl, are you all right?"

Then I heard a man give out a yell and someone began to crash through the brush after me.

I ran and ran toward home, as fast as I could until I could no longer hear anyone behind me. I found a deer trail in case they tried to follow me up the creek. I was stunned at how far I'd walked downhill; it had felt like only a few moments, but it took me forever to get back home, running up and up the hill, out of breath, my legs cramping. All I could think was, Pater told me so. He told me not to wander around daydreaming or I'd get too close.

For one small moment, I thought maybe seeing the great blue heron was worth it. But then I saw Pater's face as he saw me, panicked and running into camp, and I wished I could take that thought back.

# 3

Jess adjusted the bulky flak vest under her uniform shirt and strapped on her duty belt. The locker room was empty except for her. She was late for her afternoon shift, late for roll call, and the more she hurried, the longer it took to get on all her gear. She'd lost track of time shopping that morning, and then had to buy groceries for her mother, pick up Clara's prescriptions and drop them off before finally rushing to the station house in bad traffic.

With gear in place, Jess glanced at her blue polyester behind in the mirror on the opposite wall. Even without all the equipment, her butt would look huge in the unflattering man pants. She sighed and slammed her locker shut, then sprinted out the door and up the steps to the briefing room, boots clunking loudly as she twisted her dark hair back into an elastic band. Maybe it was good to always be on the run. She was thirty-eight and couldn't just skip a dinner or two anymore to get back into size twelve uniform pants.

Sergeant Everett was doing the briefing, his drone recognizable through the closed door. Jess stopped, took a breath, then pushed into the conference room. Everyone looked up. She mumbled an apology and slid into an empty seat at the end of the table next to Officer Ellis Jenkins. He'd been her partner when the city still had enough money to send them out in pairs, and he was still her closest friend on the force.

The sergeant shot Jess a look from the front of the room, then returned to his report. From across the table, Officer Ann Madison handed her a stack of composite drawings that had already circulated.

"Thanks, Maddy," Jess whispered, and thumbed through the drawings. There he was, right on top: the six-foot-tall sex-assault suspect in various iterations, based on three frightened and traumatized girls' memories. His MO was to nab his victim as she was walking home from school, assault her in his car, then dump her in a park or forested area. The violence involved had been increasing; the last girl had been strangled almost to death. Jess studied his penciled features, looking for something that couldn't be seen in a drawing. She shook her head. He looked like the generic example of "man" in an encyclopedia.

Next was a suspect in the rash of burglaries from unlocked garages in the White Oak neighborhood, then a convicted pimp who had been reported doing business along MLK Boulevard. Jess had booked him a year before for beating up one of his workers. She knew there were probably plenty of other women he'd brutalized who'd never reported it.

Everett rumbled on about a new lead in the hit-and-run at

last month's Fourth of July symphony concert in City Park. Even though technically that case belonged to the main precinct downtown, all five precincts wanted to find the driver, bad. There'd been a wildfire of press about the department not catching the guy despite fourteen thousand witnesses, and this on top of two recent police shootings and an allegation of sexual misconduct under investigation by internal affairs. The department had been taking a beating for the past decade—under three separate chiefs—for some good reasons and some not so good. Jess wished the concerned citizens who complained the loudest would go on a graveyard-shift ride-along. They had no idea what cops dealt with every day.

"That's it," Everett said. "The search team for the girl in Joseph Woods will be assembling in the parking lot at"—he raised his wrist—"sixteen twenty. In ten minutes."

Jess raised her hand.

"The late Officer Villareal." He pronounced her name in the anglicized way: "Villa-reel." She never corrected him.

"What's the deal with the girl?" she asked. "Has she been reported missing, or . . ."

"We've already covered it. Get here on time."

"Come on, Sarge. I'm the most prompt person in the room. You never give Jenkins half the crap when he's late, and he's late all the damn time. Aren't you, Ellis?"

She turned to Jenkins and winked. He blushed under his dark skin and said, "I cannot help that I have two kids who are involved in every activity known to man. Take it up with my wife."

Everyone laughed.

Jess turned back to Everett. "Besides, I was trying to find a birthday gift for Mateo. He's turning three on Saturday, and starting preschool this fall. Can you believe it?"

Everett softened, as he did whenever she mentioned Mateo or Nina. He had a daughter too, in college now. Jess had met her once at the annual picnic, and her opinion of Everett had changed for the better, seeing the way he watched her when she spoke, that look of pride and wonder in his eyes when she made the crowd of cops laugh at a joke.

The sergeant cleared his throat. "Unaccompanied female juvenile was sighted at approximately eleven hundred hours today north of the wildlife sanctuary property, pretty far up and off trail. Witness says she's between ten and twelve years old. She didn't get a good look, even though she had a pair of god-damn binoculars in her hand at the time. Says the girl was wearing a silver cocktail dress—whatever that means—way too big on her. Long dark hair, slight build. Fled when spotted. 'Ran like her life depended on it' was what the witness actually said. Another witness chased after her but didn't get very far. That's about it."

"Do we think she's another one of the sex-assault victims?" Jess asked, even though the other three girls ran toward people who could help them, not away. Victims varied in their reactions to the crimes against them, of course. It was possible that this girl's reaction to trauma was to run.

"We don't know," the sergeant said. "Could just be transient. Could be a runaway. That's what we're going to find out."

Jess nodded. It wasn't uncommon to find transients living in the forested foothills that abutted the city. She had hiked up into the woods to smoke them out on more than a few occasions. It was part of her beat. Transient camps were not pleasant places—drugs and alcohol, mental illness and extreme hard luck, and always a disgusting lack of sanitary conditions. Once Jess had slipped in a pile of feces, mistakenly assuming it to be from a dog until she realized there were no dogs in the area. Not many things made her vomit on the job anymore, but that had.

Jess knew everyone else in the room was thinking what she was. It was unlikely the girl was up there voluntarily. Runaway juveniles lived in packs under the viaducts and in alleyways, staying close to the city to panhandle, prostitute themselves, buy drugs. She shot her hand back into the air.

"What?" Sergeant Everett gathered his papers.

"I want to be on the search team for the girl."

"We've already assembled the team."

"With a female?"

Maddy sighed. "Lucky me. Sarge knows how I love to hike." The other patrol officers on duty, all male this day, laughed. Nobody liked to hike, but Maddy was a large woman, and particularly averse to anything but cruiser work. The city was so desperate for police officers they'd dropped most fitness requirements other than the ability to breathe. The North Station House had the baddest hoods, making it even less desirable to the best and brightest. Most of the cops assigned there were either doing time after pissing off a former CO at another precinct, or just holding on until they could figure out how to get transferred downtown, a more prestigious posting, or out in the suburbs, an easier one. But Jess liked working the North. At least she didn't spend her days getting cats out of trees and settling squabbles between bickering neighbors.

She leaned forward in her seat. "Let me go instead of Maddy, Sarge. My butt needs the exercise."

Sergeant Everett studied her, then nodded. "Fine. You're off the hook, Officer Madison."

"Thanks, V," Maddy said.

Jess leaned back in her seat, heart pounding, even though nothing scared her anymore, and hadn't in years. She didn't know why, exactly, but she needed to find this girl, and make sure she was okay.

AT ELEVEN YEARS OLD, JESS knew she was going to be a cop. It came to her like Jesus comes to some people, calling them to duty. For Jess it happened late one night while waiting in a hospital emergency room, sitting with her mother, Clara, and three older brothers in a row of hard plastic chairs, wondering if her father would live or die. Either way, she knew that night she was meant to follow his path. If he lived, he would be so proud of her. If he died, she would take his place, doing what he loved.

Her dad had been on the force nearly fifteen years when a car full of teenagers returning from a homecoming dance plowed headlong into his cruiser on Highway 319. Two of the teenagers died, the girls, and the boys walked away with dislocated ribs and bruises.

Jess's father's head hit the patrol car's windshield so hard, he shattered the front part of his skull and shook the contents like jelly. The steering wheel crushed his chest and the engine pinned him inside the car and severed his spinal column. If he lived, he would be paralyzed. He'd never again go out on patrol, and Jess knew that would kill him even if the injuries didn't.

As they waited for word on his condition that night, the television in the waiting room looped through grainy images of men wearing blindfolds, men who looked like they could be her father or his fellow officers at the station in their street clothes. They were being marched by other young men with slightly darker skin through the door of a building and out into the open. A newsman came on, saying "crisis" and "embassy" and "day sixteen."

It was day one of her family's crisis, and Jess wondered if her father would be taken away like these young men, leaving the family alone to fend for themselves. Her mother sat four chairs away with eyes closed, rosary beads clenched in bloodless fingers, and Jess decided to pray along with her. Clara was loving but not strong, and Jess knew her mother was not capable of taking care of four children alone.

When the doctor finally came out and shook his head, her mother stood and fell to her knees on the tile floor, bruising them badly. The purple never went away, leaving permanent stigmata that Clara oddly cherished.

The funeral was a blur of uniforms and flags, hugs from other cops' wives, frightened stares from their children. Jess's mother retreated into rituals of prayer and sobbing behind closed doors, and slowly deteriorated from the day of her husband's death, shrinking, deflating, becoming absorbed by the brown tweed La-Z-Boy that had been his. She acquired a sizable list of ailments and diagnoses that made it increasingly difficult for her to take care of much of anything, let alone her kids or herself. Jess took over, cooking meals when they needed to be made, hunting for quarters in the dryer or beneath couch cushions when she needed lunch money and Clara's coin purse was empty.

No one expected Jess to go to college, but she found scholarships and school loans to offset most of the cost of her criminal justice degree at the same school her father had gone to. When she told her mother her plans, Clara shook her head, repeating the line that had become her summation of life after her husband's death: "Just remember, you can't do good in this world without being hurt by it."

To Jess's disappointment, it took her six and a half years to complete her degree rather than four, because she got pregnant at nineteen and married the father. Her Catholic upbringing made it the only option she even considered. She struggled through school with an infant to care for, and then arranged day care and went to work full-time on the Columbia force. Her life was hectic, but she felt a deep sense of comfort in having replaced her dad on the job.

Rick, her husband, worked part-time selling car stereos, and spent too much time away from home, drinking with friends. After ten contentious years together and one really bad night, Jess finally came to her senses. Nine-year-old Nina hated Jess for making him move out.

Nina's anger accumulated, mushrooming into a dark cloud of misbehavior as she reached adolescence, and then she got pregnant at sixteen. Jess lost it. Maybe it had been the years of sacrifice, or the pent-up emotion of dealing with a difficult child alone, but they fought horribly, destructively. Jess said things she never would have believed could come from her mouth. Nina left, moved in with her dad, and cut Jess out of her life. After Mateo was born, they moved to Tacoma to be closer to Rick's family, and even though Jess apologized endlessly, she became even further removed from their lives, paying for her sins.

Jess tried not to wallow in the past, though. She concentrated her energy in the present, where she felt needed. The nice part about that was it left her little time to think about anything other than what was next. The driving motivations of duty and love were so intermixed in Jess's mind that it didn't matter anymore why she helped someone. It only mattered that she did.

# 4

We came to Oregon after Pater got back from the war. He was called Private First Class Raymond Wiggs when he was in Iraq. He signed up to go because his younger brother did, and Pater wanted to make sure he was there to take care of him. Crystal didn't like that. She said he loved his brother more than he loved her, or else he'd have stayed in Denver and protected her from the terrorists there instead. She didn't mention me, but I could have used protecting, too. Especially once he was gone.

Pater's brother hadn't even graduated from high school when he enlisted. Pater says it's a crime for the military to be allowed on school grounds, twisting the minds of kids who don't know what they want yet. He was worried the Marines wouldn't take him because he was older than his brother and most of the other men enlisting, but they did. By that time, he said, they'd take just about anyone.

Pater's brother's name was Robert, but we don't say it any-more. We visited his grave at Fort Logan when Pater first got back. I couldn't tell it apart from all the other white markers, rows and rows of them, stretching over the snow-covered hill forever into the blue velvet sky, but Pater looked at his map from the office and walked right up to it. He wiped a crust of hard snow from the front so that we could read: PFC Robert Wiggs, United States Marine, 1986–2004. He was only ten years older than me, and Pater was ten years older than him. I liked that, the orderliness of those numbers, how I fit so neatly in the chain. I only met Robert once, right before they went off to Iraq, but I liked him. He laughed more than Pater, and he called me Lindy-Lou. I called him Robbie.

We came to Oregon for a job Pater got with a big con-struction company, one where he could drive around in a truck and not hurt his back more, but when we got here and they found out about his disability, they got mad and said no way would they give him a job. I was still very young, but I remem-ber that day. I thought we might be in real trouble. He came back to the motel room and sat on the shiny brown bedspread and stared at the wall for a long time. Outside it was raining, and cars kept zooming by, big loud trucks, like nothing was wrong at all in the world. I'd never seen so much rain in my life, especially in the winter, and the gray made it seem even colder than Colorado.

When I got up my nerve, I asked Pater if I could watch cartoons and he nodded, but I kept the sound down, not really seeing the funny characters that had always made me laugh before. I never really watched cartoons after that because we couldn't stay at the motel, and then we started camping, and then we built our place. Television became a memory, except for the ones we see inside restaurants when we walk through town, and those TVs are always playing football games and news shows. They don't show cartoons in those kinds of places, but I don't think I would like them anymore, anyway.

If we are walking at our normal pace, it takes Pater and me thirty-three minutes to get from our camp to the trail through the wildlife sanctuary property, and then sixteen more minutes behind the fancy houses down to where we pass more fancy houses, and then there are stores and restaurants. We have never eaten in a real restaurant, but once, for my tenth birthday, we walked all the way to the Jack in the Box near the highway. Pater seemed happier than me to eat a hamburger and french fries. We shared a vanilla milk shake, and I got sick afterward. I tried not to think about the money I was barfing into the bushes on our way home. Pater didn't mention it either, just warmed up some chicken broth on the camp stove for me when we got back.

There is no easy way to get to our campsite. There are no trails to it, not even animal trails. We vary our route each time we go to town, stepping lightly, careful not to pack down dirt or break foliage. Pater walks the periphery every day, making sure we're undetectable.

We are up a steep embankment. The easiest way to our camp is to walk up along our little creek, which we sometimes do, but then you get wet, especially in the rainy season when the creek is fuller than in summer. It joins with a bigger creek about a quarter mile away. Pater has worked hard to transplant sword and deer ferns and horsetail and sedge and all manner of thick bushy plants where the two creeks meet, then up toward our place. He plants them in such a way that the leaves and fronds hang over the edges of our little creek so that it doesn't look much like a creek at all. We tend the plants like we tend our vegetable garden, and they thrive and grow and help us, because we take good care of them. The creek provides us with drinking water, which we boil, and cold water for food storage, and a bathing pool that Pater made by digging out a hole and a trench, then using rocks to line it and direct the water into it.

Pater does a lot of thinking. He thinks of everything.

Our little library is on Baneberry Street, so we usually go there on our Wednesday trips to town. Pater makes sure we're always dressed nice so no one will think we're homeless. We have a real library card, because we got it as soon as we arrived in Columbia, when we had an address. Nobody cared that it was a motel. Lots of people live in motels. Sometimes people who live in houses don't know that, but the ladies at the library do. I think the ladies at the library like us because we always return our books in good condition and on time, every week.

When we want to find a book the little library doesn't have, we take the bus to the central library, down where the big buildings are. The central library is my favorite building. It's like going to a palace full of books. I feel like a princess or an important person when I walk up the steps toward that huge brick building with its pretty windows and a roof that looks like a steeple, and go inside the tall oak doors, and the man in the uniform smiles and says, "Good afternoon." I feel even more like royalty when we glide across the shiny stone floor. Everything is so elegant that I want to just stand and look but Pater always says to hurry along. He says when we're in town we need to act like the other people, who all seem to be rushing to somewhere else, even when they're already where they're going.

Everyone but the mean group of homeless people who hang out on the steps of the central library. They're slow, and smelly, and not nice. They say mean things to Pater, like, *Think you're better than me? Think you're hot shit, asshole?* They use foul language, and they scare me. They don't say anything mean to me anymore, not since Pater got in a fight with one and made his face bleed.

We are not homeless; we have a home. Pater says we're citizens. Still, I don't feel like the other people when we are in town, even though they must think they're citizens, too.

At the central library, sometimes we go to the reference room, where there are books you can't check out, but you can read when you're there. That is where I first saw all twenty-two volumes of the *Encyclopedia of Science and Nature*. Every time we go to the reference room, I find where I left off the last time we were there and read as long as I can before Pater finishes on the computer and comes to get me. Right now I am on Volume IX. The last part I read was about igneous rock formations. The Cascade Mountain range is a string of dormant and active volcanoes, so we have a lot of igneous rock where we live: basalt, andesite, tuffs, and breccia. I can now identify them all.

This is why I don't need to go to a regular school, Pater says. My school is books. My school is the forest. My school is Pater.

When we first came here, all the night sounds—the whispery, crackly ones, the screeches and scratching noises of the nocturnals—they'd keep me awake all night long. That was before we built the tree house and we slept in an old smelly tent. I would try to sneak onto Pater's mat, not even into his sleeping bag, just to lie next to him. He'd wake up and make me go back to my own pad, which was much nicer and more comfortable, but it didn't feel safe, not at first.

Now I feel safer sleeping here than I ever did in a city, in a town, where there are bad people and all the things that make them that way: drugs and liquor and stress and jobs and useless jerk doctors and places where they try to keep certain people locked up. Pater shows me places like that when we walk in for supplies on Monday, or the library on Wednesday, or the park on Friday. The church on Sunday. Sometimes we walk by the redbrick building for sick people, the hospital. Pater doesn't like hospitals. They steal your dignity, he says, and people just get sicker there. People die there, he says.

Sometimes we walk by the tall, skinny buildings where businesspeople have to go every day to work at desks and make money so they can keep paying for all the stuff they don't need, the big houses where rooms sit empty for most of the day, or all the time, even. Pater says some people have rooms in their houses with lots of fancy furniture for when company comes over, only company doesn't come over much, so dust gets all over the furniture and then they pay someone to come clean it all up, just in case someone comes over. He says they had a room like that in his house when he was growing up.

We don't have any extra rooms now, not by definition of a room in Webster's, which is "a part of a building enclosed by walls, a floor, and a ceiling." However, if you use the second definition, "space that can be occupied where something can be done, especially viewed in terms of whether there is enough," then we do.

I lived in the other kind of rooms, in buildings, in towns, but we all lived in just one room, no matter what that building was: a motel, an apartment, sometimes a small house that might have a separate room for sleeping. There were always lots of others there with Crystal and me, when Pater was in the war. I knew even then, even though I was too young to know it, that the people were doing bad things—the things that make them crazy and dangerous and have to go live in shelters and hospitals, like the ones we walk by. I knew then and I know now, I don't ever want to be a person like that. That's the gift of your beginning, Pater says, that right there: knowing that.

5

At 16:19, Jess stood on the hot asphalt of the North Station House parking lot. The sun fried the top of her dark head and her feet baked in her boots as she talked with her old partner Ellis Jenkins and their fellow officer Steven Takei. The three made the perfect poster for diversity in the workplace, she thought: one black man, one Asian man, and one half-breed Hispanic woman.

Sweat already pooled in the small of her back beneath the heavy flak vest. They'd changed into their black tactical uniforms, which were somewhat looser and cooler than regulation uniforms, but it was closing in on ninety degrees. She fanned herself with her cap. They were expecting a K9 unit and another patrol officer from the South Station House, and Sergeant Everett had already ordered the search helicopter up. Now he was over by the garage, hands on hips, talking with Darryl, the station's transportation wrangler.

"What about the ATVs?" Jess asked the others.

"Already tried that right after the call came in," Jenkins said, sticking a piece of Juicy Fruit into his mouth. "They couldn't even get close. Too steep. Almost rolled them when they tried to go off-road." He chuckled and offered Jess and Takei gum from the pack. Takei shook his head once and adjusted the AR-15 in its sling on his shoulder. Jess hadn't yet gone for certification on the semiautomatic weapon, but she'd be lugging a shotgun, like everyone else, meaning she'd need ice on her neck before bed. She reached for a piece of gum, slipped it from its powdery enclosure, and stuck it into her mouth. The sticky-sweet taste reminded her of a time when she didn't have to worry about things like icing her neck from carrying a heavy shotgun and the possibility of having to shoot someone.

"Why all the gear?" Jess asked.

Takei grunted—he was just happy to have his AR-15 strapped on—and Jenkins shrugged.

Sergeant Everett strode over in his stiff-gaited way and Jess wondered how he was going to get up an incline an ATV couldn't. He shouldn't even be going out—he was the sergeant on duty but he'd reassigned that job immediately. He constantly nursed a bad case of sciatica and was probably over sixty, but he was stubborn. Stubborn like her dad had been. Maybe that would be enough to help him keep up with the younger officers.

She knew why he picked Officer Takei. He was the best shooter they had. Jenkins was fit and levelheaded. She was female, and while not exactly fit, Jess knew she was a far better choice than Madison. Everett knew it, too, but he'd been pissed off that she was late.

"Takei wants to know why all the gear, Sarge." Jess knew she shouldn't tease her fellow officer, but she couldn't help it. He was so easy.

"I didn't say that, sir. She did." Takei kept his eyes forward, standing at attention.

Everett ignored them. "I'll brief you when everyone's here."

They waited in uncomfortable silence until the squad car from South pulled up at the curb a few minutes later. The passenger door opened and Everett muttered, "Shit."

Jess felt the same. She'd worked at South years before with Officer David Greiner, and he was a pain in the ass, a short guy with a complex. It was rumored that he'd leaked information to the press on a rash of internal investigation cases, resulting in more than a few firings. Jess guessed he made up for his lack of height by thinking he was some kind of secret vigilante, not that she or anyone could prove it. Sure, he was certified to use an AR-15, which she guessed was the reason he'd been included on the search team, but Jess couldn't think of anyone she'd less like to see attached to an automatic weapon.

"Where's Fields? I asked for Officer Fields," Everett yelled, shaking his head.

"He was out on a DCS—a big one, eighteen kilos. He couldn't get back in time," Greiner said. "They said you wanted a good shooter."

"Get over here. You're four minutes late."

"My fault," called the other cop, the K9 officer, as he swung the driver's-side door shut. "Larry here got into some chicken bones last night and he's been crapping about every five minutes. I think he's okay now." He reached a hand through the small opening in the back window and patted the large German shepherd sitting there, pink tongue hanging like a slice of bologna in the heat. "Aren't you, Larry boy? You're good, huh?"

"He'd better be good," Everett said. "What's your name, boy?"

"Zusmanovich, sir."

Everett shook his head. "Ah, Christ. I don't have time to learn that. We're calling you Zoo, dog man."

Jess studied the younger cop walking toward them; he didn't seem to take offense. "I've been called worse," he said. He sported a close-shaved scalp even though his dark hairline went right to the front of his head—no signs of premature baldness. Probably ex-military, Jess decided, then changed her mind when she saw the blue ink on the tops of his knuckles. Ex-gang, with a name like Zusmanovich? She looked at his hand as she reached to shake it. The homemade letters spelled out "WWBD."

"What would . . ." She tried to figure out what the "B" stood for.

His cheeks colored. "'Batman,' originally. I was an idiot when I was fourteen. Now I go with 'Buddha,' or 'Bozo,' depending on what the situation calls for."

She laughed, loudly, then felt embarrassed and crossed her arms across her chest as Everett began to speak.

"Listen up. There's a little detail I didn't want to be too loosey-goosey about in front of too many people. This is for the search team only at this point, and I don't want any of you letting this out, not yet. Not till we know what's going on."

"What little de—" Jess began.

"Gee-yawd, Villareal, I'm getting to it already." He shook his jowly face and Jess took a deep breath, holding it till he began again.

"One of the bird-watchers gave chase to the juvenile. Didn't get very far, being a goddamn bird-watcher, and he probably helped run her off, but he found this. Said she dropped it."

From his chest pocket he extracted a folded half sheet of paper with "Condo for Sale" information on one side. He flipped it over and handed it to Jenkins next to him.

Jess could see that someone had drawn pictures of flowers and birds, much in the style Nina had in years past—everything curlicued and sweet. There was writing on the page, and Jess would have bet that the "I's" were dotted with tiny circles.

Jenkins drew a deep breath and handed the paper to Jess.

Her heart stopped. Mixed in among the flowers and birds were sweetly drawn swastikas and stars of David and Christian crosses, decorated with flowers, and yes, hearts. And there were discomfiting words: *Pater loves me, I love Pater. Crystal loves me, I love Crystal.* Crystal was meth. What was Pater? A title used by Nazis? Skinheads?

"Holy sh—" she said.

"You're right, holy shit," Everett said. "So, Villareal, we're gearing up in case something goes shitty. Which it won't. Right, Takei? Right, Greiner?"

Both men nodded.

"But if it does go shitty, commit." Everett paused, looking each officer in the eye. Jess nodded when he looked at her. "If a shot's fired," he said, "we shoot until we've got the situation under control. We don't back off until then. Right?"

"Right," they each said.

Jess had never been involved in a shooting, but she knew Sergeant Everett had. Twice, one fatal. Nine years earlier, he'd killed a kid who was trying to run him and two other officers

down with an Oldsmobile. Broke a femur on one of the officers, but Everett and the other cop were okay. Turned out the
kid had enough crack in his system to fuel Oregon Gas & Electric for two days. The problem was, he was only fifteen and his
only weapon was the car. After two years of media mudsling-
ing, Everett had been cleared, but his name was forever sul-
lied in the public forum. "Columbia police sergeant William
Everett" was equivalent to everything from "bad cop" to "white-
establishment pig who kills black kids." It wasn't fair, necessar-
ily; it just was.

Everett continued. "Our goal is to find the girl, whatever
that takes, and make sure she's safe. However long it takes.
Now, luckily we've got light for another five or so hours, but
it's late in the day to be starting out. So, mount up. We'll take
three vehicles, including the dog man's, and meet the birders at
the wildlife sanctuary parking lot. Let's go."

Jess's heart began to thump. She sent a prayer to her dad. She
didn't know if she believed in god even though she pretended
she did to her mother, but she prayed every once in a while,
when she knew she was no longer in control of anything.
*Please*, she prayed now, *keep everyone safe, and help us do the right
thing.*

BY 17:00 HOURS, THE GROUP of officers marched along the hiking trail with the bird-watchers, a stout older woman and her
quiet REI-clad brother. Jess knew she was thinking what every
other police officer was; this was going to be like trying to find
a tiny silver needle in a, well, in a densely overgrown forest.
The search helicopter orbited loudly overhead, but the canopy

was thick and vigorous. Jess wondered how they'd ever see anything from up there.

Even though the sun shone hot white in the city, the light in Joseph Woods State Park was filtered down to green-hued murkiness, close with humidity from the lush plant life and creeks, laced with spiderwebs. Jess stifled each shriek when she walked through them, even when the spider's dead-bug prey stuck to her clothes, in her hair. She put her cap on, though it made her scalp sweat, along with the rest of her.

The regimented regularity of so many boots hitting dirt and gravel felt comforting. Larry panted beside Zoo at the front with Everett, alongside the woman chattering and worrying that they wouldn't find the girl. The other witness, her brother, was silent. Jess looked at him more closely. His face remained impassive, his cheeks hollow and body gaunt, but he strode purposefully.

"It's very soon now," the woman said, holding a rumpled tissue to her nose. "Oh, I wish she'd just let us talk to her. Why did she have to run?" she asked, not seeming to expect an answer. "And that heron, my land, it was so unusual to see it here, and then the girl, and to think she might be . . . well, living like that, among those kind of people, and she's so young, and . . ." She went silent, and when Jess looked up, tears streamed down the woman's ruddy face.

Jess closed her eyes against the immediate heat she felt behind them. *Don't*, she thought, blinking, clearing her throat. Stealing a sideways look at Jenkins, she saw his lips tighten, his Adam's apple rise and fall. She turned her eyes back to the front. He had kids, too, young ones, five and seven. A girl and a boy.

"Here," the brother said, stopping. "It was here."

"No, was it?" The woman palmed her face. "It wasn't a little farther? Weren't there maidenhair ferns? I seem to remember maidenhair ferns."

"Sheesh, they don't have a clue," Jenkins whispered.

"It was here," the brother said again. He was soft-spoken and dressed in the too-pocketed khakis of a safari hunter, but Jess believed him. "Come stand over here; you'll see the ferns."

His sister moved to his side. "Yes," she said, sighing and leaned her head against his bony shoulder. "I'm sorry I'm so emotional," she said to no one in particular, wiping her eyes with her tissue. "I lost a daughter thirty-two years ago."

He put his arm around her, then pointed with the other hand into a small clearing, a narrow shaft of sun creating diamond light in the water of a slow-moving stream. "The bird was right there, next to that big rock in the crik, see, and then all of a sudden the girl stepped out from behind that cedar, sparkling like a fairy or something. Damnedest thing. Then the heron flew straight up to roost in that hemlock, right there in front of us. See that big branch? Right there. Still had his mating plumage. Quite a sight."

It was the most they'd heard from him and he seemed as mesmerized by the memory of the bird as the girl.

Officer Greiner shifted his AR-15 on his back and kicked his boot in the packed dirt. "Sergeant," he said, but stopped when Everett shot him a look.

The sergeant took off his cap and wiped his forehead with his sleeve, pushing sweat into his graying hairline. "And the girl, what exactly did she do?"

"She just looked at us," the woman said, "like she'd never seen people before. She looked so frightened. And I said something to her—lord knows what—and she turned and ran like a little deer back up that hill. Just scampered over those rocks, even in that big silver dress. Just bunched it up in her hands. I tried to run after her, but my baby brother here stopped me on account of my knees, and took off through all this brush you see here. Well, you can see, where the maidenhair is flattened out, all the way down to there." She pointed at the ground. "And he crossed the clearing quick as a wink, jumped the creek, but she'd already disappeared." She turned to her brother again, gave him a hug. "I didn't know you still had it in you, you old son of a gun."

She stopped and drew a breath, voice starting to shake. "And when he came back all out of breath and white as a ghost and showed us that piece of paper, my land, I've never been so scared in my life. That's when I called you folks. That poor girl. Do you think she's being held hostage by Nazis or something? Do you think it's that fellow that's been taking young girls?"

Everett snugged his cap back on. "Does no good to speculate, but we're going to find her. And if she isn't safe, we're going to make sure she will be. Now, do me a favor and don't go spreading this around, not until you hear from us again. All right? Especially not to the media." He looked at her sternly. "And tell all your bird-watching buddies the same. We don't want anything getting in the way of finding her."

The woman nodded, looking worried, and began to cry again.

Everett softened. "Now, can you two get back to the wild-life sanctuary, or do you need someone to go with you?"

"No, mercy, no, we walk these trails all the time. We'll be fine." She reached up to hug the sergeant, who turned stiff as a two-by-four and blushed.

Then the brother and sister turned to walk back the way they'd come, her shoulders heaving. He put his arm around her. Her sobbing silenced the twittering birds.

# 6

The worst thing I've ever done in my life was to steal the dress from Crystal. I was in a panic, trying to gather up all my clothes and toys, my toothbrush and comb and barrettes, my books and school supplies. We were in such a hurry, and Pater was upset like he gets, especially when he first came home from the war, and I wanted to have something of Crystal's so that I would never forget her. I loved that dress, because it made her beautiful, even after she lost her tooth and would only smile with her mouth closed. Even when her face got scarred from the sores. I grabbed the sparkling silver from the hanger in the back of the closet and stuffed it down deep in the plastic bag that was my suitcase until Pater bought us each a backpack at the Army Surplus. I put my snow boots in the bag and Pater said I wouldn't need those boots where we were going, so I pulled them back out and left them in the middle of the floor. The room was a mess anyway.

Crystal and her friend Jack had left the motel after a big fight with Pater. Pater had told her he knew what was going on, had been going on the whole time he was gone, serving our country for crying out loud, and here she'd turned into a tweaker and a lying, cheating whore, not taking care of their daughter, exposing her to all of this. It was the only time I've ever heard him use foul language. He was crazy. His eyes were a mix of fire and hurt feelings, and his arms were all veiny as he flailed them at the mess of pizza boxes and beer cans, other people's clothes and cigarettes and liquor bottles, blankets and pillows everywhere for everyone to lie on or sleep on after they'd been smoking their glass pipes and cigarettes and drinking their liquor all night. I didn't want to tell Pater that people did other things on those pillows, mostly under the blankets but not always. I was worried he was going to hurt Crystal.

Fine, she yelled at him as she grabbed her fake fur coat. You take her then. You see how easy it is to raise a kid by yourself. And then she looked at me with eyes crazier than Pater's and said, I'm sorry, kitten, but I just can't do it anymore, and ran into the snowy night after Jack, who'd run out already.

I knew she didn't mean it, not really—it was just the way she got sometimes—because she sent a letter to Pater's mother a few months later, saying she wanted me back and she'd sue him for every red cent he had, even though it wasn't much. His mother said we should come back home. That was the last time Pater called her. He said we didn't need any more bad news in our lives.

I don't remember a lot about driving here from Colorado, only that I was happy when it quit snowing and the car quit slipping and sliding on all those ice-packed curves in the dark.

We ate white powdered doughnuts from 7-Eleven for break-fast, and then I slept for a long, long time in the backseat, and when I woke up again, the radio was on, playing a song I liked, and Pater seemed calmer. I sat up and tapped my fingers on the armrest, and he said into the mirror, You like Green Day? I nodded, and he smiled. Daddy's girl, all right, he said; then he told me about the job in Oregon, said it didn't matter if Crystal didn't come with us. We'd make a new life without her. We'd get a house; I'd go to school regular for once and make friends. And I would never have to see all those things I'd seen ever again.

We pulled off the road into a rest area so I could use the ladies' room and brush my teeth and Pater could stretch his back, and when I returned to the car, he looked at me all serious. I have to ask you a question, he said, and I'll only ask you once. Did any of those people ever do anything to you they shouldn't have? Did anyone hurt you?

His eyes were all sad and crazy again, and I felt sad inside, too, but now that I was safe with him, I could forget the past. Nothing had happened that was worth him feeling so awful.

I shook my head no. We got back in the car, neither one of us talking, and headed west, driving for what seemed like forever. I was asleep again when we hit Columbia.

# 7

Once they left the hiking path, there were no trails. Somehow, Jess had envisioned trails. They'd gotten nothing other than a general direction from the bird-watchers. There were no consistent clusters of broken plants beyond where the bird-watcher had crushed them with his hiking boots. The forest became thicker and more tangled. Ever-larger spiderwebs stretched between ever-larger trees. As they left civilization behind, muffled quiet surrounded them, except for the sounds of six heavily armed, booted police officers and a dog crashing through waist-high foliage, and the occasional deafening fly-over of the helicopter.

"Anybody would hear us coming a mile away," Jenkins said softly so only Jess could hear.

They didn't spread out as widely as they would have if it were a standard search for a missing person. If they were walking into a hostile situation, which Sergeant Everett obviously assumed they were, they tried to stay within a few yards of one another, each scanning the dense growth for any signs of human activity. Jess knew Everett fancied himself a great outdoorsman—he had a twenty-six-foot fishing boat and an RV the size of a locomotive—but none of them was prepared for these conditions, boots slipping off fern-obscured logs, having to grab spindly trees for handholds on steep inclines and declines, falling into foliage-covered holes and through rotten logs, tripping over god knew what. Up one steep embankment they'd go, then down, up another, down. Everett checked his compass and GPS unit every few minutes. It was worse than the stair-stepper machine at the gym, but Jess wasn't going to complain, not after she'd asked for the assignment.

"Do you think we know where we're going?" Jenkins murmured when they crested the next hill. Everett decided to scout ahead, telling everyone to hold. He looked again at his compass, his GPS—For what? Jess wondered—then walked along a ridge until he was out of sight. She took off her shotgun to ease the twinge in her neck, cradling it in her arm, barrel down. Jenkins did the same, but Takei and Greiner kept their firearms firmly in place.

No matter their fitness levels, everyone huffed and puffed, even the dog. Larry seemed amiable, happy, and steadfast—qualities she'd always admired in animals and humans.

"You can pet him," Zoo said. He crouched beside the dog, scratching his ears. "He's a good boy. He'll stay focused. Won't you, Larry?" He buried his face in the ruff of fur around the dog's neck.

Jess walked over. "You don't really want us to call you Zoo, do you?"

"Doesn't bother me," he said. "Some people call me Z. Some people call me Stupid. And some people actually call me Chris."

"Z is good," she said, stooping in the small clearing Larry had found to lie in. "Better than Zoo." She ran her hand down the thick fur of the dog's back, giving a good scratch on his flank. He swung his head around in appreciation, panting, mouth dripping with drool. What fascinated Jess about search dogs was their intense work ethic. When they smelled their target, they pointed like a laser beam at the spot. Even in the inevitable maelstrom of human craziness when police officers confronted perpetrators, they held their ground.

"So," Z said, "what do people call you when they're not calling you Villareel? J-Lo? You kind of look like her, you know. Your eyes, I mean."

Jess shook her head. What a line. The only thing she had in common with J-Lo was the big behind, but on Jess it was not an asset. Why did so many cops—male and female—assume it was okay to hit on one another, to engage in late-night trysts while on duty and bored? It happened more than the public would ever guess, even to Jess, and she tried to shut down any invitation as quickly as she could. She set herself apart from her comrades in most ways. Jenkins was her only friend on the force because he embodied more of the cop spirit than anyone Jess had ever known, next to her dad. And he'd never once been inappropriate or made a suggestive remark.

"Vee-ah-ray-ALL," she said, rolling the R. "Or Grandma." She stood and walked in the direction Sergeant Everett had taken.

She came upon him standing on the other side of an upright dead cedar, and it was only after she said, "Hey, Sarge," that she realized he was urinating.

"Sorry. God." She turned back the way she'd come.

"I'm done, Villareal. Get back over here," he said, and she heard the sound of a zipper; then he stepped out from behind the tree. "I might have got us good and lost," he said, waving the compass uselessly at the quiet vastness before them: the trees, the deep ferns and sticker bushes, the steep inclines and downed trunks that blocked their every step. The light suddenly dimmed to green-gray. Jess hoped it was a cloud drifting over the sun. She looked at her watch. It was still only 18:20. They'd been hiking nearly an hour and a half. They had at least three hours of daylight.

"Nah, we're not lost," she said. "We can always find our way back with your GPS."

"We're not going back. Not till we find her."

"Yeah." Jess pulled her lips tight. "I know."

In spite of the heat and the sweat-soaked flak vest encircling her torso, Jess felt a chill run up her sternum. Maybe it was the dimming light, the unearthly silence, the sergeant admitting he didn't know what he was doing, but everything had taken on an eerie, surreal quality, as if they'd left the real world behind. As if they were in a movie or docudrama, only there was no director yelling cut, no one telling them what to do next.

"This doesn't feel like any other case I've ever been on," she said. Her pulse pattered nervously in her neck—she rarely talked so personally with him.

Everett sighed. "No," he agreed, "it doesn't."

"All we can do is keep going."

"Right," he said, then again more firmly, "Right," and they walked back toward the group.

They set out again, crossing the small creek that wound its way from where they'd started, through gullies and ravines, ever higher. When the forest opened up, they'd spread out more, some going straight up hillsides while the others traversed them, reuniting as they tried to pick their way carefully through without falling, but everyone fell, multiple times. It was grueling work made worse by the fact that they were searching blind. The girl could be anywhere. She could be out of the woods by now, for all they knew. She might have been with a group of other kids, partying, getting high, and afraid of getting caught, or she could be a runaway, running blind herself. But Jess didn't think so. No one would come to this part of the forest for no good reason; it was too much work.

As it approached 19:00 hours, Jess felt tension building in her jaw, and tried to relax her bite. Her shift ended at 02:00, but not if they didn't find this girl, soon. At their next rest break, Jenkins pulled out his cell phone to call his wife, Maggie. Z and Larry lay on the ground, Z's head on the dog's torso. Takei stood at attention, surveying the creek ahead. Even though she'd worked with him for over a year, Takei was not forthcoming about personal details and she had no idea if he had a family, a wife, kids. Did Z? she wondered.

Jess wished she had someone at home who would worry. She could call her mother, just in case something should go awry. She couldn't shake the feeling that something was so different about this day, this place. Of course, she would first have to figure out how to tell Clara what was going on without causing her to freak out. Her mother had few other responses to anything in life.

On the final day of Jess's marriage, she'd made the mistake of calling her mother. Jess had never been more certain that her marriage was over, but her mother cried, worrying that Jess and Nina would end up broke and on the streets, imploring her to give Rick another chance, even after Jess told her what happened. He'd gone out drinking after work, even after he'd agreed to pick up Nina and her friend Blaine from the cineplex at the mall.

Jess had been on duty that night. She called Rick to make sure he didn't forget to go get them. She heard voices and the sounds of a public place in the background and assumed he was already there.

"Oh, good, you remembered," she'd said, and she could tell by his silence that he hadn't.

"Remembered—" he tried.

"You're not at the mall?" she asked, shaking her head. "Where are you then?"

"I just needed to pull over and get some gas, hon. That's all."

Jess took a deep breath. He never called her "hon."

"Those girls have been out of the movie for ten minutes. You need to get over there now."

In retrospect, what still killed her was that she knew he wasn't at the gas station. The sounds were convivial, social. But she said, "You need to get over there now" instead of "Are you out drinking?"

It sank in a half hour later, when the radio dispatcher requested a patrol car to respond to a bar fight out of her jurisdiction. A chill descended upon her, almost as if from above, and she radioed her commanding officer, told him she had an emergency at home, and could she take the cruiser? Of course, he said, but let me get someone out on the street to replace you first. She called Rick while she waited, parked behind a Safeway store.

"Hello?" he answered, his voice rising too grandly at the end, and she knew. He was drunk.

"Are the girls with you?" she asked.

He laughed. "Yeah, of course they are. Geez, give a guy a break." She knew he was mugging it up for Nina and Blaine, who probably weren't in seat belts.

"Where are you?"

"We stopped for ice cream at the Dairy Queen by the high school. Neenie's having a twist."

"Stay right there," Jess said. "I'm going to take a break and meet you, okay? It'll be fifteen minutes."

She didn't want to tip her hand. He'd get angry and his driving would be even worse.

"Really? Hey, Neen, Mom's coming to meet us!"

It finally hit her that the only time her husband ever sounded happy was when he drank.

Her CO radioed back that she was clear to go, and she arrived at Dairy Queen within ten minutes. Nina and Blaine watched wide-eyed from their outdoor table as Jess got out of the car in her uniform, slammed the door, and strode over to Rick. He was the only one who didn't see her anger.

She leaned down and he thought she wanted to kiss him. He grabbed at her playfully, the reek of alcohol so strong she shuddered. She pushed him away and straightened up, finally accepting that she never should have married him in the first place.

"You just lost your family," she said.

Nina looked like she'd been hit, her eyes wide and awful.

"Come on, girls," Jess said. "Let's go for a ride in a police car."

# 8

After I ran back into the camp, Pater had a look on his face like he wanted to be sick, like the feeling I had after the vanilla milk shake. He wasn't mad at me. He should have been, but he wasn't. He said, Well, then, I guess it's time to see if the Emergency Plan works.

This is our Emergency Plan:

1. Extinguish the campfire with the bucket of dirt beside it. If it is nighttime, blow out all candles.
2. Pack emergency backpacks with two changes of clothes (including socks and underwear), toothbrush, soap, comb, and any other personal effects. Wear your coat and boots, even in summer.
3. We are allowed two books each and I am allowed one toy (although I've outgrown most of them). I am in charge of my schoolwork and Pater is in charge of our

Bible, papers, and money (I have a folded-up copy of my birth certificate and an emergency twenty-dollar bill at all times in my sock), water, and some food. We each must strap our sleeping bags to our backpacks.

4. Make sure we've left nothing behind that can identify us. Pull up the rope ladder and jump down from the tree house.

5. Sweep the campsite thoroughly, including our footsteps, as we leave. Hide the broom in dense foliage.

6. Retreat to either the fallen cedar up and over the hill, where we have cleared a nice space that fits us both comfortably, or exit the park down the steep north route (which Pater says no one else in their right minds will ever go up or down) in case of extreme emergency.

7. If we are separated, we are to meet as soon as possible at church. I am to ask Reverend Rosetta for shelter if Pater doesn't arrive right away. If he doesn't arrive in one week, I am to ask Reverend Rosetta for bus fare to Denver.

8. Once I am in Denver, I am to call Pater's mother, whose phone number is written on the back of my birth certificate. She is, at heart, a good woman, Pater says, and will take me in to live with her until Pater can join us. Ask her to send a check to Reverend Rosetta covering bus fare and any expenses I've incurred. He means food when he says this, but I like the way he says it better. It sounds more like an official plan.

Our Emergency Plan is a secret. We've added to it since but we started it a long time ago, back when we didn't have our tree house yet, or candles, or lanterns, or anything to do once it got dark at night but sit in our tent, or if it wasn't raining, out by the fire—always a small enough fire to put out quickly.

Pater would tell me stories about all kinds of things, like how he used to go camping with his dad and brother, Robert, in Colorado when he was a boy, and fish for trout in the Platte River, how the fish would spew their eggs all over the place when he and Robert were trying to take them off the hook. His dad would fry them with their heads on with some potatoes and onions, and Pater said that was some of the best food he'd ever eaten. Once he even told me about when his father left to go live with another woman in Nebraska, how his mother had run after his Ford Bronco for half a mile. Pater laughed like that was funny, but his eyes didn't look happy. His dad came back to live with them after a few months, and they were all supposed to act like it had never happened. I was surprised that these were the same people I knew as Grandma and Grandpa Wiggs, who I'd always thought were the most upstanding people in the world, but I also felt special, being told this story. It meant I was growing up, even though it made me realize that there weren't perfect people in the world, the way I had always thought.

I told Pater things, too. I told him what I'd learned in school while he was away at the war, showing off my times tables and tongue twisters. I'd also tell him stories I made up on the spot: silly ones about enchanted animals and princesses, or scary stories about monsters and dark caves. I never told him everything about while he was gone, though. Even when I was young, I knew better than to get him all riled up. Now that it was just the two of us, it was peaceful, and I wanted more than anything to keep it that way.

Memorizing the Emergency Plan was a game we played, like "identify the birdcalls" or "how many words can you think of that start with the letter R?" When I messed up, Pater never got angry. He'd just remind me how the next part started, and then I could remember the rest. I never thought of it as something real, something we may have to do someday. We heard campers and hikers every once in a while, but only because they're noisy. They were never very near and we were always quiet, so they'd never have found us.

But now, here we were, packing our emergency backpacks and making sure we had everything that might identify us. Pater reached down and pulled all of my writings from the book crate by my mattress. We can't leave these here, he said. You can take as much as you're willing to carry, but you know what we have to do with the rest.

Tears prickled my eyes and the heaviness of what I'd done sank harder into my chest. I took the pile of papers from his hands, all mismatched and different colors, my pencil markings smudged on the backs of "Work from Home" and "Lose Weight Now—Ask Me How!" flyers and used envelopes. His voice softened. Why don't you pick a couple of favorites? he said. Then we'll hide the rest. Maybe they'll still be okay when we come back for them. But you have to hurry, Lindy.

I picked a report I'd done on the Swainson's thrush because Pater marked it with an A+, and a poem I wrote about Crystal a long time ago when I still missed her. I folded them neatly and slid them into my backpack next to my books and school papers. Pater took the rest and put them in a paper bag, then stuffed it into his pack. Any other day and I would have kept the story about the princess and the great blue heron who turns into a boy, but I most especially wanted to get rid of that story.

Pater pulled up the rope ladder and threw our backpacks to the ground. He looked at me and said, No matter what happens, stick to the plan, okay, Lindy? Everything will turn out all right if we stick to the plan.

My heart was pounding, but I nodded and then he turned and jumped down like a flying squirrel with his arms wide, his camouflage jacket stretched between them like forest skin. He landed with a hard thud and a gasp. His back. That was how he hurt it in the first place in the war, by jumping from a building that was exploding. At least he was luckier than his brother. Robert died before he had the chance to jump, and that hurts Pater even more than his back, I know, because he only went to Iraq to take care of his brother. I think that's why he tries extra-hard to take good care of me.

"Are you all right?" I cried.

He waved his hand, like, Don't worry, though he stayed hunched over too long before straightening up. Come on then, he said. His face was expressionless, but an odd color, like the inside of a green grape when you peel it.

I've never liked jumping from high places, even though Pater taught me how to land on my feet, then tuck and roll. I'm always afraid I will spin out of control as I'm falling, that I won't land the right way and I'll break something, and then we'll really be in trouble because we have no money for doctors. I sat on the edge of the platform, trying to make myself push off the way Pater had. I began to shake and I wanted to be sick, and I thought Pater would hate me for being so afraid, but he kept looking up at me, talking smooth and low, saying, It's okay Lindy. I'm right here. I'm not going to let anything bad happen to you.

Even after I'd ruined everything.

I turned to give Sweetie-pie one last look. She was watching me, and blinked twice before closing her eyes and swiveling her head away from me. Everything about a bird is made for flight: the way they breathe, the shape and design of their bodies, their weight. I wished I could fly, but even if I were covered with feathers, I would not be able to avoid gravity.

Finally, I shoved the heels of my hands as hard as I could against the wood and then I was as close to flying as I could be, greens and browns whirling around me before the rush of air blew the silver dress up over my head so that all I could see were sparkles, and morels falling from the pocket, landing with soft pocks all around me as I hit the ground feetfirst and tucked and rolled.

I sat up and pulled the dress off over my head. I looked up at Pater and he was laughing, shaking his head. His face was the right color again. That dress has got to go, he said. It's just going to trip you up if we have to move quickly. I nodded and stuffed it deep inside my pack. Maybe I would throw it away next time we passed a Dumpster. It wasn't beautiful anymore, not with all the wear and tear it got, and maybe it never was. Maybe it was just my wanting it to be that had made it so.

It was Wednesday, our day to go to the library, but Pater said we should go to our hiding place instead, up over the ridge from our camp, behind the huge fallen cedar. Pater says the cedar is probably one of the most ancient trees in the forest, it's so big around, and must have fallen right before we got here five years ago, because back then it still looked like a normal tree. Now the bark falls away in strips, and the pileated wood-peckers have gotten to it, carving out rectangular holes with their pecking, trying to get at insects, leaving places for other, smaller birds to roost. Red sawdust carpets the ground around it, scenting the air with cedar perfume.

Our forest has very few areas of old-growth trees left. I studied this in Miss Frischmann's book; I even taught some-thing to Pater, because he did not know this before. We live in the next highest stage to old growth, where the trees are eighty to two hundred fifty years old. That makes them very tall, and when you look up, you see long, naked trees reaching to the sky, and only then are there leaves or boughs of needles. It's like the green stuff needs to be on top, where there is brighter light. Down where we are the light is always silvery gray and the air moist and cool. It's like being inside the biggest, most beautiful church in the world, especially on a sunny day when the sun is shining way up high through the top branches, making green and blue windows of light.

We sat in our cleared-out space behind the big cedar on a blanket, eating dried apples and peanut butter sandwiches. It was like being on a picnic until we heard the chopper coming.

Pater looked up. We stayed very quiet. It moved slowly overhead, so slowly that I thought it had stopped. All they can see is canopy, Pater said, but he was saying it to himself, like he sometimes does when he's nervous about us getting caught. His forehead was shiny with sweat. Finally, the chopper moved away, and it was quiet again.

I couldn't believe that anyone would go to such lengths to

look for me. Why would they? I wasn't lost. I wasn't in trouble. Everything was fine. But somehow I knew it was looking for me. I finished my sandwich and lay on the blanket, tucking myself tight up against the length of the tree, inhaling its scent. I would have fallen asleep if it hadn't been for the chopper coming back, then going away, back and forth, back and forth.

Pater sat with his back to the tree, pretending to whittle something with his penknife, staring up at the sky, sometimes saying how there was no way they could see us. At first I thought we'd have to wait there for a while until they gave up, until we were sure no one was coming, and then we could go back to our tree house, and Pater would climb up and throw down the rope ladder, and then we would go to bed, and in the morning everything would be the way it had always been. That's what waiting a long time does to you, makes you start to invent stories to make yourself feel better. I'd been making up stories my whole life, but I started to realize this one wasn't going to come true. The chopper kept coming back, and Pater shook his head, said they probably wouldn't stop until they found us.

The last thing I heard him say before I fell asleep was, "Get some rest. We'll walk out after dark."

# 9

At nearly 20:00 hours, the light turned a duller shade of green; the air cooled to lukewarm. Jess, Jenkins, and Takei walked along the creek now, shoes muddy and pants soaked from the knees down, while the others climbed the ridge above them.

"We've only got an hour of light left," Jenkins said, stopping and removing his cap. His short, wiry hair glistened with sweat against his scalp. "We still have to find our way out of here. Looks like we'll be doing that in the dark." He ran his hand over his head, wiped his face with his forearm and pulled his cap back on.

It didn't matter to Jess; they weren't going to stop. How could you ever stop, knowing a kid might be in trouble?

They came upon a swampy spot that looked like it might connect to another stream. "Let's try this way," Jess said, and the two men followed her, even though it led them farther away from the others. They followed the soupy depression until it became an actual creek, though a tiny one, only three to four inches at its widest spots. Jess knew her choice was popular, though, as the stream was surrounded by good flat earth to walk along, with foliage so beautiful she wanted to tiptoe through the ferns and leafy plants that nature tended so meticulously. Was it bad karma to step on them? Would she come back as a plant in her next life and be trodden upon by some boot-clomping hiker? Jess shook her head. She was getting punchy. The sense she'd had earlier, that they were traveling through some other world, some other time and place, shimmered in the periphery.

They tracked the creek for a few hundred yards, their footfalls remarkably loud in the still of the forest.

Jenkins slipped and fell to one knee in the creek, cursing, then laughing. "Damn. We're never going to sneak up on anyone like this."

"Whoa," Takei said. Jess felt her heart lurch as she saw what he was looking at: a slice of blue farther ahead.

"Oh, my god," she said. Not only blue but man-made blue, like a tarp, or a tent, a startling sight after so many hours of green upon green. They reached for their firearms and rifles. Takei held the AR-15 at his side, staying in the lead.

"How far away are the others?" Jess asked in a low voice, but no one replied. They hadn't heard them since they turned up the smaller creek. Jess reached for the radio on her shoulder. "Villareal to Everett. Come in."

It occurred to her that this must be what it felt like to be a foot soldier in a war, trudging through a foreign land, wondering at every turn whether someone was hiding in the underbrush—someone more familiar with the territory than you and not wanting you there, fingers on their own triggers.

They proceeded toward the object, scanning the surrounding woods with each step. The earth around them suddenly became hard-packed and clear of growth—smooth to the point of seeming swept of loose dirt. Jess wondered if the others could hear the blood slamming through her veins, if they felt as frightened as she did. The clearing widened, and indeed a blue tarp covered a large woodpile. Fir boughs had been laid across the top to camouflage it, but the tarp had slipped a stubborn few inches below.

They stopped. All around them were signs of human habitation. Jess tightened her grip on the shotgun. To their left, the tiny stream had been diverted by a short wall of rocks into two pools: one shallow, one deeper.

"Look," Jess said. The shallow pool held a plastic gallon container of milk, plastic bags of carrots and apples. A tub of the same canola oil margarine she used. She tried to swallow and couldn't.

Jenkins called out, "Police! Everyone out here in front of us, now, hands in the air!" They waited, then proceeded uphill on the hard-packed ground, passing a raised vegetable garden with an enviable crop of chard and spinach, a few broccoli and cauliflower plants beside the thick stems of those that had already been cut, rambling pea vines, tall flowering onions.

At the far-right edge of the site, between the clearing and the forest, a crude lean-to covered a hole in the ground.

"What's that?" Jenkins asked.

"Latrine," Takei said.

"Oh." Jenkins nodded. "Yeah."

They climbed a short set of log steps, and Jess stopped. "Look, a tire swing," she said. The dirt beneath it, and the dirt in front of them, was smooth and untracked. The only footprints were theirs. It felt as if they were caught in a spell, bewitched by whoever lived in this place. Jess could feel them there, somehow, even though they were no doubt long gone.

"This is freaky," she said, then called out, "Columbia Police! Anybody here?"

Takei walked ahead, then called back to them, "There's a camp kitchen up here. Pretty well stocked. They've been here a while."

"I'll try Everett again," Jess said.

"Hey," Jenkins said, "look up there. A tree fort." He sounded like a kid, and swung his shotgun back on its sling to climb the tree. Jess had seen him this way at barbecues and holiday parties, but never on the job.

"Nice move, Jenkins," Takei said, walking back down the hill. "You're not even covered." He raised his rifle and peered through the sight. "Go ahead."

"Villareal to Everett," Jess said into the radio clipped to her shoulder. "We've found a camp. Over."

She watched Jenkins climb, ringing his arms around the big trunk, using knots as footholds, then pulling himself onto a large limb to rest. He grinned down at them.

Jess felt queasy. "Villareal to Everett. Come in."

Jenkins stood on the limb, reached up to the platform with both hands and scrambled until he was on his knees in the structure, probably a good fifteen feet off the ground. "Man, you should see all the books," he said, and then screamed as something large and white flew out past him, streaking like a comet out and down over Takei's head, then into the woods.

"Ellis, are you okay?" Jess gasped. Takei had begun to laugh. "Why are you laughing?" Jess yelled at him. "What the hell was that?"

Jenkins still had his arms over his head as he turned to face them. "I don't know but it was fucking huge! Motherfucker!"

"Owl," Takei said, grinning, the most animated Jess had ever seen him. "It was just an owl. And you screamed like a little girl."

"Where the hell did you wander off to? What's going on? What's that noise?" Everett's voice crackled from Jess's radio. She must have tensed her hand on the TALK button when Jenkins screamed, held down the button, a reflex.

"Um, that would be Officer Jenkins screaming like a girl, sir," she said into the radio, smiling at Takei, who smiled back. It seemed they had all become enchanted in this forest.

Jenkins yelled, "Hey now!" then shook his head and threw down a ladder made of rope and wood dowels.

"What? Why the hell is he screaming?" Everett growled. "What's going on? Where are you?"

"We found a camp, no inhabitants, but looks like they've been here recently." She did her best to direct them to where they were and signed off, swinging her shotgun back on its sling.

"Can I come up?" she called to Jenkins, walking to the tree. "Will it hold both of us?"

"Yeah. Whoever built this thing wasn't fooling around. It's

rock solid." He jumped twice, heavy boots hitting the platform with firm thuds. "That ladder looks tricky, though. Be careful."

"I'm not a complete klutz," Jess muttered, grabbing the side ropes, putting a boot tentatively on the first rung, then her weight. She swung in toward the tree and almost lost her footing. Clutching tighter, she stepped onto the next rung, swung back out, then the next rung. Halfway up she looked down, closing her eyes for a moment before continuing. At the top, Jenkins offered a hand to help her, but she hoisted herself, her duty belt, her shotgun, and her butt up onto the platform.

"Check it out, V," Jenkins said.

She turned to look behind her, then scrambled to her feet. Two sleeping platforms edged the small space, empty except for yellowed foam pads, separated by a makeshift shelf filled with old books and encyclopedias. Above the shelf, clothes hung from a series of hooks: men's flannel shirts, a pair of army fatigues to the right, a girl's rose-colored sweater and assorted tops and jeans to the left. Beneath the sleeping platform on that side, a pair of white Reeboks with purple hearts peeked out.

"Nina wore those years ago," Jess said. "That exact shoe. She loved those things." Her throat almost closed in on itself. "We scared them away," she said. "Damn it."

"Look at this," Jenkins said. "Goddamn owl."

Another thick dowel protruded from the timber wall toward the front, a bird perch. Beneath it sat a newspaper-lined box with a few droppings and puffy white feathers.

"It must be a pet," Jess said, sighing.

"Pretty weird pet."

Jess smiled. "You should have seen yourself," she teased. "You looked like you saw a ghost."

"That thing was worse than a damn ghost, if ghosts even existed."

"I don't know, Ellis. Maybe this place is haunted," she teased, trying to make the mood light, but everything felt heavy. Not only her duty belt, or her shotgun, or her body. The air was heavy, the ever-graying light around them. Were they capable of handling this? What would her father have done if he'd been in this situation?

Jess breathed in deeply, holding the stillness of the moment as long as she could. She wanted to find this girl. She had to. The thought that she had been so close and now was gone felt like punishment, somehow. This could have been her own worst nightmare: Nina could have been abducted like this if Jess hadn't been so careful.

She shook her head. It didn't matter who you were; it could happen to anyone. Nina was lost to her now anyway; all Jess's efforts to protect her had failed.

After Jess made Rick move out, Nina had just hated her—angry, tearful accusations were their only communication for months. Even though just nine years old, Nina had a surprising capacity for fury. Where Jess had stuffed her emotions after her father's death, Nina practically vomited them.

As Nina entered puberty, Jess's sense of protection went on hyperalert; she could admit this now. Sure, she'd probably been overzealous, but she'd wanted Nina to be safe. Whole and complete.

But Nina couldn't stand how protective Jess was. As a young

teen, she started to lie about where she was going, to sneak out to see certain friends Jess thought inappropriate. She came home later in the afternoons from school, and Jess wondered if she'd been smoking pot or drinking beer. When Jess tried to clamp down on her, restrict her, ground her, Nina pulled farther away, ignoring Jess's demands. It was tough being a working single parent. She could only keep an eye on her daughter so much, and Clara was hopeless when watching Nina.

It all came to an end on an autumn day when Nina was sixteen. In retrospect, Jess now realized Nina had wanted it to happen. They shared the only bathroom in the house, and Jess couldn't have missed the Clear Blue Easy package Nina left in the wastebasket.

"It's none of your business," Nina had snapped when Jess confronted her after school, and pushed past Jess toward her bedroom.

"Then why did you leave it where I would find it?" Jess demanded, following Nina to her room, holding out her arm to fend off the slamming door. "You're not getting off that easy. What was the result, Nina?"

Her daughter would not look at her, would not even face her. She flung her school bag into the far corner of the room, wrestled off her long black sweatshirt and threw it on top. She stood with her back to Jess, knees against the edge of the bed, slim arms wrapped around her torso, looking out the window as if she'd like to fly right through it and away for good.

"Nina Marie, after all the talks we've had. You know how difficult my life was. That's why I told you about my own experience, so you wouldn't—"

"So I wouldn't have sex?" Her daughter's voice was acid.
"You did."

"So you wouldn't get *pregnant*." Jess heard her own tone. It
was just as harsh, just as angry, but goddamn it, she'd done everything she could so this wouldn't happen. She'd talked openly
about sex and the risks of disease and pregnancy from the time
Nina had first asked about it: how to say no, how to get away
from sexual predators. She'd brought home books, pamphlets
from the doctor's office. She'd even offered to take Nina to the
doctor for birth control when she got serious about her first
boyfriend the year before. Nina had refused, and wouldn't even
talk with her about anything related to the topic, saying that
Jess was invading her privacy. Nina never wanted to talk with
her about anything. Jess didn't even know when she had her
first big breakup until Rick mentioned something on the
phone, asking how Nina was dealing with being dumped.

"How far along are you?" Jess asked.

Nina's back softened from rigid to slumping, her shoulders
shaking. Jess walked up behind her, tried to embrace her, but
Nina jerked away.

Jess sighed. Surely it wasn't that far along. "Honey, there are
choices. You don't have to go through with this. One of the
doctors I know through work is very good at this sort of thing,
and she's very nice. It's not that big of a deal anymore, just a
simple medical procedure."

"What?" Nina whirled around, hair whipping, eyes fiery,
angry fists grazing Jess's abdomen and hip. "You want me to get
rid of it? Because that's what you wanted to do with me? Why
didn't you, then? Why didn't you just kill me before I could
ever come out?"

Jess tried to draw a breath, but it felt as though her lungs were deflating. She groped her way toward the bed and sat on it before her legs could give out. Nina was still looking at her that way, that horrible, hateful way.

How could she have said such a thing?

How could her own daughter despise her so much?

Jess's breath came back, then her voice, words measured and precise: "I—did—*everything*—for—you."

Nina yelled, her mouth red and wounded, her eyes narrowed and searing, but Jess didn't hear her, only her own words, growing louder and angrier.

"I carried you inside me for ten months, Nina, not nine. I gave long, hard birth to you, forty hours with no drugs, so you wouldn't start life with chemicals in your system. I sat up every night with you when you were colicky, when you were sick, when you were afraid of the tree outside your window that whole year when you were six. Even when your dad still lived here, it was always me, Nina. Always. I went to school around your schedule. I was always home to wake up with you and to be there after school. I put my needs aside and bought you clothes I couldn't afford, sent you on school trips I had to take out loans for. Why would I do these things?"

Nina had stopped yelling, her mouth agape, but Jess couldn't stop this ugly lament. Something had opened up inside her, and it wouldn't go away until she was cleared out.

"I protected you. I tried to keep you safe from bad people, from bad situations. And nothing bad has ever happened to you except that your parents got divorced. Well, forgive me, Nina, but I married a man who was a spoiled, selfish child, and I did that for you, too. Goddamn it, I gave up my whole fucking life for you. How dare you say I would do anything less?"

Nina started to sob. Jess would normally have stopped herself long before it got to this point, calmed down, and tried to hug her daughter at the sight and sound of her crying, but she couldn't. Not until this was straightened out. Not until she got Nina to understand. It was too important.

"You *hate me*," Nina said, voice shaking, incredulous.

"For god's sake, Nina, I love you." How did the kid not see that? "I just want you to make the best decision, for god's sake. You can have the baby and put it up for adoption, if you want to. You have choices, Nina. That's all I'm trying to say."

Nina ran past her into the kitchen. After a moment, Jess could hear her on the phone, pleading with her father to rescue her from this evil monster that hated her and was trying to make her abort her baby.

Jess stalked to the bathroom and sat on the closed toilet, trying to calm her anger before talking to Nina again. By the time she opened the door and walked back out into the living room, Nina was packing and Rick was on his way to pick her up. At the time Jess thought it was for a cooling-off period, but Nina never came home again.

After Teo was born, Rick moved the three of them four hours north to Tacoma, to be closer to his family, who would help take care of the baby when Nina went to school and, later, to work. Whoever the father had been had either fled from the responsibility or had been shut out, as Jess was, stripped of the privilege to be a mother, a grandmother. And every day, still, she tried in vain not to think about all she was missing.

# 10

I woke with a jump, drool on my cheek, and Pater put a hand on my shoulder. *Shhh,* he said very quietly. We could hear them, far away at first, down by the big creek. A man and a woman talking and crunching their feet down on all of our beautiful plants. We'd have to replant when they left. I wiped my face and hoped they wouldn't turn up our way, but their voices got closer. We could hear them slip and splash and curse, and then laugh.

"We sure aren't going to sneak up on anyone like this," the man said.

Pater pocketed his knife and slid down lower against the tree. We barely breathed as we listened to them.

Suddenly the woman said, "Oh, my god." The sound of her voice made chills run up and down my body; I even had goose bumps on my neck and my cheeks—everywhere. She sounded scared, like she'd found something horrible, but she couldn't have. It was just our forest, just our home.

"Police!" the man's voice called out.

I gasped. I'd thought these were the people who'd seen me by the trail.

We barely breathed. We were up and over the ridge, and they were down in our camp, but it felt like they were right there. If we could hear them so well, they would be able to hear us.

"Everyone out here in front of us, now, hands in the air!" the man shouted.

My stomach cramped. I suddenly had to go to the bathroom, really bad, but I stayed silent next to Pater, who'd closed his eyes. I think he was praying.

We heard them walking through our camp, remarking on everything we owned like they were in the Columbia Museum of Natural History or something, looking at dioramas of cave dwellers and native tribes.

"This must be how they refrigerate their food."

"God, do you think this is where they bathe?"

"Look, a stove!"

"How on earth do they keep everything so clean?"

It was like they expected us to be filthy creatures that ate raw squirrel meat or something. I tucked my head down and burrowed into Pater, just to feel his arms protecting me. *Please,* I prayed, *make these people go away and leave us alone.*

When Sweetie-pie flew out and made the man scream, Pater and I smiled at each other, me trying hard not to giggle. Then we heard another voice, like from a television, and the woman talking to it. She was on a radio, and we stopped

smiling. There were more coming. They weren't leaving anytime soon.

After a while the chopper went away for good, and I was
glad, because I know Pater hates that sound. He hates a lot of
sounds—sounds that come from big machines, trucks backfir-
ing, and jackhammers breaking up sidewalks in town. When
we have to walk past them, he gets a mean look on his face and
plugs up his ears, walking so fast to pass them that sometimes I
have to run to catch up. He doesn't talk to me until we've gotten somewhere quiet again, and then he'll look embarrassed
and ask me if I'm hungry, or thirsty, or if I need a restroom.
Pater doesn't like me to see him that way, but I know it's from
the war. He wasn't that way before he left.

We used to have a book with photographs in it, pictures of
all kinds of things: me as a big-eyed baby with a weird stand of
dark hair right on top of my pink head. A young Pater and
Crystal standing on skis in the snow in parkas and gloves, leaning forward on ski poles. Crystal's dark hair was blowing completely sideways, but they were smiling. There was a picture of
my grandpa and grandma Wiggs sitting on a couch, two-year-
old me between them grinning like a monkey.

There was also a photo of my grandparents' big house near
the reservoir, and a picture from when Crystal and Pater took
me swimming there when I was very young. I remember that
day, certain things about it, anyway. Most of the other pictures
became my memories, but this one I remembered first, and
could add details to, like the way the day was so hot, the smell
of suntan lotion on my arms, the feel of the wet towel on the
sand and me lying on it, digging my bottom and heels and el-
bows down to make an impression that fit only me. The sound

of Crystal laughing and the beer bottle clinking against her teeth. Pater running into the water like a crazy man, waving his arms and acting funny for me and Crystal. He was funny before he went to the war.

Nothing scared him back then.

He went to the war soon after that day at the reservoir. Crystal and I lived with Grandma and Grandpa Wiggs for a while, but she always fought with them, and then we moved into one of Crystal's friends' apartments in Glendale, but they fought, too, and then we lived in a motel room in Aurora, and then there were too many places to remember. Just like with the pictures: some I remember the smells and sounds and what it was like to be there, and others I just can't remember anymore. Who would want to remember them, or the people who came every night, or the sounds when it was dark?

There was a sound I always loved, though, and I imagine it every night before I go to sleep. When Crystal wasn't sick, she'd lie beside me on the couch or floor or wherever I was sleeping and put her arm around me and whisper, "Sweet dreams, kitten."

# 11

Jess and Jenkins climbed back down the rope ladder and joined Takei in scouring the encampment, making notes and diagrams, taking rough measurements. What could they find that would tell them where the camp's inhabitants had gone? Jess had looked through all the clothes and books before she came down from the tree, hoping to find clues, loose papers, but there was none. The person behind all this was ingenious. A survivalist, no doubt, or someone who'd been in the military. Jess held hope that he wasn't a sexual deviant, wasn't the sexual predator they'd been looking for recently, and so far nothing indicated he was: separate sleeping areas, and no—well—no stains anywhere, no porn. Nothing gross. Everything was tidy and clean, considering it was all out-of-doors.

It was 20:38 when they heard the others above them, uphill, the unmistakable freight-train sound of six boots crunching and sliding down on rock and dirt and woody flora, the grunt-ing, breathless conversation of men not accustomed to such strenuous conditions.

"Oh, yeah, they heard us coming all right," Jenkins said.

Jess wondered how far away the inhabitants were by now, and if they'd ever come back. She shook her head and walked toward the sounds of the other officers. They were descending a steep ridge southwest of the camp, and she wondered how she and Jenkins and Takei had gotten ahead of them. The others had been headed north when they parted.

"Ah, Christ," a weary male voice said, followed by the un-mistakable sound of bodies suddenly sliding and scrambling down the tangle of vines and brambles on the steep face of the ridge. Finally they came into view.

"Sarge, over here!" Jess waved.

He was red-faced and muddy down one side, as was Z, but Larry looked relaxed and happy, his tongue lolling to the side of his mouth as he picked his way carefully down the hill.

Z looked at her and smiled sheepishly. He was handsome; she'd give him that. He couldn't be over thirty-five. She didn't return his smile. That was the last thing she needed: another crush on someone she worked with. She'd been through that, on both sides of that, too many times to think it would ever be anything but a bad idea. The police force was like the dating service from hell, officers dating and mating indiscriminately; even married officers wanted to participate.

She turned away. They'd find their way now.

As she rejoined Jenkins and Takei, a human scream tore through the woods, followed by loud, desperate cursing. The three of them grabbed their weapons off their backs and ran north toward the sound, just past the camp.

A male voice yelled, "What the fuck is this? What the fuck?" The sound came from above them, where the hillside was vertical, and there was Greiner, lying nearly upside down, his foot and leg caught in a trench that had been dug in what looked like a stone wall, though it was just the earth cleared of foliage.

Everett, Z, and Larry were closer now but still descending. They'd stopped and drawn their weapons, too.

"It's okay!" Jenkins shouted, lowering his shotgun. "It's just Greiner. He fell."

"I didn't fall. I'm caught in some kind of booby trap," he cried. "Goddamn it! What the fuck is this?"

"Oh, man," Takei said quietly.

Jess looked at him, then back at where Greiner had fallen. "Oh, no," she said. "Oh, god."

Jenkins climbed toward Greiner to help him down, not seeing what he was climbing through on the vertical face.

"I guess it's them," Takei said.

Greiner's leg was stuck in the upper-right quadrant of the biggest swastika Jess had ever seen—maybe twenty feet across—carved deep into the earth.

Once Jenkins had Greiner's boot unstuck from the swastika, he helped him slide down to the bottom, then checked his ankle and leg. "It's not broken," he said, "but you'll probably have a pretty good sprain." Jenkins helped him to his feet, took his arm, and Jess realized how small David Greiner really was. He came only to Jenkins's armpit. Granted, Jenkins was well over six feet, a gentle giant, and it was clear he had kids from the tone of his voice. "Can you put weight on it? Does that hurt?"

"What do you think?" Greiner said, but he let Jenkins help him downhill to join the others.

They'd all gathered near the shelter that housed the camp kitchen. Takei pointed out the tree house, the latrine, the garden. They couldn't see the pools from where they stood, but Takei explained how they'd seen the tarp first, then the way the rock wall had been used to divert the creek for refrigeration and bathing. Jenkins and Jess showed them their diagrams and explained what they'd found so far.

"Okay, then," Everett said, folding his arms over his chest. Any hesitation or vulnerability Jess had witnessed earlier in him was gone. "Girl plus adult male plus encampment plus goddamn swastika equals dig-in time. We're here for the duration, folks."

No one objected. Jess gave silent thanks to the men around her. She blew the breath she'd been holding out into the silver dusky air—the same air the girl had breathed, was breathing maybe. Jess closed her eyes, as if to try to feel her presence in the forest.

The tug deep inside her abdomen was so forceful that Jess opened her eyes. No, this girl wasn't Nina, but she would find her, and do the right thing by her, no matter what.

They broke into pairs to search the surrounding area before it was completely dark. *Maybe they dropped something in their hurry*, Jess thought. She imagined bread crumbs, Hansel and Gretel; if the girl was being held against her will, she might think to leave something behind.

Z had found a way to pair with Jess; she wasn't sure how it

had happened. She'd have normally teamed up with Jenkins, but it seemed Greiner had taken a liking to his rescuer. She switched on her Maglite, and the three of them, Larry in the lead, headed away from the others in the murky dusk, moving generally north by northwest. At nearly 21:00, it was going dark. Jess hadn't eaten since a quick sandwich at lunch, but she wasn't hungry.

The others' voices faded as they climbed, taking it slowly. Z was in good shape and could have climbed the ridge like a mountain goat, but he took his cues from the dog, letting him sniff everything in a wide circle around them. Jess shone her flashlight so they could see what Larry intuitively knew was there, in dark recesses, around trees. They saw the occasional arc of others' flashlights, heard when they tripped and cursed, but it seemed the police officers were the only humans in the forest.

"Where are you, sweetie?" Jess said under her breath, wishing, hoping they'd somehow find her.

Ahead, Z and Larry crested the top of the steep ridge and suddenly there was commotion as they disappeared over the other side.

Jess's scalp tingled, as if electrical currents were flying through the air, and she raced uphill to join them. Her boot struck something large and solid, and she tumbled backward, somersaulting, sharp, hard things gouging her back, her right shoulder, the side of her face, until she came to a rest, panting. "Ow," she moaned, rubbing her shoulder. She opened and closed her hand, raised and lowered her arm. Nothing seemed broken, but the inside of her shoulder was on fire.

From above, Z yelled, "Backup! Backup!"

Jess scrambled to her feet. Adrenaline kicked in and she pulled herself up the steep face until she came upon Z just over the top of the ridge. He restrained a determined Larry, and pointed his flashlight at a huge downed log fifteen yards below them. She quickly drew her sidearm from her holster and held it with both hands in front of her, pointing at nothing, wondering what had happened to her shotgun when she fell. She couldn't feel it on her back. *Damn,* she cursed herself. The sharp, hard things.

"Police!" Jess yelled. "Get your hands up and get the hell out here where we can see you."

Who knew if they were facing a lone survivalist or a band of Nazi skinheads? Probably just one—the camp conditions indicated only one adult male—but they couldn't be sure. They heard movement in the brush, a whimper, then a shushing. It was a girl and she sounded distressed.

"Now, goddamn it!" Jess shouted more adamantly. "Get out here now!"

Z tucked his flashlight under one arm and radioed the others for backup, holding the dog back with the other hand.

Where the hell were these people? Jess quickly scanned back and forth in the murky light, seeing only a gray-scale forest, but then she saw it, the shape of a head just behind the downed tree. Keeping her sidearm trained on the shape, she reached carefully for her Maglite, clicked it on, pointed it there, and watched the back of a blond head duck out of sight. A girl's voice cried out, "Oh, no!"

"We've got them!" Z yelled. "Backup! Top of the ridge!" He dropped the radio and trained his flashlight back at the log.

They could hear the others scrambling below now, panting, trying their best to get to them as quickly as they could.

Jess advanced a step, trying to see better, and yelled down at the suspect, "Get out from behind that tree, now! We've got you surrounded! Give it up!"

The only sounds, the only movement, came from the other side of the hill as her comrades thrashed over brush and boulders to reach them, rays of LED light careening through the trees.

"Shit. What now?" Jess whispered to Z.

"I don't know. You're doing pretty good. Larry'll nail the guy if they run."

Everett reached them first, apoplectic from exertion. He had his sidearm drawn. "Where?" he panted.

"Spotted the top of a head just to the left of that branch," Jess said, pointing with the light beam. "Heard a female voice."

The others joined them and took tactical positions, Takei and Greiner drawing their AR-15s, Jenkins his shotgun. Jess and Z kept their lights focused on the log.

"Forward," Everett ordered, and they advanced, carefully, a step at a time. "Columbia Police!" he shouted. "Get the hell out here where we can see you."

Ten yards from the tree the light was better, the last of the dusky twilight filtering down through thinner treetops. Another two yards and they could see over the top of the log into a depression dug out on the other side, the back of a man huddled around what appeared to be an adolescent female. The two held on to each other with clawlike hands.

Jess gripped her weapon tighter. She hoped to god the man was unarmed.

"Hands up! Hands up!

"Get your goddamn hands in the air!"

"Police! Hands up!"

They all yelled at once, the surge of adrenaline racing through everyone. Even Larry lunged at the people, Z caught off guard and pulling hard to restrain him.

"Now! Get your motherfucking hands up now!" Greiner screamed especially frantically, and Jess winced at his choice of language in front of the girl.

The man and girl whipped their faces toward them. They looked like ghosts, the man lean and bearded, the girl small and wan, crying now.

"No!" she sobbed. "Don't kill us! Please don't shoot us!"

Bile rose in Jess's throat. She'd pointed her weapon at juveniles before, but never one who looked so very much like her own daughter.

Everett boomed, "Shut up! Everyone shut the fuck up!" and everyone did.

"Now, you," he said to the man, "get your goddamn hands up before we have to do something you don't want us to, not in front of the girl."

"No!" she screamed, hiding her face in the man's shoulder.

He cocked his head at Everett with a look of indignation, then turned to the girl and spoke gently. "They're not going to shoot us, Lindy. They don't shoot people who haven't done anything wrong." He turned toward them. "Right? Tell my daughter you don't shoot innocent, unarmed people."

Jess's hands trembled, but she kept her light and weapon trained on him.

Everett spoke in a normal tone: "Then get those hands up and step away from the girl, and send her out first."

The girl collapsed against the man's side, trembling and sobbing, and he looked back at Everett. "Promise you won't separate us. We've done nothing wrong."

"You do what we say and we—" Everett started, but Greiner advanced toward the man.

"Get your hands the fuck up, asshole, like the sergeant said!" He trained the barrel of his assault weapon dead on him. The man threw his arms in front of his face, cowering, and the girl screamed.

"Greiner!" Everett shouted. "Back the hell off!"

Greiner refused to back away or lower his rifle, agitated, and Jess guessed he was still pissed off at having fallen in the swastika. "Sergeant," he said, "we have no idea if he's armed or—"

"Drop your goddamn weapon!" Everett bellowed.

Greiner lowered his weapon, seething, but he said nothing more.

"Let's all take a deep breath," Everett said.

The girl calmed to whimpering, and the man finally raised his hands. The situation could still go bad, but Jess had new respect for the sergeant.

"Good," Everett said, never taking his eyes from the man. "Now, young lady," he said, "you come on out here, and we need your hands up, too."

She looked at the man. He turned to her. "Do what they say."

She rose to her feet and walked slowly around the log, her small hands raised, palms out. Her long brown hair was tangled on one side, like she'd been sleeping, and she wore a pink hoodie and jeans on her slight frame. Jess guessed she was eleven, maybe twelve. *She could be Nina at that age,* she thought. *She could be any kid getting off the school bus, or hanging out at the mall.*

Jess edged closer as the girl cleared the tree.

"No! Don't take me away from my father!" The girl flexed as if she might bolt.

Jess stopped. "It's okay. We're not going to take you anywhere. We're just going to talk to both of you."

Everett sighed and said to the man, "Go ahead and come on out now."

The man moved slowly, rising from his knees into a standing position as if it pained him.

"Hands behind your head," Everett said.

The man complied. He wore an olive green T-shirt and jeans, his beard on the scruffy side. He had no visible tattoos, and he didn't look like an addict, Jess thought. He was clean, healthy-looking. Except for the eyes. They had an unsettled look to them.

As soon as he cleared the log, Jenkins and Greiner were on him, each grabbing an arm and pushing him toward the nearest tree. The girl gasped. They forced him into a leaning position against it, bracing with his hands, and kicked his legs apart to search him as Z kept a light trained on them. The man kept looking back over his shoulder at the girl and she cried out, "Don't hurt my father, please! Don't take him away!"

"Calm down, now," Everett said. "We're just going to ask both of you some questions. See this nice lady here? This is Officer Villareal. She's going to find a place for you two to sit and talk."

Jess holstered her weapon and walked toward her, lighting the rocky path between them. The girl started to scream again.

Jess turned to Everett, who raised his light until her face was illuminated. "Wipe the blood off your forehead, Villareal. How'd that happen, for god's sake?"

Jess reached up and felt stickiness on her right temple, then wiped it as best she could with her sleeve. "I fell, Sarge, just like everybody else." To Lindy, she said, "It's nothing serious. I just fell down. It's tricky walking around here, you know? Especially in the dark, and especially for someone like me who doesn't get out in the woods much. I bet you never fall down, do you?"

The girl shook her head, keeping her eyes trained on her father, her pink-sleeved arms shaking as she held them in the air. She was slight but not unhealthily thin. She had pink in her cheeks and clean clothes, clean hair. Jess had a feeling that if she could see the girl's fingernails, they'd be clean, too.

"Look, I'm sorry, but I need you to unzip your hoodie and hold it open so I can see that you don't have anything under there."

The girl unzipped her sweatshirt with delicate, trembling fingers, then looked at her the same way Nina had whenever she'd been hurt, or experienced a disappointment, or didn't understand how the world could be so awful.

Jess had to take a deep breath before she could say, "Thanks, sweetie. Now pull it wide-open and turn around for me."

The girl complied, exposing an equally pink T-shirt.

"Thank you," Jess said. "You can zip back up. I have to look through your stuff, okay?"

The girl nodded but didn't come closer. After all the screaming, she'd gone mute.

Jess walked over to the log the girl and the man had been behind, seeing over it now with her flashlight: their blanket and backpacks and sleeping bags, a camouflage jacket and a girl's pale blue parka, the leftovers of a picnic. No visible weapons.

The backpacks held clothing, including the silver dress, toothbrushes, small towels, books, a Bible. A copy of *The Wind in the Willows*. Jess looked up at the girl and said, "That used to be my favorite."

The girl averted her eyes.

Jess called over to Everett, "Okay, Sarge. We're good."

# 12

I t felt like a dream, the worst bad dream, when they all pointed their guns at us and yelled. I couldn't understand their words. I couldn't think. My mind was bright white, lightning flashes, blood and murder. I thought they were going to kill us. I thought Pater and I were going to die right there, and I could even feel the heat of bullets in my chest, the sensation of metal exploding my heart. Why else would they point their guns at us if they didn't mean to kill us? All I could do was hold tight to Pater and scream for our lives.

After they put down their guns, after they searched us like criminals and made Pater sadder than I think I've ever seen him, they turned from nightmare monsters back into people. They spoke in normal voices, and asked us to do things that were odd, but they were mostly nice about it, even funny. The black man was the funniest, and the nicest. But the woman was nice, too.

She followed me down the hill to our camp, pointing her

flashlight in front of her, but I knew the way in the dark. I wondered if she had her gun drawn again.

We sat on the log stools that Pater and I made last winter, chiseling out the tops and smoothing them with sandpaper to fit our bottoms more comfortably. She sat in Pater's, but she didn't look comfortable.

"Okay, Lindy, right? Can you tell me your full name?" She held her big flashlight between her arm and her side, and wrote something in a blue notebook, waiting for my answer.

The two policemen who'd grabbed Pater brought him by the arms down the hill.

"Are they going to hurt him?" I asked.

"No, of course not," the policewoman said. "They're just going to ask him the same questions I'm asking you."

I kept watching them. They finally let go of his arms when they'd sat at our table beneath the cook tent, and then a lantern began to glow. Pater looked over at me and nodded. I tried to smile back.

"So," the policewoman said, "let's do this. Your full name?"

"Melinda Faith Wiggs." My voice was quiet. I wanted to hear what they were asking Pater, but I couldn't.

"Date of birth?"

"August eighteenth."

"Well, happy belated birthday," she said. "What year were you born?"

"Nineteen ninety-six."

She looked surprised. "You're thirteen?"

"But I do high school math and reading."

She squinted at me like I was a jigsaw puzzle she was trying to find the right piece for.

"Okay, Melinda. Lindy. What are you doing up here? Are you being held against your will?"

I rolled my lips together and shifted on my stump. I looked at the other police officers and that big, mean dog, everyone kicking up dirt, ruining my sweeping. There would be dust all over our books and our pots and pans. Everything would be dirty now. Everything would have to be cleaned.

The policewoman sighed and said, "Let's start with something else, then. Like . . ." She glanced around. "How about the bird that lives in your, uh, your tree fort, is it? Is it a pet? Whatever it is, it sure scared us a while ago." She smiled.

I shrugged and tried not to cry. Everything was ruined. I'd ruined everything. She flipped the page in her notebook, and handed it to me with her pen. "Maybe you'd feel more comfortable if you wrote it down."

I didn't know if she was trying to trick me, but I wrote:

*That isn't a tree fort. It's our house.*

She waited for me to write more.

*And Sweetie-pie isn't a bird. She's a barn owl. I don't know why she scared you because her wing feathers are fringed at the edges so they slice the air silently, not like other birds whose flapping you can hear coming from a mile away.*

*Just like we could hear you*, I thought, but didn't write. I handed the notebook back to her.

She pointed the flashlight at what I'd written, read it, and laughed. "You keep the notebook. You have a way with words.

I'll just keep my pages." She flipped back and tore out a few pages of notes and maps and diagrams, a bunch of blank ones for her to write on, then handed the notebook back to me. "Consider it a gift," she said, her head tilted. She looked at me in a way that felt like she knew what I was thinking, how I was feeling. I had to turn away.

"I'm sorry, Lindy. We just need to know more about you so we can determine if you're safe here. I have a daughter, too, and if she were in trouble, I'd want people like me to help her. We're just here to help you, okay?"

We both waited for something. I looked at Pater in the dimming light, his shiny blond hair held back in a rubber band. His beard needed trimming. I had been planning to do it after dinner. He was talking to the black police officer now, but he was watching me. He'd already forgiven me. I turned back to the policewoman. She had dark eyes like my mother. Like Sweetie-pie.

"What's your name?" I asked.

"Officer Villareal," she said, a name more beautiful than I could imagine or remember how to pronounce. "But you can call me Jess, if you want."

"Please don't let them hurt him. Promise me. Cross your heart. Promise?"

She looked at me that way again, but I didn't turn away this time. "We won't hurt him if he doesn't do anything that makes us have to," she said. "Has he, Lindy? Has he done anything to you that he shouldn't have? Anything inappropriate or sexual?"

"No!" I practically shouted.

Pater half rose from his seat across the way, and the short police officer jumped up.

It's okay, I mouthed to him, then looked back at the woman and whispered, "Why would you even say that?"

"Only to make sure you're safe," she said. "He can't hear us over here, Lindy. You can write it in the notebook. He'll never know what you've told me. Is this man really your father? Has he harmed you in any way?"

"Of course he's my father," I said, tears on the sides of my face. My nose was all runny. "He would never hurt me."

"His full name?"

I couldn't. I shook my head.

"How about your mother? Where is she?"

I'd probably already revealed enough for her to find out everything about me. Pater says our identities are not our own unless we keep them to ourselves. Was he telling them his name? About Crystal? About our lives? I looked over again. He was talking and the black officer was writing in his own notebook.

I turned back to the policewoman.

"If I tell you, do you promise to leave us alone?"

"I can't do that." She gave me a sad kind of smile. "But I can promise to make you safe."

"I am safe. We were safe, right here. We were fine."

"Then tell me about that, Lindy. Tell me about your life here, how you got here. Tell me why you think you're safe here."

We talked for a long time, just as Pater and the other officer did over in the cook tent. He kept looking over at me, like he was saying it was all right.

The telling wasn't as bad as I thought it would be, and after so much of the truth was out, I started to believe it might help Pater and me stay here in our forest, or I never would have told it.

"Okay, Lindy," Officer Villareal finally said, "I have to ask you one more important question."

I was glad it was nearly over. I just wanted to climb up into my bed and go to sleep for a long time, and wake up in the morning to find that this had just been an awful dream.

She paused, like she was trying to find the right words. "So, what is that over there, carved into the dirt?"

I thought everyone knew what it was. I told her as much.

She looked perturbed with me for the first time. "But, what does it mean to you, exactly?"

"It's our good-luck charm. It protects us."

I started to cry again. No matter what all those ancient people believed, the svastika had failed us.

# 13

As the dark grew denser, things that had become familiar to Jess—jutting tree limbs, rustling leaves, sticky webs—were startling once more. With only a fingernail clipping of moon and no clouds, not even Columbia's pink sodium city light could penetrate the treetops. The police officers' flashlights veered and dove like giant fireflies as they finished questioning the man and girl, wrote their notes, wandered into the woods to relieve themselves, and in Jess's case, to quickly retrieve her lost shotgun while the girl used the latrine.

Jenkins turned the man, one Raymond Wiggs, over to Takei for safekeeping, then went to join the other officers assembling out of earshot. They hadn't cuffed Wiggs, but Takei kept his automatic rifle at his side rather than on his back. The two stood silently in the cook tent under an old Coleman lantern, the cool glow lighting a ten-foot-diameter circle of dirt. The sergeant had yet to determine how to proceed.

Technically, they should charge Wiggs with recklessly endangering and/or failing to supervise a child. They were squatters. The girl had inadequate shelter and was truant. The law didn't take into account whether a parent had the means to provide what the state thought of as proper shelter; that was where social services came in, as lousy as that system could sometimes be.

What the letter of the law lacked was human consideration, Jess thought, the weighing of consequences. Compassion. That was why it was good that cops were real people, with families and lives and hardships of their own. They could interpret the law and try to apply it in a way that was best for the people involved, whether that was getting a drug dealer out of a neighborhood or releasing a drunken teenager to a parent who promised to get the kid help. If Jess hadn't believed in that her entire career, she would have gone into nursing or, god forbid, social work. The aim was to help, not to hurt.

She was glad Wiggs had decided to settle down and cooperate. Even though he apparently disdained society and anything that smelled of authority, he seemed to be holding it together for his daughter. Jess wondered what the consequences would be if they separated the two, placing the girl in foster care. Would that help her, or would it just rip apart an already struggling family?

Jess walked the girl over to her father. "We're going to have a meeting to decide what to do next, so you and your dad need to hang out here with Officer Takei, all right?" The girl had dark smudges under her eyes now. It was 22:30, probably past her bedtime.

"Don't worry," Jess said. "It shouldn't take too long. Are you hungry? Do you need some food?" The girl shook her head. Jess realized she herself was starving.

Lindy walked into her father's embrace. He leaned down and laid his cheek against the top of her dark head, face lingering there. "Put your coat on," he said, then looked up at Jess. "I should make a fire. She's cold."

The temperature had dropped with the dark. Jess looked at Takei. He shrugged. He had the situation under control. "Sure," she said.

Somehow this man had maintained his dignity in front of his daughter through all of this. He'd been screamed at, held at gunpoint, threatened, searched, interrogated—things that might make another man feel powerless or broken.

Lindy still clutched the notebook, along with Jess's favorite pen. The man nodded at Jess—a silent thanks, she guessed. His eyes no longer looked distant or crazy. He was just a dad, glad to have his daughter safe beside him.

Jess nodded back, then turned away. If the sergeant decided to take Lindy into protective services, she and her father would be separated for days, maybe weeks. Maybe forever, if they determined he wasn't a fit parent. Lindy looked young, but she was obviously wiser than her years. She might have been lacking in the ways of teens raised in more conventional settings, but Jess didn't think that was such a bad thing.

The girl was intelligent and articulate, and she had a compassion for nature and living things that left Jess feeling both awed and guilty. Had she exposed Nina to enough of the world, to nature that didn't exist in a zoo or a Disney animated film? Had she expected enough of her, or had she let her skate the easy suburban route through life, watching too much TV, never developing interests in anything except for the gender-specific fluff society presented her with, clothes and gossip and boys? Was that where she'd let Nina go wrong?

There'd been a time when Jess thought she'd be the kind of parent who took her child to museums and libraries, on hikes and vacations to national parks. In fact, she'd promised Nina a trip to Disney World for years. They'd gotten as far as the Oregon coast on a small handful of occasions, up into the mountains once or twice. *Why didn't I just make it happen?* she wondered. Why hadn't she done a lot of things?

Jess stood in the dark forest, as far removed as she could be from the day Nina left three years earlier. The old grief still haunted her, still gripped her chest like a claw, and made her ask the big question: *Why didn't I do more to make her stay?*

She shook her head, drew a breath. She had to focus; she had to get on with the job at hand. The shushing of tree boughs eddied around her, midway between the man and girl and the group of officers assembled at the other side of the camp.

Jess forced herself to repeat her mantra: *I am not the worst parent in the world.* She'd seen far worse, of course, and Nina had turned out okay. She hadn't ended up a druggie or an alcoholic or even a smoker; thank god she had never cut herself or had other self-destructive tendencies. She'd graduated from high school only one semester late and found an administrative job she liked with an insurance agency in Tacoma. And now she'd saved enough money so that she and Teo could live in their own apartment. She was a computer-savvy young woman, attuned to American culture, to society, and she knew how to survive in the world she was inheriting. That world would probably make hamburger of Lindy, if she were forced back into it. Jess drew a deep breath and held it, then went to join the other officers.

They'd convened on the log steps she, Jenkins, and Takei had first walked up. She took a seat next to Z and the dog on the top step. Greiner and Jenkins stood behind them and Everett stood facing the group at the bottom. They each shone their flashlights at a central spot between them, their own campfire of sorts.

She and Jenkins had compared notes earlier, and now shared the man's and the girl's stories with the group. The parity of their statements made even Everett shake his head and whistle. Their histories of moving from Colorado to Oregon after the father came home from Iraq, the mother's apparent drug use and negligence, the anxiety they both felt over her trying to find them, their daily routines—the seemingly normal routines of a father doing an admirable job raising a daughter with no help, no money, and no home.

It didn't happen this way, that two stories matched so exactly, not when those being questioned hadn't had time to put their heads together, and not when one of them was a juvenile.

After debriefing, radioing in for results on the background checks, and compiling their data, now they needed to come to some kind of conclusion. It was gut-check time.

Jess reached to pet the scruff of Larry's warm furry neck. If it hadn't been for him, they might never have found Ray and Lindy. They were well camouflaged, well hidden, and it had only been their scent that drew the dog to them. He'd done his job admirably, no matter what the consequences.

"Good puppy," Jess said softly. Even in his sleep, he sighed and his body stretched in contentment at the compliment. Her own body ached, especially her right shoulder, and hamstrings, and feet. Her temple throbbed, and she was famished. Everyone else had to be feeling worse for wear, too, but no one complained.

"Let's wrap up," Everett said. "The facts as you see them, Officer Villareal."

"Well," Jess said, determined to argue her case persuasively, "we've verified they're who they say they are, Raymond and Melinda Wiggs, formerly of Aurora, Colorado. Mother is out of the picture and seems to be a practicing drug addict, hasn't filed for custody or pressed any charges that we've been able to track down. Father has no outstanding warrants, no priors, and one tour of duty in Iraq. The girl appears healthy, well educated, well adjusted, and their relationship seems appropriate and beneficial to her. Other than camping illegally, I have to say I'm searching my brain for what they've done wrong. I mean, is she really in danger?"

Z nodded beside her.

From behind them Jenkins cleared his throat. Jess turned to look at him.

"Officer Jenkins?" Everett pointed his flashlight high enough so they could see Jenkins's face.

"Well, to be honest, I do think we have a child in danger here. She's living out in the open. She's not enrolled in school. They have no visible means of support other than a small disability pension. And, uh, we haven't actually ascertained yet whether or not there's been any sexual or physical abuse." He shrugged. "That's how I see it."

Jess drew her lips tight against her teeth, trying to nod. He was entitled to his opinion.

"What about the swastika?" Greiner said. "Isn't anyone going to mention that?"

"It's moot," Z said. "How often do you get two separate stories that line up like this? I mean, they each said it was a symbol of good luck and protection and happiness and all that stuff. That's how they view it, and as far as I know, freedom of expression still exists."

"Barely," Jess muttered, and Z smiled, glancing at her sideways.

"But—" Greiner tried.

"It checked out when I had them Google it at the station," Jenkins said. "Svastika, an ancient Sanskrit symbol, an ancient Native American symbol, an ancient—"

"That doesn't matter," Greiner said. "Not since Hitler. Everyone knows what it's a symbol for now. Maybe not the girl, but I don't buy that this guy doesn't mean it exactly the way everyone means it now. He's a survivalist. He's from freaking Colorado. I mean, don't they breed white supremacists there?"

"Sarge," Jess complained. How was this a sane and rational discussion between police officers?

Greiner wouldn't stop. "And give me a break. The guy's obviously got some pretty serious post-traumatic stress going on. Isn't anyone concerned about that?"

"We get it, Officer," Everett snapped. "And there aren't many boys coming back without some shell shock. He's clearly competent."

"And how about the press?" Greiner continued. "They're gonna have—"

"Enough," Everett barked. "The press isn't going to hear about this. Not if I can help it. Not yet anyway. Agreed?" He shone his light in each officer's direction, and they all nodded, except Greiner.

"Agreed?" Everett steadied the beam of light on Greiner's face. "We're not going to do either of these people any good by selling them out to the media or by leaking rumors. You're a professional, Officer Greiner, and you'd damn well better act like one, or I will personally kick your ass. Do I have your cooperation?"

Greiner flinched and nodded.

Everett dropped the light to the center and blew a long breath. "Jenkins is right, though. We can't let them keep on living here. Even though it's a clean, well thought-out camp, it's a camp. I think we might overlook the illegal camping charge, but we can't let a kid live like this. We have to get DHS involved . . ."

There was a collective groan.

"I know," Everett said. "DHS isn't perfect, but nothing is. So, I want to take a poll. Anybody think we should charge Wiggs with child endangerment?"

Greiner twitched, but no one moved.

*Thank god,* Jess thought.

Everett continued. "Okay, then, who thinks the girl should be in foster care?"

Feet shuffled. Jess held her breath, hoping no one would say anything, but Greiner said, "I do."

After a moment, Jenkins said, "Ah, hell. I do, too."

Everett shone his light at Larry, who slept soundly. "Dog man? Villareal?"

Jess looked at Z. He had his hand on the dog's back, watching it rise and fall as Larry breathed in and out.

"I guess we should," he said, looking back at Jess. She turned away.

"Villareal?" Everett asked again.

Her jaw tightened. "I disagree."

"I had a feeling."

"Not because I'm female."

"I know that, Villareal," he said. "It's because you're difficult."

Everyone laughed and Larry stirred. Jess put her hand on his head. It was as soft as a baby's blanket.

"Could we just let them get a good night's sleep?" she asked. "Come back for them tomorrow?" Even she could hear it— this wasn't Officer Villareal talking. It was Jess the mom, and she clamped her teeth together to prevent any further outbursts.

"No way," Greiner said. "They'll bolt."

"It's gotta be tonight," Everett said, "but first we have to get Wiggs to agree to walk out. Jenkins, I want you and Villareal on that. You've established the relationships with them. Tell Mr. Wiggs we can't let them camp here illegally, but we'll help them out all we can with housing and public assistance, school, all that stuff. Don't tell him about taking the girl away, though. Let's break that one to him when we get to the vehicles. No need to make it any more traumatic than it has to be for either of them."

The meeting broke and Jess watched Jenkins walk toward the small campfire Ray had built.

She turned to Everett. "Sarge, can I talk to you alone for a minute?"

He looked at her in the dim light filtering up from their lowered flashlights. Was it the Halloween trick of light, or did he look older than he had when they started out that day? He nodded, and they walked down the log steps toward the creek.

"I'm concerned," Jess said quietly. "What do you think this guy's going to do when we take her from him? What if he grabs one of our weapons? What if he takes her hostage, tries to run off with her? Are we going to give chase? How hard are we going to pursue him?"

"I know, I know," Everett said. "We still have to do it. We're trained public-safety officers, Villareal. We don't lose control of our weapons"—he'd known all along, and Jess felt the sting of shame he intended—"and we don't let him near the girl once we're near the vehicles."

"No further discussion?"

"No further discussion."

"Yes, sir." Jess turned and walked back up the steps, waiting until she was far enough away in the dark to shake her head. Why not just take them to a shelter? That would be least damaging thing for the girl, and the most humane thing to do for both of them. And if they were going to split them up, they should at least wait until they were back at the station.

As she neared the campfire, she patted her shirt pockets, her pants pockets, looking for her cell phone. It must have gone flying when she fell. She had to go find it. The route was becoming familiar now, even in the dark.

"I'll be right back, Ellis," she called to Jenkins.

He nodded his chin at her and turned back to Takei, Ray, and Lindy on log stools around the fire, everyone smiling, even Takei. That damn Jenkins—he'd probably told them the goofy frog joke, the one he dragged out whenever dealing with scared juveniles. She'd always loved that about him, but this time it was only going to make things worse for the girl, building her trust in them just to snatch it away.

Climbing back up the embankment she'd tumbled down, Jess felt every muscle in her thighs and calves and feet working overtime; she hadn't tortured them this much since she'd tried out for track in high school. She pushed herself up every step with a hand on each thigh. When she got to the area where she'd found her weapon, she stooped over, breathing heavily. She'd have to take half a bottle of ibuprofen to get any sleep when she got home.

Slowly panning the flashlight back and forth across the ground, she stopped at the jutting rock that had tripped her, looking for the glint of plastic that would be her phone. She got down on her knees, feeling through the foliage, raking her fingernails against dirt, afraid she might grab something reptilian or buggy, but nothing. She moved back, expanding the search area, skimming the light over more crumpled ferns and digging through vines and pine needles. She'd have to borrow someone else's phone, call her number to hear it ring. Wouldn't her fellow officers love that? Maybe if she asked Jenkins, he'd keep quiet about it.

"Damn," she said, pushing on her thighs again to stand up.

Small creatures skittered in the dark; a breeze rushed through the branches overhead, sending down more pine needles and their woody aroma. She was about to give up when she heard a comforting sound, the *beep beep*ing of her phone, notifying her she had a message. She followed the sound with her flashlight until she saw the phone resting against the root of a tree many yards downhill from where she'd hit the ground. No wonder she hurt so much.

Quickly, she picked it up and dialed voice mail.

"Jessica?" Her mother's voice, as if expecting her to speak. "Oh, well, I just wanted you to know that Nina called tonight—"

Jess's heart stopped.

"—and she's thinking about driving down with Mateo for his birthday this weekend. He told her that's what he wants, to see his grammy and great-grammy. Isn't that the sweetest thing? That child . . ."

Jess clicked off and scrolled through her missed calls. Nina hadn't even tried calling her. She punched her mother's number up and hit SEND.

"Oh," Clara said. "Hello?" As if she didn't know what a phone was for.

Jess took a breath to steady herself, trying to calm the tension in her voice, erase the stress of the night's events, of the strained relationship between them.

"Hey, Ma. Great news about Teo and Nina. Maybe we can have a party or something. I'm on a crazy one tonight. I'll call you tomorrow." She needed to get back.

"Is everything all right, Jessica? What's going on?"

"No, it's fine." Why had she said "crazy"? "Just a case."

Her mother harrumphed. "You're too old to be on patrol. It's too dangerous. Why can't you just take that detective test or find some other kind of job? I hate having to worry about you every single night."

"Then don't, please, okay?" It was a recurring conversation Jess hated. "You should go to bed. It's late."

"Do you have any idea how it feels to wonder if your daughter has been hurt, or in an accident, or—"

"Do you think I don't worry about Nina? That I don't worry about that girl and Teo every single day, still? How can you even say that?"

Her mother was silent.

"I mean . . . come on, Ma."

"Please, don't. I'm just so worried about you, all the time. Every night is a nightmare for me, wondering if you'll . . . if it will . . ." Her voice broke and Jess knew she should apologize, but couldn't bring herself to.

"It's not gonna happen again, Ma. No god would let it happen twice." Of course this wasn't about Jess, not really. It was about her father.

After a long moment and the sound of her mother blowing her nose, Jess said, "Look, I'm sorry. Can we just talk tomorrow? I have to get back."

"Call me in the morning to let me know you're all right."

Jess wished she hadn't snapped at her almost as much as she wished she hadn't called her back. It had been a weak moment at the mention of Nina and Teo.

As she returned to the group around the fire, a long, loud screech burst across the sky. Jess screamed much the way Jenkins had earlier in the day—like a terrified little girl.

"What the—" Jenkins yelled now, and they all turned to track the sound across the camp and into the trees as it died out, replaced by the sound of something so lovely that Jess thought maybe she was dreaming. It was Lindy laughing.

She looked at the girl, her small, pretty face lit by amber light. She'd clapped her hand over her mouth the way young teen girls did probably the world around. Takei tried not to smile as he shook his head; Jenkins had his forehead in his hand. Ray looked at the fire, amused, it seemed.

"Stupid owl," Jenkins muttered.

Lindy's face was animated now, the tired smudges gone from her eyes. "Isn't that the most horrifying sound?"

"Well, yeah!" Jess put her hand over her heart. "That is definitely something. Was that Sweetie-pie?"

Lindy shrugged and leaned sideways into Ray. "Probably, but there are other owls in the woods, you know."

He gently knocked his knuckles against her knee. "Don't be rude, Lindy. Respect your elders."

"Sorry," she said, but still she smiled.

Ray shook his head, a smile lurking but not quite materializing, and he and Jess briefly made eye contact over the fire. He looked away and said, "We'll be needing more of our belongings."

"Well, whatever you two can carry yourselves," Jenkins said. "Ten minutes, okay?"

Ray nodded and stood. "Come on, Lindy. Bring your pack." The two of them stood and slipped their arms beneath their backpack straps, then walked to the base of the tree and climbed easily up the rope ladder, Lindy first and Ray following when she'd arrived at the top.

Jess turned to Jenkins. "How'd you get him to walk out?" she whispered.

"I just told him we couldn't let them stay here, and that

we'd help them find a new place to live. He didn't like it much, but he seems to be on board."

"Good job," she said. Maybe she had Ray all wrong.

"Takei," the sergeant barked from across the camp, "over here for a minute." Takei stood and walked to the sergeant, and they slipped into the dark, their voices a low murmur.

"Everett must be polling him. No way Takei is going to sway the vote," Jenkins said. "He's a nice guy and all, but, man, I've never seen anyone more regulation than him."

"I don't know," Jess said, rubbing her sore shoulder. "I think there may be a human buried in there somewhere."

Jenkins sighed and took a seat on the log Lindy had vacated. "I just kept picturing my kids, you know?" He held his palms in front of the small fire. "What if they had to live like this? I mean sure, Troy would probably love camping out for life, but . . ." He sighed. "I'm sorry, but I had to vote the way I did."

"Shut up, Ellis," Jess said, kicking dirt toward him. "You gotta do what you gotta do. I know that." She watched as a light began to glow from the tree house, another lantern, and Ray's and Lindy's shadows stretched tall across the structure and trees and into the dark. "We all have to. I just hope this goes well." She looked back at Jenkins and made a grim face. "You know?"

"Yeah, I know," he said. "It will. We'll make sure."

"That's what we do."

"That is what we goddamn do," Jenkins said. "We make sure everything and everybody are all right. All the time. Every day. Every minute." He stared into the fire, then sat up and stretched. "I'm beat."

Jess stifled a yawn. "Me, too."

"And hungry."

"I was starving but now I think I'm past it," Jess said.

"And sore! Are you sore?" Jenkins rubbed his lower back with both hands. "I thought I was in shape. I've been lifting, and run—"

He stopped. They heard rustling behind them and swung around. Greiner materialized out of the dark.

"Maybe we could cut the chitchat and put out that fire," he said. "I'd like to get the hell out of here before midnight." He stood outside the warm glow of light.

"Hey, lighten up, buddy," Jenkins said, and Jess marveled at how he could make such sentences sound almost congenial. "Take a load off. It'll only be a few minutes. They're packing up some of their stuff. It'd be hard to leave everything behind. This is their life."

"Yeah, well—" Greiner lowered his voice and sidled closer. "They probably stole half this crap anyway."

Jess met Jenkins's eyes for a long moment, but neither spoke.

Greiner stomped his boot down on the embers, sparks flying up and dying out, turning into dust.

# 14

When Pater and I climbed into the tree house to pack more stuff, he sat me down on my bed first, before he even lit the lantern. He asked me in a whisper if I was doing okay and he said he was sorry this was happening. I started to cry again, because I was the one who'd caused it, but he took my hand in the dark. No, Lindy, he said. It's not your fault. You wouldn't even be here if I was working, if we had a place. I shouldn't have given up so easily.

I knew he felt ashamed, but I remember those first few years when he was always looking for a job like he had before the war, doing construction, and being told no. Nobody would even let him wash dishes or pump gasoline. He said it was because everybody was afraid of being sued when his back acted up.

I asked him where they were going to take us, and what they were going to do with us. I really wanted to ask when we'd be able to come home, but I was too afraid of the answer to let those words come out.

He was quiet for a moment, then said, I don't know yet, but the Emergency Plan is still in effect. Pay attention. If there is an opportunity, I will let you know.

I stopped crying and nodded, even though he couldn't see me. I needed to be strong. I needed to be ready for anything. I could already feel Reverend Rosetta's cool, plump arms around me and smell her baby-powder scent. And when Reverend Rosetta sings, you know there is a god who will watch over you and take care of you, even if the people in your life can't anymore.

Back when we still lived in the motel, Pater and I would walk to the tiny, dusty grocery store I liked on Martin Luther King Jr. Boulevard to stock up on apples and bananas, Rice Krispies and milk, cheese and saltines—things we didn't have to cook. Back in room 116 we had a Styrofoam cooler filled with ice from the machine by the motel office.

One morning, we set out for the store because the rain had stopped, finally, but we kept getting splashed by cars racing through puddles beside us like we didn't even exist. I was mad at the drivers, and upset about getting wet when it wasn't even raining and I'd put on my favorite sweater, but Pater said, They're just not thinking, Lindy. We're all guilty of it from time to time.

It had to have been a Sunday because we could hear singing, the church kind of singing, but not like we'd ever heard in Colorado at the church Grandma and Grandpa Wiggs went to. The sound of ten thousand angels filled the steeple of the big gray church coming into view, and their voices were soaring

out into the sunny morning. Pater stopped, and he got a look
on his face I hadn't seen in a long time. Since his job had fallen
through, he'd been wearing a blank expression, the one that
meant something was wrong but he wasn't going to tell me. He
looked down and pinched my nose; then we walked right past
the grocery store and through the doors of the City of Refuge
United Church of Christ.

I don't remember much about our first time there, other
than the singing and my childish amazement that so many black
people could be in one place, but I do remember the feeling I
got, and the one I still get every time we set foot through the
big purple doors and under the rainbow banner inside: over-
whelming happiness and peace. Pater said we were called there
for a reason, and pity the man who doesn't answer his calling.

# 15

They assembled once again on the steps to walk out, Ray and Lindy each wearing overstuffed backpacks, bedrolls strapped beneath, and carrying their own flashlights. Jess wanted to tell them they wouldn't need their sleeping bags, that shelters and foster homes had beds and blankets, but she knew this was what they had to do—assume they were in control of their own destinies for as long as possible. It was what everyone wanted, every suspect she'd ever cuffed, every dirtbag she'd ever testified against, every apologetic speeder she'd let off the hook. If only she were in charge tonight. She'd have talked with them, listened to their story, then thanked them and walked way. Who were they hurting by living there illegally? Jess wasn't usually one to turn a blind eye to the law, but everything was different this night, even her.

Lindy turned to look at her over the bobbing beams of flashlights, struggling to get her backpack into place. Jess would have worried about the girl carrying that much, but she was strong and lithe. She had her dad's wiry build. Five years of traversing the rugged terrain, of climbing up to bed each night, down each morning, of carrying supplies in from town clearly had made her strong. Even the task of making a meal must have been arduous, ferrying food and water up the hill every single time. Nina had always complained when Jess asked her to help unload groceries from the car in the garage.

"I'm guessing you have a better route out of here than we do," Everett said to Ray, who shrugged.

"It's steep."

"Hell, we've been doing steep all day. If it'll get us down faster, let's do it. It's going to be pretty treacherous for us in the dark, though, so let's take it easy. I don't want anyone getting hurt."

"Yes, sir," Ray said. Military training, Jess knew, and perhaps a religious upbringing, but she sensed genuine respect there, too. She respected Sergeant Everett herself. How many commanding officers would ask each officer for his or her opinion on a case like this? He was being as fair as he could. As much as she didn't want to do what the sergeant had ordered, she had to. She was a good police officer, and good cops, like good soldiers, followed orders and respected their senior officers. She'd known that all her life—it was her father's creed.

"Move out," Everett said, and they began to move forward, forming a single line with Ray at the lead, then Lindy, then Everett close behind. Jess guessed the sergeant imagined he could catch them if they ran off. He should have put Z next, or Jenkins or Takei, but the man had a healthy ego. Jess almost hoped they would run off, but who knew what would happen then? There was a lot of firepower among the search team and at least one hair trigger.

The walk down was steeper than steep, vertical in many spots. They each shone their lights at the feet in front of them so that everyone had a good view of what was coming next, but it didn't matter. Each step presented a new challenge, and Jess's thighs ached with the tension.

Ray and Lindy nimbly picked their way among loose rocks and dirt, through knee- to waist-high brambles, never once grabbing at the slim alder trunks or for handfuls of fern fronds as the rest of them did. And they did this while wearing heavy backpacks, no less. At one point they veered out of sight to stay on whatever path they somehow saw, and Everett slid downhill past them, not quick enough to recover. The rest of the officers rushed forward, skidding, sliding down the near vertical face until they caught back up to Ray and Lindy, who still descended steadily. Greiner had to be shitting himself that they weren't just running off, Jess thought.

After thirty minutes they found themselves on a hiking path far less steep and far more easily navigated. Jess shone her light at a small wood sign at the side of the path: "Chickaree Trail." They were now in the wildlife sanctuary trail system and would probably be at the parking lot soon. They might even have walked this path coming up, when it was daylight and beautiful. Stars glimmered through the treetops, and Jess thought she could hear the soft *who-hoot*ing of an owl in the distance. She tried not to let emotion overrun her sense of logic; there were many owls in the woods, as Lindy had said. But she couldn't help wondering if Sweetie-pie had followed them down to keep an eye on the girl or to say goodbye.

They walked quietly now, no more grunting or falling, only the regimented marching of boots. They'd survived the forest, the night. They'd each go back to their homes, to their families, to their familiar beds, and wake to familiar faces. Everyone, of course, but Ray and Lindy.

AS THE EXTERIOR LIGHTING OF the wildlife sanctuary came into view, Jess grew uneasy once again, wondering what would happen next. She looked at her watch. It was a quarter till midnight.

"Damn, that only took forty-five minutes," Jenkins said. They walked in a formless group now; the trail had widened into a paved superhighway for bird-watchers and hikers.

"It usually takes us only thirty-three minutes," Lindy said, and Jess saw Ray nudging her, telling her to mind her manners.

Maybe everything would work out. Maybe Lindy would be fast-tracked through the system, seeing as she did have such a capable parent. Maybe they'd let Ray visit her every day. When the juvenile court decided to let her go, maybe they'd have a fresh shot at a life in civilization, with help from Uncle Sam.

*Right,* Jess thought, trying to imagine what the family-court judge would make of Ray's choices heretofore, of the decision to leave Colorado and Lindy's mother behind, without court-approved custody arrangements in place. The mother was undoubtedly an unfit parent, but she had no convictions, no record—they'd already checked. If worse came to worst, DHS might even ship Lindy back to Colorado and let the family courts there wrangle with the case.

They reached the parking lot, three shiny patrol cars parked in a row. The sergeant was going to have to act quickly to get Ray and Lindy separated somehow. Everyone seemed nervous now: the officers watching Everett, Ray watching the officers, Lindy watching Ray.

"All right, listen up," Everett said, and they grew still. The overhead light cast deep shadows beneath his eyes and turned his skin sallow. "Now, we have to take care of some procedural matters here."

This was it.

Jess tried to catch Lindy's eye to smile at her, to send a message that she would help her and be on her side, but the girl clung to her father's hand and didn't take her eyes from him.

Everett continued. "What we're going to do is ask you, Ray, if you'll consent to letting us fingerprint both you and Lindy back at the station. That way we follow procedure and make my commanding officer happy that you're who you say you are."

The sergeant was lying. Jess sighed, but she knew he was trying to make the situation safer before separating them. He had the authority to let them go, even now, but he had no intention of letting that happen. Could Ray tell? She looked at him, but he appeared calm. He touched Lindy's shoulder, as if to assure her.

Everett ushered the two into the sterile plastic backseat of Jenkins's squad car and closed the car door, then walked back over to the others. Once the father and daughter were inside behind the car's closed door, the officers breathed a little easier.

Jenkins had driven Takei in one cruiser, and Jess had brought the sergeant in another. She was surprised Everett didn't put the Wiggses in her car so he could ride back with them.

"All righty, then, Officers," Everett said, clapping his hands together, "good job tonight. You're relieved of duty. Greiner and Z, you can go on back to South. Jenkins and I will take these folks into North and print them. Takei and Villareal, clock out early when you get back to the station and go home. Don't worry. You'll be paid for a full shift."

Jess looked at Jenkins, who shrugged. Why did he get to stick with the case, she wondered, and not her?

"And don't go talking about this, not to anyone. Keep it on the q.t. for now. Let's not make it a circus for these folks. We're going to try to let them get back on with their lives as best they can."

"I'd like to complete my shift and help with the girl, Sarge," Jess said, feeling the jut of her chin. Her brothers had always called it her tough-chick face, the face she wore to get them to stop teasing her or tormenting her with slugs. The face she now wore whenever things started to go south and it felt that only she could fix it. She didn't know what was happening, exactly, but she had a feeling Lindy might need her.

Everett cocked his head at Jess. "I said you're relieved, Officer. Go on. Skedaddle."

His tone was dismissive. Sarcastic. Her hands trembled; she balled them into fists. "Sir, I'd like to see this through. I have a good rapport with the girl, and I think she trusts me."

He studied her for a moment, then lowered his voice. "You're on board, then?"

Jess jerked her head in what she hoped he'd interpret as a nod.

"Fine. You can take her to foster care after we've checked out their prints." He turned toward the cars.

She knew Ray and Lindy couldn't hear him from where they sat in the closed squad car, but still she cringed, hearing him say it out loud. "Sarge?"

"What?" he snapped without looking at her.

"Did Takei vote to let her go? Is that why you were sending us home?"

"Gee-yawd, Villareal, this is why I do not enjoy the company of females, other than my daughter. Just go to the station."

"Yes, sir," she said, and headed toward her car. At the sound of his car door opening, she stopped. "And by the way, Sergeant, I won't turn you in for sexual discrimination. I'm sure you're just tired and didn't mean to say that."

His car door slammed as she dropped into the driver's seat next to Takei. Her hands wouldn't stop shaking.

"That wasn't too bright," Takei said, head turned away. "I thought you were smarter than that, Officer."

"Oh, bite me, Steven," she said, fumbling her seat belt buckle into place. "He's trying to get rid of us because we voted against reporting her to DHS. Just what other ramifications do you think our honesty might have on our careers? I mean, why ask if you're going to use the answers against us?"

"How do you know how I voted?" he asked, turning to look at her now. The other cars pulled away, red taillights disappearing into the dark. Jess rotated the key in the ignition.

"Call it a wild-ass guess," she said, and put the car in drive.

It took only twelve minutes to drive back to the station house. Jess pulled in behind Jenkins's car and switched off the ignition. The others had already gone inside. Darryl the car wrangler walked over and leaned down. She lowered her window as Takei got out of the other side. "Hey, Darryl," she said, "how's your night going?"

"Not so good. Had a puker tonight, and a bleeder. I hope your car's clean."

"Pristine," she said as he opened the door for her. She started to climb out and felt every muscle she'd overtaxed in the woods. "Damn," she said. "No wonder Maddy hates to hike." In the short ride back, she'd stiffened up like a corpse.

"You guys had a rough one, I hear," he said. "That's why I like my job, other than cleaning up puke and blood and shit. I just polish up these babies, feed 'em some oil, rotate the tires, and my day is done."

"Yeah," Jess said, shouldering the shotgun on her good side. "That would be nice. I envy you, Darryl." She smiled and limped after Takei toward the employee entrance.

After quick stops to stow her shotgun, use the restroom, and wash the grime from her face and hands, Jess headed up to check in with the lab on the prints.

She passed Jenkins in the hall. "What's up?" she asked. "Where're you going?"

"Home," he said, smiling. "Sarge said I could clock out early. Thank you for volunteering to stay. I'm going to have me a nice long shower, a big old beer, then hit the hay."

Jess smiled. "Say hi to Maggie for me."

Jenkins clopped down the steps. "I will do more than say hi to my wife, thank you very much. I might just get lucky. Hell, it's only . . . Damn, it's past midnight. I gotta hurry!"

"You go, Ellis," Jess said, wishing she'd have someone waiting for her at home, a warm body to nuzzle up to at the end of this long, long day. But she'd been going home to an empty house for so long, she wondered if she even could sleep with someone else in her bed anymore.

Jess passed the conference room on her way to the lab, and saw Lindy busily writing in the notebook she'd given her, Ray sitting and staring at nothing. Maybe she could find him a newspaper or something to read, at least.

Inside the lab, the bored tech glanced up from her computer. "Still running," she said, so Jess ducked into Sergeant Everett's office. He was on the phone but nodded toward a chair. Jess sat, her quadriceps aching as she did. Everett doodled on his desk pad, listening intently to whoever was at the other end.

"Duly noted," he said, "but I'm still not making any comment." He hung up and looked at her. "That was fucking KCMB-TV. Goddamn fucking son of a bitch."

"Who blabbed?" she asked, but she knew.

"Guess," he said.

She shook her head. "That was fast. What now?" This was not good news for anyone. Not Ray and Lindy, not the department. The public scrutiny of everyone involved began now.

"We gotta do everything on the up-and-up, no favors, no emotional decisions. We should probably just go ahead and book Ray for child endangerment. It'll be overturned. This is goddamn Oregon. Then they get on with their lives and forget this ever happened."

"Sarge, with all due respect, you know that's not going to happen. The system will grind them into mincemeat. I mean, the media alone—"

"Goddamn it, Villareal, you don't think I know that? What the hell am I supposed to do about it now? Jesus H. Christ."

She took a breath. "What do you need me to do?"

"Sit tight. I'm waiting for a couple of guys from graveyard so we have some more muscle around here. Just in case. I still have to talk with the chief, who will love that I'm waking him up at this hour with such good news. I'll page you. We'll meet here, then talk to them in the conference room."

"What if—"

"What if we do this my way, Officer? I've had enough of your great ideas for one day."

Jess felt her mouth drop open and tried to close it quickly. "Yes, sir," she said. "If this has anything to do with what I said—"

"I didn't hear anything you said, Villareal. I have calls to make, if you'll excuse me."

Jess stood. Everett picked up the phone to dial. She hoped he was calling David Greiner's CO to tell him to reprimand him, to do something to the jerk. Just because he wanted to feel important—and, Jess suspected, because he'd felt bullied by Everett—he'd messed with two people's lives in ways no one could yet comprehend.

She found Ray and Lindy in the conference room, waiting for results. Ray studied his ink-stained fingertips while Lindy lay sleeping across two seats, her head on his thigh.

"Hey," Jess said softly. Ray looked up. "Believe it or not, all of this will be over eventually, and you'll be able to get back on with your life."

"What kind of life?" he asked. "At least I didn't have to worry about drug dealers and child molesters, living up in the woods, but your sergeant will make sure that's no longer an option. I already know all about social services, how much they help people like me. We'll be living on the streets."

They looked at each other in silence until Ray looked away.

She could pull strings at City Lights, the one shelter in Columbia that took families. A whole slew of low-income apartments had just been built along the edge of the industrial district, and there were the older projects in the city center, but essentially, Ray was right. Lindy had been safer in the woods than she would be in the city. Shelters and public-assisted housing projects were often crime factories, and with Ray's issues with authority, Lindy and he might not last very long in any kind of governmental setting.

"Listen, we'll do . . . I'll do everything I can to help." Jess shifted from one leg to the other, looked behind her. "If we can get through all of this, this crap we have to put you through, I promise I will do everything I can to get you two back to the kind of life you want."

He looked at her coolly for a moment, eyes intractable, then stroked Lindy's dark hair away from her face, tucked it behind her ear. "Why?"

"I don't know. Because I'm a mom. I have a daughter, and . . ." She faltered, her pulse quickening, her eyes welling. She stopped to take a breath, to get her emotions under control, and looked around again. "I don't know. I . . . I just want to help." She shrugged, embarrassed. "Please don't run off or do anything . . ." She paused. "Just try to trust me."

He went back to studying his fingers. How did you tell someone—a father, a survivalist, a war vet for god's sake—not to freak out when someone was threatening his family? She didn't know what she was promising him, not really, but she wanted to do everything she was capable of to make this situation turn out the way it should.

Ten minutes later, Jess was sitting in the break room nursing a Diet Pepsi when the lab tech tracked her down and told her that Ray's and Lindy's fingerprints had come back clean. Jess hoped Sergeant Everett would change his mind now. They could give them a voucher for a room at the Best Western, a cab ride there. Or she could take them on her way home.

Everett's static growl came through her radio. "Villareal, Madison, report to my office." Jess pushed herself from her chair, her thighs and glutes in agony.

Maddy and two large uniformed sides of beef were already waiting in Everett's office. They all nodded, introduced themselves, but Jess immediately forgot the two guys' names. The rate at which new officers rotated through the North Station House made it useless to try.

Everett looked grim. He was going to go through with it. He was going to split them up for no good reason. "We'll take the girl to the foster home in Wood Dock," he said, "but we're letting Mr. Wiggs go if he doesn't get crazy on us. Take it easy on him, on both of them. They've been through a lot tonight. We all have."

He made brief eye contact with Jess. She averted her eyes. She should be thankful that he wasn't going to arrest Ray, but who knew how the guy was going to react? She tried not to think of how betrayed Lindy would feel. If all went well, there'd be no need for force, but all Jess could think of was the way Ray and Lindy had clung to each other, had screamed at the officers even with all of their weapons drawn. They lived in survival mode; when something threatened them, their instincts were unpredictable.

Jess looked at Maddy; Maddy pursed her lips and gave a slight shake of her head. Jess nodded back. Her head tingled; her vision grew blurry until she took a deep breath. She had to focus. She had to stay aware of every motion, every sound. She had to do her job and make this go well, at least as well as it could.

Everett broke them down along gender lines; the bruisers would take care of Ray; Maddy and Villareal would handle the girl.

The two male officers lurked outside the conference room door as Everett strode in and went straight to Ray and sleeping Lindy, followed by Jess and Maddy. He cleared his throat, and Ray shook Lindy gently awake. She opened her eyes and, seeing them all standing around her, sat up quickly, wide-eyed and blinking.

"Well, son," Everett said, "the good news is we're not going to issue you a ticket for camping illegally, and your prints check out, so we'd like to get you two somewhere safe and warm for the night. We've found a bed for you at the Y, but they, uh, don't take children."

Ray's eyes went dark. Jess looked from him to the sergeant. She couldn't believe he was screwing this up, separating them without even explaining why.

"Not to worry, not to worry," the sergeant said quickly, as if he were calming someone over a bag of burned popcorn. "Officer Villareal will take your daughter up to Wood Dock, where we have a real nice foster family who helps us out like this, and they'll have a warm bed for her, a shower, a hot meal in the morning."

"I don't want to go," Lindy said. "I want to stay with my father." She gripped his camouflage jacket.

"Can I go get her first thing tomorrow?" Ray's eyes darted from the sergeant to the bruisers in the doorway. On cue, they walked toward him, hands in that ready position that makes even the innocent want to run or start punching.

"Well, Ray, we'll have to see what DHS says," the sergeant continued, a commanding tone in his voice that Jess knew pushed every button Ray Wiggs had. "Once we put her in foster care, she's out of our jurisdiction."

Jess wanted to interject, to stop this thing from happening this way. Why hadn't the sergeant sat down with Ray alone, human to human, and explained the situation if he felt so strongly that Lindy needed to be in foster care? Why had he sprung it on him like this? Now that the decision was made and witnessed and documented, it was too late for negotiation, for warnings—actions Jess would have thought far more appropriate in a case like this.

"Unfortunately," Everett blustered on, "we've determined that we need to get DHS involved in this one. See, there's this ordinance that says you can't put someone else's life in danger, especially a minor who's in your care. The girl should be living in a safe environment, going to school. Now, we're not going to detain you, but—"

"Don't do this," Ray said, voice rising. "We have our own money. We can find a place to sleep on our own." He started to stand but the male officers moved in quickly, each grabbing one of Ray's arms and yanking him out of his chair. Ray struggled, grimacing as his arms were forced behind him.

"You're hurting him!" Lindy cried, trying to rush for him but Maddy stepped in to block her, wrapping an iron arm around the girl to restrain her.

"Calm down, now," the sergeant said. "It's just a matter of procedure, for Lindy's own good."

"The best thing for my daughter is to be with her father." Ray struggled, trying to twist from their grip. "We haven't done anything wrong."

"Well, actually, Mr. Wiggs," Everett said, annoyed now, "you were camped illegally on state park lands, and that's no place to raise a young girl. There's a whole lot of charges we could be throwing at you, and if you want me to add resisting—"

Jess stepped between them. "Ray, Ray, don't fight," she said, moving closer, holding her palms up to him. "Please, don't fight. I'll be with Lindy every step of the way. I'll take as good care of her as I would my own daughter." She fought to catch his eyes; if she could only convey to him that she would work this out, somehow, even though she wasn't sure yet what that meant. He looked at her finally, his gray eyes distraught, wary, but he quit struggling, and she kept talking, trying to calm him. "Really, I promise. I'll stay on this until we can get you two back together, as quickly as we can. I'll give you my cell phone number and you can call me anytime, night or day, and check on her."

Lindy let out a long wail and lunged at her father. Maddy grabbed for her but the sergeant shook his head. "Aw, let them say goodbye," he said. "Just for a minute."

The officers dropped Ray's arms and he pulled Lindy to him, whispering into her hair as she cried. After a moment he pulled back and looked at her, saying steadily, "It's all right, Lindy. You're okay."

"No," she cried, "I want to stay with you."

"Please, Lindy," he said, then looked at Jess.

She stepped closer, put a hand on Lindy's heaving shoulders, fingers trembling at how warm the girl was. "Honey, I'm going to take the very best care of you I can and get you through all of this as quickly as possible. We'll get you back to your dad real soon. Cross my heart." Jess looked at Ray. "I promise," she said.

"Be a good girl, Lindy," Ray said, taking her chin gently in his hand and looking into her eyes. "Come on now. You can do it. I know you can."

Lindy nodded, still snuffling, and let Jess lead her away.

JESS SAT IN THE WOMEN'S locker room, waiting for Lindy to finish up in the toilet. She'd been in there a long time. If it hadn't been a secure facility, Jess would have gone in looking for her.

All that was left to do was drive Lindy to the foster home, get her checked in, then bring the cruiser back to the station and clock out, change out of her uniform and go home. Considering what they'd been through this day, it would be an uneventful and routine resolution, all on the level and according to Oregon statute. Even with media scrutiny, the department would be above rebuke.

Jess opened her locker. Her civvies hung on the pegs inside; her sandals sat on the shelf with her earrings. She sighed. She'd driven other children to the foster home in Wood Dock, a few miles north of the station, but they'd been kids with no good options. Kids with unfit parents, abusive parents. No parents. It usually made sense. This didn't. It was late; everyone was tired and just wanted it to be over. She wanted to get home, get some sleep, but she'd never felt this way about a case, had never felt she had to do something so wrong and against all common sense. There was no logical reason to separate Ray and Lindy, and she knew DHS would prove that over time. They'd arrange a physical for Lindy, a mental-health evaluation and find she was a normal, or above average, healthy thirteen-year-old. Jess knew when something wasn't right between parent and child— she'd witnessed it hundreds of times (especially in her own household)—and this was not one of those cases. If only she could prove it now, tonight, before they did irreversible damage to a kid whose only desire was to be with her dad.

Even though Jess had never gotten to know her own father as anything more than the heroic figure in their family, she knew how Lindy felt. Her dad had always made sure things went all right in the family when their mother couldn't. Sure, he was gone a lot, but when he was home, he was really there. Making waffles on Sunday mornings before church. Waxing the station wagon in the driveway, giving the boys and Jess chamois cloths to buff out their own territories on the car. The boys got the good parts: the fenders, the doors, the hood. Jess usually got the hubcaps, but she made them shine like mirrors, just to hear her dad say, "Good job." They had all depended on his approval, his normalness. After the accident, after her father's death, everyone wandered in different directions and became solitary. Her brothers lived in different states now. Her mother lived inside her own little world. Once torn apart, they'd never felt that idyllic cohesion of family again.

Jess shook her head, closed her eyes for a moment, then changed into her street clothes. She grabbed her purse, banged the locker door shut, and looked around, but no one would be coming in until the end of the shift. It was still only one thirty. Adrenaline filtered back into her system. She'd thought the night's events had depleted her lifetime supply.

She knocked at the bathroom door. "Lindy? Are you okay in there?"

"Yes, Officer Villareal, I'm fine. I'm just washing my hands."

The door swung open. "Oh, you look so pretty." Lindy seemed surprised that Jess turned into a regular woman without the uniform, the weapons.

"Sweetie, I need you to be very quiet as we leave. We're going to do something a little different than we should, so we need to hurry to my car, which isn't in the same parking lot we came from. It's around the other side of the building, okay?"

Lindy nodded, swinging the huge backpack to her shoulders. She seemed to understand everything Jess was saying, everything Jess was implying. The girl looked prepared for whatever came next, whatever it took to get back to her dad.

Jess wasn't at all sure she was ready for what lay ahead, but she did know she was in the worst trouble of her life. She could only imagine all the charges a district attorney would dream up for her absconding with Lindy: disobeying direct orders, reckless endangerment of a juvenile, abusing a position of trust, certainly. Worse, she could be charged with kidnapping.

But Lindy's fate was in her hands. Jess wanted to cross

herself, to pray to god and Jesus and the saints and the Virgin of Guadalupe to protect them both, to deliver them safely, wherever they needed to be.

"Follow me," she said, and Lindy smiled. They stole quietly away, through the empty lobby, the glass security doors, and out into the dark.

# 16

Nocturnal birds are rare in the Pacific Northwest, other than owls, of course, so when I looked out the car window and saw the gull flying alongside us, a white flash against the dark, I knew it was a sign. If he could fly at night, so far from water, I could do this hard thing, too.

The policewoman was nice. She kept saying I could call her Jess but I liked calling her Officer Villareal. It sounded important and beautiful all at once. We took her car, not the police car, and I was glad. Her car was small and messy, and I had to scoot things out of the way just to sit, like shopping bags and mail and a hairbrush, but it felt more like I was with a real person than with a police officer. "Sorry." She tossed the bags into the backseat. "Presents for my grandson," she explained.

"You can't be a grandmother!"

Her face went from smiling to about to cry and back to smiling again. I noticed that about her up in the woods, too, when she was questioning me, and at the police station. Her face told all of her feelings, like Crystal's did. I can never tell what Pater's feelings are half as well.

I felt bad about blurting that out. "I mean, aren't you too young to have a grandson?" Pater always said I needed to work more on my manners.

She smiled. "Thanks for the compliment, but I am indeed a grandma. I have a three-year-old grandson named Mateo."

"Mateo," I said, to feel the shape of it in my mouth.

"We mostly call him Teo for short," she said. "Like you're called Lindy, right?"

I nodded and settled back.

"Buckle up," she said. "We're not going to Wood Dock."

I already knew that, but I just smiled. She was taking me to meet Pater at the place they were sending him. I just knew it.

On her dashboard there was a small statue that looked like Jesus' mother except more colorful. She saw me looking at it. "That's Our Lady of Guadalupe," she said. "Mexico's version of the Virgin Mary. My mother makes me keep it in my car, for protection." She looked over her shoulder to back out of the parking lot, and then turned onto the street.

"Like my svastika?" I asked.

She kind of laughed. "Yeah. I guess so."

"Do you believe in her?" I reached forward and touched her tiny praying hands.

"Sometimes," she said. "Like right now? Oh, yeah."

We drove for a few minutes, then turned in the direction of my little library, and then past it, pulling into the parking lot of the big redbrick building for sick people. The hospital.

"Is this where they're taking Pater?" My voice was high and

panicky. It was his worst nightmare, he always said, ending up in a hospital.

"No, of course not, Lindy. What makes you say that?"

"Aren't we going to meet him, if you're not taking me to the other place?"

She turned in her seat, touched her lips with her fingers, watching me.

"What?" I asked. I couldn't help being rude.

"I know you said no before, but it's just me and you now, and I have to ask you again. Has your father ever touched you in a way that made you uncomfortable, or tried to do anything inappropriate?"

I felt blood burn in my cheeks. Why did she keep asking me this? "No! He's my father. He wouldn't."

She studied me some more. "Would you be willing to help me prove it?"

I didn't understand what she was asking me to do, but slowly I nodded.

"How long since you've been to the doctor?"

I couldn't remember ever going, not for me, anyway. Sometimes when Pater had trouble with his back, we'd go to the VA clinic to see Dr. Toby, the only doctor Pater trusted. I shrugged. "I don't know," I said. "Is that what you want me to do? To see a doctor?"

"I want you to have a checkup to prove you're healthy. If you want, I'll stay with you the whole time, and explain everything to you." She touched my arm. "Sweetie, they'll want to examine you down there. It's not fun, but I've had it done a bunch of times, and it'll be over quickly. Personally, I'd be more scared of spending the night in the woods." She smiled. "Don't you ever get scared of wild animals up there? There was that bear sighting at the west end of the woods not too long ago."

I laughed, snorting through my nose, which was embarrassing, but I couldn't help it. "Bears only come around when they want food. They don't want to hurt anyone."

"Well, sure," she said. "But what if a hungry one came into your camp, even if it was just looking for food? Don't you worry you might bump into something big and scary up there in the woods?"

"Officer Villareal, you have to respect Nature enough not to go walking around in the dark and letting something bump into you."

"Okay," she said, kind of laughing. "You got me. So, you've never been scared of anything up there?"

"Only people," I said.

She was quiet then. I looked out the window. At night, the city seemed dim and dirty, more frightening than the forest had ever felt.

"So?" She touched my arm. "Will you do it?"

I didn't want someone looking at me there, touching me there, but I had a feeling we weren't going anywhere until I did.

"If I do, will you take me to Pater?"

"If you do, I will have an easier time making sure that happens as soon as possible."

I unbuckled my seat belt. "Then let's go."

Inside the building, we walked down long, shiny halls until we came to a tall desk with nurses behind it. Officer Villareal asked, "Is Dr. Yamin on tonight?"

"Third-floor lounge, next to the chapel," one of them said. "Slow night. She's catching up on paperwork."

"Thanks," Officer Villareal said, and we walked to the elevator. On the ride to the third floor, she said, "Dr. Yamin is a friend of mine. I think you'll like her."

I tried to smile. The elevator made me feel sick, or maybe it was the idea of someone looking at my private areas. I just kept thinking, *This is what I have to do to get back to Pater.* So far, it seemed better than trying to escape and run away, like he wanted me to, and meet him at our church. But if I had to, I would.

Dr. Yamin was nice. She was younger than I thought doctors were allowed to be, and had pretty dark eyes and long black hair, almost as long as mine.

Officer Villareal introduced us, and she shook my hand.

"This young woman needs a physical," Officer Villareal said, "including a pelvic."

The doctor looked concerned. "Have you been assaulted?" she asked me, and the way she spoke I knew she was from a land far away, her words musical and soft.

Officer Villareal shook her head. "No, it's a custody case," she said. "We just need to prove Lindy's healthy, and hasn't been abused."

The doctor nodded and led us to a small, dark room. When she turned on the lights, there sat a paper-covered bed, like at the VA clinic, but cleaner. Whiter. She opened a drawer beneath it and pulled out something that looked like old people's pajamas, explaining that I had to take off all of my clothes, even my underwear, and put the thing on backward, so that the opening was behind me. She and Officer Villareal left while I did this, then knocked on the door to see if I was ready.

I sat on the edge of a plastic chair, trying to keep the gown wrapped tightly around me. The shiny floor felt cold on my bare feet. "Okay," I said.

They both came in, and Dr. Yamin asked if I'd like Officer Villareal to stay. I nodded, and she sat in the chair next to me while Dr. Yamin walked to a counter and sink to wash her hands, then put on a pair of see-through gloves.

"Now, Lindy, sit on the end of the table, just here, while I check your heart and your lungs."

She talked the whole time she was examining me, explaining everything she did in her pretty voice. Her hands were warm through the gloves, but the things she used to check my heartbeat and blood pressure and ears were cold, even after she tried to warm them in her hand.

When it came time to lie back, I started to feel sick again. I put my feet in the metal holders at the end of the table. She pulled a paper blanket out of another drawer under the bed, placed it over me, tucked me in almost, smiling down at me. "Please relax. This really won't take long at all, but you'll feel some pressure, and perhaps a little embarrassed. I'm sorry for that."

How could I relax, no matter how nice she was? There had been another soft voice I trusted. "Just relax, kitten," Crystal had said, "for Mommy. It'll all be over soon."

I was frozen, trying not to remember Crystal's "friend." I looked at Officer Villareal, and her face went all soft.

"Are you all right?" she asked. I couldn't answer. She held my hand. I held my breath. Was it lying not to tell her that I did know what this felt like, kind of, like from a dream, a really bad dream?

When the thing went inside me, I closed my eyes and let her squeeze my hand. I tried so hard not to make a sound, but one escaped me, a baby-crying sound. I squeezed my eyes tighter, quit breathing almost, and when it was over, Dr. Yamin pulled the gloves off with a snap and looked at Officer Villareal. "No injuries, no trauma. This is one healthy girl, Jess. I'll write up a report for you."

I felt like I had passed a test of some kind, like when Pater has me lead us back to camp from an unfamiliar entry point in the woods, or identify poisonous berries. Even though I'd done nothing but lie on that hard table, though, this test was the worst I'd ever taken, and I hoped I'd never have to do it again.

When we got back to the car, Officer Villareal opened my door for me, touching my shoulder as I stepped inside. Once she was in her seat, she turned to me, a troubled look on her face. "Honey," she said, "has someone hurt you?"

I closed my eyes. The sound of screeching, like a hundred eagles, filled my ears, or maybe it was all the screaming I never let out before. I clenched my teeth together as hard as they would go, squeezed my eyes tighter so tears wouldn't leak, but my nose kept running no matter how hard I sniffed. I heard the sound of rummaging, of keys and coins clinking, and then felt a tissue in my hand.

I opened my eyes and felt the water run down my cheeks. If I didn't tell her, I'd never see Pater again.

"It was a long time ago, when Pater was in the war." I pressed the tissue against my face, trying to hide in it. I wanted to stifle the gulping noises that sounded like someone else, but were coming from me. "One of Crystal's boyfriends touched me, but that wasn't even as bad as when Dr. Yamin put that thing inside me. That hurt."

I cried harder. It had hurt, but it had done something else. The doctor had been right. It had embarrassed me just like back then. It had made me want to fly far away from everything, from my own body, even.

"Oh, Lindy," Officer Villareal said, "I'm so sorry," and I felt her hand on my head, like Reverend Rosetta's when I am praying for forgiveness on Sunday.

I looked up at her. "Pater never hurt me. He was gone when it happened. When he came back, he saved me."

She blinked rapidly. Her eyes were moist, and she took her own tissue from the packet and held it to her nose. "I am so sorry," she said again. "Do you want to talk about it?"

I shook my head, and blew my nose. "No, thank you," I said, and she tilted her head and smiled. It was that sad kind of smile, but it made me feel better.

She studied me for a moment, chewing her bottom lip. "So, in case you're wondering, I'm not exactly following the rules, here."

I'd figured that out when we first left the police station. "Are you taking me to where Pater is now?" I asked.

She shook her head. "Not just yet."

"Are you taking me to your house?" I was surprised to realize that as much as I wanted to go find Pater, the thought of going to her home was almost too exciting to imagine.

"I'm sorry. I can't. I'd be in even bigger trouble than I am now."

"Then where are we going?"

"Well, I'm kind of figuring this out as we go." Her cell phone rang; she pulled it from her purse, looked at the screen, and then hit a button that made it stop ringing. "Well, the sergeant's on to me," she said. "The foster parents must have called looking for us."

My heart banged harder now. I was so tired of being afraid, of people looking for me. I reached over the seat and grabbed my backpack and pulled out the notebook she gave me. While we were waiting at the police station, I'd started writing our story in it, remembering the questions she'd asked me. It felt good to have the words somewhere real, where I could find them when I needed them. I opened the notebook to a page where I'd written about the Emergency Plan, about meeting at the church, and handed it to her.

"Oh, wow," she said, thumbing through all the pages. "You wrote a lot while you were waiting, didn't you?" She looked at the page again. "Lindy, you probably shouldn't draw these anymore, not on anything that might get into someone else's hands." She meant the svastikas mixed with the hearts and birds and flowers.

"But they're like pinwheels," I said, "like wind and lightning bolts, like the intersection of two birds crossing paths. I love that symbol."

She sighed. "I know, but—"

"Just like your mother gave you the statue. Pater taught me all about the svastika, about how the Persians, and the Hindus, and the Native Americans all used it in their religions and their pottery and stuff, and it was as beautiful to them as a cross is to people who love Jesus. We have a cross up there, too, you know, if you would have looked farther up the hill, and a peace symbol down by the creek. I asked Pater to make them for me, and he did."

"But did he teach you about Hitler and the Nazis?"

"Of course he did, but before that, people thought the svastika brought happiness and good luck for thousands of years. Why should one evil man change all of that?"

She looked at me, then away. "Because that's what evil does."

"Not to me, not to Pater. It still meant something good in the woods, without other people around." I knew I sounded angry, and I was. Why did they have to take away everything that made us happy? Why did they have to make us leave our home? Why did they have to break us apart?

"I don't mean to sound impatient, Officer Villareal, but are you going to read what I wrote?"

"Oh, sorry," she said, reaching to turn on the overhead light. When she finished, she looked at me. "You think your father will go there?"

I nodded fast, head like a woodpecker's.

A breeze came through her open window, the smell of linden flowers and some kind of smoke, and she turned toward it, eyes closed for a moment. Then she started the car. "Buckle up," she said.

As we drove, I looked for the gull, hoping to see it again, flying alongside us, but there were no birds. Amid ugly dark buildings, a tall spire glowed like the green sea glass Pater and I found when we went to the ocean, right after we first got to Oregon, before we had to sell the car. I'd seen that building in the daytime when it looked ugly but unusual. At night it became beautiful.

We turned and drove along a wide street lined with closed stores and homeless people either shuffling along or lying in doorways. I'd never been on this street before, and I didn't want to be now.

"Where are we going?" I asked. "This isn't the way to the church."

"I know. I'm taking you to a place that will take good care of you until morning, and then we can arrange to meet up with your dad tomorrow. Okay? I just think it's better this way."

I closed my eyes, trying not to be sick. I felt her hand on my arm.

"You know how Dr. Yamin was my friend, and she was nice and wanted to help us? I have another friend who runs a safe house, a place where women and girls, mothers and daughters live when they need shelter. I'll be back for you first thing in the morning, I swear. I bet your dad will have found a way to call me by then."

She wasn't going to take me to the church, even after I showed her the plan. Even after I told her everything. *Everything.* I wanted to cry again, but I wouldn't. I never should have trusted her.

Find an opportunity, Pater had whispered at the police station. There will be an opportunity, and you're going to have to recognize it, to seize it. There may not be another.

She pulled the car over in front of a plain building with no signs to tell what it was. There were bars over the windows. It looked like a prison. She took her phone from her purse, hit a few buttons, waited, then said, "This is Officer Jess Villareal with the Columbia Police. Is Wendy on tonight? Thanks. I'll hold."

I crept my hand along the armrest on the door, fingering the button to make the window go up and down. Where would the lock be? I wondered.

She glanced over at me. "It'll be okay, sweetie. I promise."

I stilled my hand.

"Hi, Wendy. It's Jess. Good, you? Listen, I have kind of an unusual case tonight. . . ."

The door lock was on the top of the doorframe, just below my right shoulder. I pretended to have an itch. Officer Villareal kept talking.

Slowly, silently, I released the latch on my seat belt, but kept it in place, wondering which bus I would catch from here to the church, wondering if buses ran this time of night or if I'd have to find somewhere to hide until morning.

I wrapped my left hand around the top strap of my backpack. Officer Villareal glanced at me, then turned away. "Really? Oh, great. You don't know how much I appre—"

Before I even knew what I had done, I was standing in the gutter outside the car beneath a dirty streetlight and ten thousand stars. I pulled my pack through the door and slammed it shut. I started to run back the way we'd come so she couldn't drive after me, slinging on the backpack as I ran.

Pater would be proud of me, I thought. I recognized the moment, and I seized it, even though I was afraid.

# 17

"Aw, shit!" Jess yelled, then said into the phone, "Damn it, she ran off. I'll call you back."

She threw the cell phone into the empty passenger seat and fought out of the seat belt, pulled keys from the ignition, and jumped from the car to chase after the girl.

"Lindy!" she yelled, dodging between parked cars to the sidewalk. "Get back here! What are you doing?"

The girl sprinted easily away, even lugging the huge pack. Jess's thigh muscles were in spasm; she ran stiff-legged like a toddler, legs burning, cheap sandals flapping uselessly on her feet. She'd left her purse behind. *Shit,* she thought. Had she locked the car?

Leaving the circle of streetlight, she stubbed her toe on uneven pavement and cried out, then continued limping forward as quickly as she could. How had she let this get so out of control, so quickly?

"Lindy, come on!" she yelled after the girl, feeling naked and vulnerable without her weapon in such a rough neighborhood, so late at night.

Over a block away now, Lindy paused, then turned left between buildings. *Toward what?* Jess wondered, then heard a scream. She ran harder, her legs responding to extra adrenaline, the sharp pain subsiding to leave a dull one she could tolerate. The slap-slapping of her sandals echoed in the dark canyon of concrete and brick. Fear propelled her now, her vision sharpening in the dark. Lindy had turned between an old stone two-story and a squat, flat-topped dry cleaner. Jess's feet found a rhythm, her arms pulling long swim strokes until she came to the space between buildings.

"Lindy, where are you?" she yelled, breathing heavily, wishing she had her flashlight. The gravel alley was dark and smelled of fetid Dumpsters. The sound of scuffling in the gravel was followed by voices, one angry and male, the other frightened and small. Lindy.

"Columbia Police! Freeze!" Jess shouted, running straight into the dark toward human figures against the wall of the stone building. "Freeze right there, motherfucker!"

"Let me go," Lindy's voice cried out. "Let me go!"

"Let her go, goddamn it, or I swear I'll shoot," Jess bluffed, and what appeared to be a lanky juvenile male spun around. For one heart-thudding moment, Jess wondered if he had a weapon, if he'd now fire at her, but he turned and sprinted farther into the dark and disappeared.

Lindy ran toward Jess, who could barely breathe. She caught the girl in her arms and leaned against the wall to catch her breath.

"Are you okay?" Jess wheezed between breaths. "Did he hurt you?"

"No, he just scared me," Lindy said into Jess's shoulder, arms clinging to her. "He said he would help me get away, but then he tried to steal my backpack. Oh, thank you, Officer Villareal. Thank you. I'm so sorry."

"Lindy, listen." *Puff, puff.* "Nothing bad"—*puff*—"is going to happen if you stay with me, I swear. I'm trying"—*cough, cough*—"to help." White dots danced before Jess's eyes in the dark.

"Are you all right?" Lindy asked, stepping back.

"No, yes. I'll be fine, but it would be much easier to find your dad if you didn't run off, if you just let me help you." Her breath was coming back to normal. Jess reached for the girl's hand and said, "Okay?"

Lindy squeezed Jess's hand with both of her small, rough ones. She had palms like a lumberjack, Jess thought, or a stonemason. Of course she did; she lived out-of-doors, performed daily physical labor. Jess thought of Nina's small, soft hands and shivered.

"Officer Villareal, could you please just take me to my church, please, please?"

Jess sighed. "How do you even know someone will be there? We haven't heard from your dad yet." Of course, the phone was now in the car. The unlocked car, probably, several blocks away, along with her purse, weapon, and badge.

Lindy's voice quavered. "He will be," she said. "He promised."

The church would be closed and locked up for the night, but if Jess took her there first, the girl might be more willing to go back to the safe house to sleep. They could call the church in the morning, and maybe they wouldn't turn Lindy over to the authorities. *Sanctuary,* Jess thought. Wasn't that what churches did? Provide sanctuary?

"Okay," Jess said. "We'll go check it out, but if it's not open, I'm taking you back to the safe house."

"Oh, thank you, Officer Villareal. Thank you. Thank you."

"Jess. Come on, call me Jess," she said. She looked at her watch. It was closing in on two a.m.

Cops couldn't make decisions like this on their own. They had to play by the rules, remain impartial. *Right,* she thought. The rules were long gone. Maybe she had gone round the maternal bend, or maybe Lindy was truly that one outstanding case that made the rules impossible to follow, but Jess was relying on dead reckoning now. She was bushwhacking, traversing territory as unfamiliar as the forest had been, and all she could do was keep moving forward, one foot in front of the other, heading in the direction she believed to be right.

Like Ray had been doing for five years. He would never give up on his daughter.

Jess felt her chest close in. Lindy was right; her dad would find his way to the church somehow. *I'll do everything I can to help,* she'd told him. *Just trust me.*

He had.

"Come on," she said. "Let's hurry up and get back to the car before someone else tries to mug us. We'll go to the church to see if your dad's there."

"Oh, thank you, Officer Villareal," Lindy said again. She skipped like a second grader all the way to the car and Jess had to smile. That would probably keep the bad guys away. If her own legs hadn't been in such agony, she might have tried it herself.

At the car, Jess unlocked the passenger door, pleased that she had indeed locked it, and helped Lindy take off her pack. She considered stowing it in the trunk so Lindy couldn't run off again, but shook her head and let the girl keep it at her feet. Then Jess slid into the driver's seat, locked the doors, and turned the key, the car shuddering to life.

"So, what's the name of this church? Where is it?"

Lindy folded her hands in her lap and looked straight ahead. "It's called City of Refuge United Church of Christ, and it's on Martin Luther King Junior Boulevard, a block past the little grocery store with the big green sign."

"Really?" Jess wished she'd kept the surprise from her voice. It actually made more sense than any other church she could think of—the City of Refuge had a longstanding tradition of assisting Columbia's downtrodden.

She blew a long breath. She was really going to do this. They had a bed for Lindy at the safe house, but the thought of leaving her there felt less palatable now. She was a fresh little flower who'd been tended to and protected by her dad for so long Jess was afraid what would happen to her if she let her out of her sight before she got her back to him.

# 18

Three years previously, Jess had responded to a call to assist other officers during an INS raid at Pacific Produce Wholesalers. Undocumented workers streamed from the building when they got wind of the raid, still wearing latex gloves and hairnets, a good many of them escaping into north Columbia's industrial warehouse catacombs. Like most of the other officers, Jess didn't try too hard to find them. The city—the entire state of Oregon—had a policy of looking the other way when it came to these workers. It was only the feds who wanted them rounded up and deported, and Oregonians didn't much care for feds.

Jess knew that if not for a little good luck, her mother's grandfather might not have made it here from Chihuahua, might not have found work at the lumber mill in Columbia and met her great-grandmother and started a family.

A small group of fleeing produce workers found their way

that day to the City of Refuge Church, a nondenominational house of worship in Columbia's oldest African-American community. The church welcomed all, delivered meals to AIDS patients, assisted the homeless and the poor. They granted the workers sanctuary and, over time, helped them immigrate legally. The feds backed off in disgust. The citizens of Columbia rejoiced, most of them anyway. Those who didn't wrote their editorials and huffed and puffed for a while, then moved on to taxation issues the next election year.

That Ray and Lindy attended the City of Refuge Church made a strange kind of sense to Jess. They were refugees, more so now than they had been before the Columbia Police had found them. She stared resolutely into the dark as she drove.

At MLK, Jess turned north. After a few blocks, Lindy's excitement became palpable in the car; she fairly glowed with it, wriggling and chattering in her seat.

A block away, Lindy exclaimed, "There it is, there it is!" She pointed out the tall spire, dark and stately against the city-light glow of sky. "Wait till you meet Reverend Rosetta!"

"Honey, it's two something in the morning," Jess said. "It's probably all locked up for the night, and even if we can get in, the reverend will surely be home in bed." She didn't mention Ray. Even if he planned on meeting her eventually, Jess doubted he could have made it there yet. What would she do with the girl? "Just don't—"

*Get your hopes up,* she was going to say, but clearly Lindy's hopes were well beyond up. Maybe coming here hadn't been such a good idea. If the doors were locked, what then?

At the church, Jess eased the car into the parking lot and came to a stop beneath a light pole, the safety of illumination not all that comforting in a neighborhood known for drug activity and drive-by shootings.

Before she'd even switched off the ignition, Lindy was out of the car with her backpack, sprinting across the lot.

Jess pushed her reluctant body out of the driver's seat, clutching her sore shoulder. "Lindy," she called, "wait!"

The big purple door appeared to be opening before Lindy even reached it, and Jess wondered if it was fatigue or shadows causing her eyes to play tricks on her, but out stepped two adult figures. They were too far away and it was too dark outside of the circle of streetlight for Jess to be sure who they were.

"Great," Jess muttered, breaking into an agonizing trot across the parking lot. This time she had her purse, her badge, and her weapon. One of the figures grabbed Lindy and Jess ran faster. As she drew nearer, she realized it was, of course, Ray. The other person she recognized from news photos. She slowed to a stiff-legged walk, even though her heart kept pumping at full throttle.

Ray either hadn't gone to the Y or had left immediately after being dropped off.

The woman was undoubtedly the notable Rosetta Norton Albert, pastor and community activist.

And Lindy had been right to trust they would be there.

Jess stopped at the edge of the church lawn. What was she supposed to do now? She had crossed some indefinable boundary, crawled to the underside of the rock, where day was night and night was day, where children were wise and adults could be clueless, and where those who were supposed to do good did more harm than she had ever let herself believe.

She could turn around, get back into her car, and drive

away. She could report that Lindy had escaped and Jess had given chase but failed to catch her. She would be disciplined. She would probably be suspended, but it would be with pay, for a while at least. She doubted she would be fired, but it was possible, in which case it would be next to impossible to work in law enforcement again. Even if she wasn't terminated, Sergeant Everett would never trust her now, nor would any other commanding officer, any other fellow patrol officer. She'd never be promoted. She'd always figured she'd at least make sergeant before retiring. But if she'd done what she was supposed to do, she'd never have forgiven herself.

Lindy moved from hugging her father to hugging Pastor Albert, then back to hugging Ray.

Jess wiped her eyes as she walked back to her car, then got in and drove away.

THE DARK QUIET JESS DROVE through occurred only at this hour in the city. After a night spent in some otherworldly enchantment she would never be able to explain to anyone, it felt as if she were now reentering the normal world. This was the time of morning she usually drove home from work; her shift ended at two and it usually took until two thirty to get out of the station house. The bars had emptied, their patrons mostly home, and the early-morning commute was still a couple hours off. Jess was glad for the emptiness of it. She had turned her phone to vibrate; she wasn't ready to talk to the sergeant. Yet. It wouldn't be lying to say Lindy ran away. The girl had escaped, after all, and might have found her way to the church somehow, if she'd survived the night on the streets.

It was Jess the mom who had taken her—safely—to the City of Refuge Church. Jess the cop had failed as soon as Lindy jumped out of the car and sprinted easily from her grasp. No, she realized. The transformation had come in the locker room, when she traded her uniform for her street clothes and stowed her duty belt. Her fate had been sealed when Lindy emerged from the restroom, looking at her with those eyes, the eyes of a child who still believes in you.

Once in her own neighborhood, driving along rows of homes with the occasional porch light glowing, Jess saw her small ranch house ahead. It was nearly three a.m. when she pulled into her driveway, and so quiet outside that the closing of her car door echoed like a shot in the night.

# 19

In all the time I've been coming to the City of Refuge Church, I never knew Reverend Rosetta had an office. She walked us down the corridor past the Sunday school rooms, past the bathrooms, and then inside a small wood-paneled office. The church caretaker, Michael, was already there, and he offered us something to drink, but I wasn't thirsty. Pater and I took seats on an old green velvet couch and the reverend sat behind a wood desk that looked like a boat, it was so big. Michael sat in a folding chair tipped back against the wall. His big tattooed hands were clasped over the top of his head, bald and gleaming like he polished it. Michael always let me help him blow out candles after Sunday services. He was gentle and easy to like, even dressed in a black leather vest and spiked wristbands.

Pater told the reverend about everything that had happened, starting with the police coming into our camp and ending with the police car dropping him off at the Y. He never went inside, he said. Instead, he waited until they were gone and then went to a nearby gas station to call Michael at the church. Then he caught the 22 bus across town. Michael had called Reverend Rosetta, and she drove right to the church, still in her purple quilted bathrobe and with her big silver hairdo flatter on one side than the other. She looked like a queen anyway, sitting regally in large gold-rimmed eyeglasses, tapping her long, pretty, dark fingers on the desktop.

"Now, sweet pea," she said to me, "are you too tired for all of this? Have you gotten any sleep tonight? You could go take a nap in the child-care center if you'd like while we figure this out with your daddy."

"No, thank you," I said. "I want to be here." I couldn't help yawning, but I stretched my eyes wide to feel more awake.

"So, let me get all this straight," she said, looking at Pater, then me. "You two have been camping out the whole time we've known you? Every Sunday when you show up for church, you've come straight from those woods?"

We nodded and she shook her head.

"Lord have mercy on you. Bless you, for finding a way to survive."

"But it's not—" I started, and Pater shushed me. *It's not a horrible place,* I wanted to say. *It's our beautiful forest.*

"And God bless that police officer for bringing you here, honey. We may need her help. What was her name again?"

"Officer Villareal," I said. I had gotten very good at pronouncing it.

Reverend Rosetta took a pen from a blue coffee cup that

said "Heaven Sent" on the side, and scrunched her brows together. "Do you know how to spell that, sugar?"

Pater dug in his pocket and pulled out Officer Villareal's card. "She gave me this, with her cell phone number."

"Praise the Lord. It's good to have a friend in the police department," Reverend Rosetta said. "That will definitely help."

"Well, she might not be on the force for too long," Michael said quietly, and brought his chair to the floor, hands together in front of him now.

"Why not?" I asked.

"Because she broke the rules," Pater said. "She didn't do what she was supposed to."

"But she was just helping us." Every time I thought things were going to be all right, something else went wrong. "She took me to the doctor and everything, to prove that everything is . . . is fine." I was too nervous to say it was to prove that Pater didn't abuse me. We couldn't even talk about my periods.

"What?" Pater turned to me. "Why didn't you tell me?"

"'Cause I just . . . I am telling you. I was going to tell you." There was too much going on, too much to say, and I felt out of words. My mind was blank and I felt like bawling. I didn't want Pater mad at me.

Michael asked, "Do you have a copy of the doctor's report, Lindy?"

I shook my head. "She gave it to Officer Villareal."

"Figures," Pater said, shaking his head.

"I think the officer will do the right thing with it," Reverend Rosetta said. "And for now, we don't need it, not where you're going."

"Where's that?" Pater asked, the muscle in his jaw jumping. He didn't like being told what to do.

"Until we find a host home, you're bunking with me," she said, looking straight at Pater. "Okay? Trust me. And why don't you let me take down the officer's details so we all know how to get in touch with her if we need to?"

He handed over the card and watched while she copied the numbers. Then he cleared his throat and said, "Thank you for taking us in, Pastor. It's been a tough day."

I smiled at him the way he smiles at me when I remember to use my good manners.

The reverend clucked and nodded, and we all stood. She herded us back out of the church and into her minivan for the drive to her house.

I was excited and nervous. If I thought being in her office was something special, what would it be like in her home?

When we arrived, I was surprised that it was so small and ordinary-looking, from the outside anyway. Once we walked through the front door, though, it was like being inside a grandmother's house in a book, all cozy with quilts and pictures of people on top of the TV, and a rocking chair, and soft white carpeting beneath our feet.

We went into the kitchen and sat at the table while she hummed and scrambled eggs. I'd never imagined that a woman as powerful as Reverend Rosetta did regular things like make eggs and butter toast, but I'd never seen her in pajamas, either, so nothing was exactly normal.

There was so much stuff in this one room; there was no space that didn't get used, not even the countertops. She had a cookie jar and a blender and a bowl of fruit, a big thing just for

holding spoons and spatulas and tools I didn't recognize, a cof-
feepot and a toaster, and a teakettle on the stove. The glass-front
cupboards and shelf over the sink were crammed full of bowls
and plates and drinking glasses, like twenty people lived there
instead of one. When she opened the refrigerator, it was filled
with things to drink—milk and juice and water and Diet
Coke—and more bowls covered with wrap. I imagined the
leftovers she must have. Now that I knew she cooked, I imagined her to be the best cook in the world. Pater and I couldn't
store leftovers, so we always made only enough to eat, and that
was usually things like rice and noodles, beans and soup. We
couldn't keep meat very well, but sometimes we'd bring home
a package of marked-down chicken thighs to grill and eat them
all—four for Pater, two for me.

Pater was hungry now, and he shoveled the scrambled eggs
into his mouth. We hadn't eaten anything for dinner but peanut butter sandwiches, and that seemed like forever ago.

The reverend watched him eat, smiling, then turned to me.
"Aren't you hungry, sugar?"

I'd never been hungrier, but I didn't like scrambled eggs
much. We always cooked them in the same oil we used for
everything else, so they tasted like onions, my least favorite
food except for Jack in the Box. The reverend, though, had
melted thick pats of butter in the frying pan and stirred cream
into the bowl with the eggs. I lifted a bite to my mouth and
heard a noise escape my throat at the smooth velvetiness, the
buttery flavor.

Reverend Rosetta smiled and went to make up beds for us
to sleep in.

Later, walking down the small, narrow hallway, she stopped

at the first door. "This is where my oldest boy, James, used to sleep," she said. "Mr. Wiggs, you'll sleep in here." There was a single bed along one wall and a desk with lots of books on the other. "This is where I write my sermons now," she said. "James's spirit seems to help me." She sighed. "He got in with the gangs, and got killed, but he was a good boy."

I wondered how Pater would feel, sleeping in a dead boy's room, but he eyed the bed as hungrily as he had the eggs.

"Lindy and I can share a room. We're used to it," he said, and the reverend hooted so loud I jumped.

"Lord, no, you won't. I have plenty of space, more than I need these days. Miss Lindy will have the guest room, thank you very much."

We walked down to the other end of the hall to see the guest room, all yellow, soft, and pillowy. I'd never seen so many pillows.

"I just finished redecorating," she said, proud. "My other boy, Robert, and his wife are expecting, and I have a feeling I'm going to have a granddaughter."

"I used to have an uncle Robert," I said without thinking. I was too tired to watch my words anymore. I looked at Pater, but he looked too tired to be sad.

"Died in Iraq," he said. "My younger brother." I'd never heard him tell anyone that before.

Her face scrunched down like she might cry, and she shook her head and gave Pater a hug. He didn't put his arms around her, but he nodded when she said, "I am so, so sorry for your loss. You must be very proud of him, serving his country."

I wanted to tell her that Pater had served it, too, and that it had done terrible things to him, but I'd made enough mistakes that day.

It had been a long time since I'd slept alone, without Pater a few feet away. I stood there, just outside the room as Pater walked back to his room.

He turned. "You'll be okay," he said. His face was ghostly. I'd put him through so much. "See you in the morning, then. Sleep tight." He went into his room and closed the door.

"The ladies' room is next door," the reverend told me. "There's a night-light on in there for you."

After she left, I tiptoed into the bathroom and turned on the light. It was yellow, too, with lots of white towels, all clean and neatly folded. I slipped out and back into my room, dug through my backpack for my toothbrush, hairbrush, and hand towel, then went back to use the toilet, wash my face, and brush my teeth, cleaning up every droplet of water I spilled.

Then I looked into the mirror to brush my hair. It was all dusty and stringy around my pale face. My eyes seemed sunken and dark and my mouth was a thin line. Pater told me I was pretty when I asked, but I wasn't. In the mirror I looked like the homeless kids who beg for money downtown, with that hard, mean look they have. That dirty, tired look they have. I didn't belong in this nice bathroom.

I hurried to my room and pulled back the bedcovers. The sheets were white, too, so white they scared me. I knew I'd turn them gray if I were to sleep on them.

I pulled the blankets back up, unfurled my sleeping bag, and lay down, pulling the bag on top of me like a giant leaf. I lay there a moment before I realized I had to turn off the light, so

I got back up, but the light switch by the door didn't work. I went back to sit on the bed and study the glass lamp on the bedside table. A gold chain dangled from below the bulb, so I pulled it, but the room didn't go completely dark. Light from another house lit it to a dull gray. I lay back down beneath the bag, then crawled inside it so I wouldn't get the nice yellow blanket dirty either. It was hot but it felt better to hide inside its wood smoke–and–cedar smell. I bunched the bag around my face and tried to pretend I was back in my bed in the cool, dark woods.

I was almost asleep when I remembered to say my prayers:

*Thank you for keeping Pater and me safe and together today. Thank you for Officer Villareal, and for bringing us to Reverend Rosetta. Please take care of Crystal, and everyone in the world who needs some extra help. And please watch over the souls of those who are departed, especially Uncle Robbie.*

I had more to say, but I wasn't sure what. *Please,* I kept thinking, but please what?

My eyes got wet.

*Please help Pater forgive me, and please, please, help us get back home.*

I rolled over on my side, into a ball, and even though the sounds inside and outside Reverend Rosetta's house were strange and unfamiliar, I slept.

# 20

J ess kicked off her sandals at the door. Her feet felt grimy from the night. She was still coated in forest dust; spiderwebs still clung to her hair. Her right shoulder ached from her fall in the forest. Her legs throbbed; her back—no, everything—hurt. She checked messages on her cell, listening to only enough of three from Sergeant Everett to know she didn't want to hear the rest. Not tonight.

She dropped her purse in the chair by the front window, and stood staring into the dark, waiting for the enormity of what she'd done to sink in. Her job. Her pension. Her reputation.

But all she could think of was Nina. Lindy had reminded her so much of her daughter. Her womb twisted in her abdomen, a strange sensation never mentioned in pregnancy and parenting books. How had she let her daughter get so far away?

A shower. She needed a shower before bed. She walked

across the living room to the hallway, turned right, headed for the bathroom at the end, but at the doorway to Nina's old bedroom, she stopped, took a breath, then turned and walked inside.

She half expected to see the small lump of Nina beneath her blankets, one slender arm hanging to the floor, but the blanket stretched tightly across the bed. The top of Nina's dresser was empty, no longer cluttered with framed photos or knickknacks or barrettes or half-empty gum packages. The ghost holes of thumbtacks remained where Nina's Christina Aguilera posters had been.

Tears filled Jess's eyes; mucus flooded her sinuses.

She sniffed and palmed her eyes. "Okay," she said to calm herself. "Okay." She needed just a moment more, here in the place where she came from time to time to torture herself.

She slid open the closet door. Nina's faded scent wafted from her clothes as Jess rummaged through them. She found the sleeve of a sweater Nina had loved almost to tatters, took it between her hands, and brought it to her face, breathing in the remnants of girl scent and wood fire from some long-ago night in the living room, just the two of them.

Jess blinked away tears as she turned her attention to Nina's desk, pulling open drawers just to see her daughter's things. They were still neatly organized with notepads and pens, old birthday cards she'd saved, the eyeglasses she was supposed to wear at school but never did because she felt ugly in them.

The first year Nina was gone, Jess had come into her room often, daily if not more, but eventually the temptation dwindled. It caused more pain than it provided solace, and Jess found the strength to fight the almost addictive pull to touch Nina's things, to sit in her desk chair, to look out her window and see what she had seen for so many years.

She looked through half-opened blinds into the neighbor's darkened yard. Running a finger along a crooked slat to straighten it, she realized it needed dusting. She'd kept the room immaculate at first, cleaning and vacuuming weekly, changing the sheets as though Nina had been sleeping between them. How long had it been since she'd cleaned in here? Why had she stopped?

It was as though she'd given up on Nina at some point, when the pain grew too tiresome, when it changed from sharp to aching.

She wanted to call Nina that very moment, to say, *Honey, I don't know what I was thinking when I let your father come and take you. I should have barricaded the door, called 911. I should have grabbed you and held on to you until you understood that I loved you.*

Jess shook her head. Nina would have fled no matter what she did. It hadn't been right between them for a very long time, Jess trying so hard to protect her that she forgot to be a mother, and Nina looking for the love she so needed in the arms and bed of a boy.

Sobbing overcame her, rounding her shoulders, tightening her abdomen, and she felt her way to Nina's bed, pulled back the blanket, and curled into a ball, the sheets soft beneath her fingers, stroking them the way she'd smoothed Nina's hair away from her face when she was small and had a fever or a nightmare.

"Oh, god," Jess moaned into the pillow. How had she let all this happen? Her family was gone, and now she might lose all that was left. In spite of everything she knew she should do or undo, she was paralyzed by grief, and could only wait until the vacancy of sleep overcame her.

IN THE MIDDLE OF A vivid nightmare in which Jess skidded her patrol car endlessly across lanes and lanes of oncoming traffic, just waiting to be crushed, the ring of the cell phone in the kitchen startled her awake.

She rushed toward the sound, plucked the phone out of its charging cradle. "Hello?" she said, clawing her way out of sleep. She looked at the clock on the stove. It was five minutes past six on Thursday morning.

"In two minutes, the goddamn chief is going to be calling you," Sergeant Everett snapped. "And you are going to explain to him, as you've refused to do with me, what in goddamn hell is going on."

Jess tried to clear her head enough to speak intelligibly. "I was going to call you last night, Sarge, but—"

"You screwed up, Villareal," he said. "Big-time. Have you turned on the news this morning? Seen the paper?"

"No, sir, I was just—"

"The media has hit like a goddamn suicide bomber. Your plan backfired. There's no way those two aren't going to be exposed to shit far worse than the social-services system now." She knew spittle was forming at the corners of his mouth. "You may not want to tell me where they are, but you're going to have to come clean with the chief. You call me back, goddamn it, after he rips you a new one. We have to fix this, and fast."

The line went dead. Yesterday's skirt and blouse had wrapped around her mummy-style. The world still felt surreal, dream-like. She trudged to the bathroom. As she sat on the toilet, the phone rang again.

"Great," she said, unspooling too much tissue, tripping over the hall runner as she sprinted back to the kitchen.

"Jessica!" her mother said, more than the usual alarm in her voice. "They're saying awful things about you on TV, that you've taken some little girl or something. You didn't, did you?"

"Ma, no, of course not. What are they saying?"

"That you haven't been seen since this girl disappeared. They're making it sound like you've done something awf—"

Call-waiting beeped. The chief. "It's not true, Ma. Believe me. I'm sorry. I have to take this, but I'll call you right back, okay?"

"But, Jess—"

She hit the button. "Hello?" She was determined to sound professional—sane, if at all possible.

"Well, hello there, Officer Outlaw," an unfamiliar male voice said. Was she already getting crackpot calls?

"Who is this?" she demanded.

"It's just me, Z. Chris. Dog man. I was just so surprised when I turned on the tele—"

The phone beeped again; another call waiting.

"I can't talk to you right now, for god's sake. I can't even talk to my mother." She clicked him off and the new call on, and tried to compose herself.

"Officer Villareal, please." It was Kathy, the chief's secretary. She and Jess sometimes went to the movies together or had coffee.

"Kathy, it's me."

"Hold for Chief Gleason, please," the woman said, then classical music replaced her voice.

Jess trembled and sat at the kitchen table, hand over her eyes. She had to calm her breathing, her heart. So she was being crucified in the press. She'd seen it happen to others but never thought it could happen to her—she'd always been too boring, too normal for that. She suddenly felt the need to cry; the heat of it waited just behind her nasal passages, in her throat. Crying was a cardinal sin in her line of work—especially for a female. She drew deep, long breaths, exhaled slowly, counted backward from one hundred—a trick she'd learned to help frightened crime victims calm down enough to answer questions.

"Gleason here," he finally said, as though she'd placed the call.

"Good morning, Chief. Let me explain."

"No," he said calmly. "Let me explain. You bring in the father and daughter, now. If there are reporters in front of your house, don't let them see you. Go out the back or through a neighbor's house. Borrow a car. Once you get them to the station, we'll talk about what we do with you. Got it?"

Jess stood to peer through her curtains. There didn't appear to be anyone outside. "But—"

"No buts. Do it, or this thing will get a whole lot uglier, and I don't think anybody wants that."

"But, sir—"

The line clicked dead. Jess pressed the OFF button, her hands shaking, and set the phone on the table. It began to ring; she walked away, then turned back and picked it up.

"Hello?"

"Is Officer Villareal available, please? I'm calling on behalf of Reverend Rosetta Norton Albert." A male voice, not Ray's. Who else knew?

"Who is this?"

"Michael Rogers. I'm with the City of Refuge Church, where you dropped Lindy Wiggs off last night. The reverend would like to meet with you this morning. This is Officer Villareal, isn't it?"

His pronunciation of her name was perfect.

"Yeah, but I . . . I can't really do that," she said.

"We think we can help you just as much as you can help us."

"How so?" she said, doubtful.

Outside, a large truck lumbered up in front of the house. She edged closer to the window and read the call letters emblazoned on the side: KCMB-TV.

"Could we talk in person about that?" the man asked.

Jess hesitated. "Who are you again?" Every bit of her training and experience told her to hang up.

"A friend, trust me."

"Well then, *friend*, give me a reason to trust you."

He paused. "You like being a cop, right?"

Tears pricked her eyes. "Of course. It's the best thing I am." Confessing it aloud did not make her feel better.

"We'd like to help you keep your job, but you have to trust us. Keep the faith, as it were."

"What, is this a syndicate? You and God or something?"

"Nope, just me and the rev," he said. "We want this situation to turn out well for everyone, for the Wiggses, for you. For us."

Jess sighed. She was too tired for all of this, for any of this. "What do you want me to do?"

"We'd rather talk with you in person. I could come get you, take you to the reverend. We can sit down together and figure this thing out."

Another truck pulled up outside. "I'm not going anywhere without being followed."

"I'll take care of that. Do you have a back door?"

"Don't you think they'll have thought of that?"

"Trust me," he said. "The Lord works in mysterious ways."

"Yeah, well, I sure hope that's who you're working for," she said, but it sounded better than any of her other options. She moved away from the window, gave him her address, and went to get ready for whatever the day might bring.

# 21

I woke when it was still dark outside, feeling hot and sticky. I was damp in the small of my back. The birds weren't even singing yet. I kicked off the sleeping bag and rolled over to look out the window, to find some cool air to breathe. The neighboring house had finally turned out its light, and all was still.

You would think I might have not known where I was—that happens in stories in books: the character wakes in a strange bed and forgets for a moment where she is until it all comes rushing back to her in a flurry of emotions—but I knew exactly where I was, and why I was there. It was hard to believe that less than twenty-four hours earlier, I'd seen my first great blue heron up close, had been foraging for morels in my beautiful forest like any other day, wearing Crystal's dress, which was now just a dirty memory. It was the only thing of hers I'd had, but I threw it away in the bathroom at the police station.

I should have thrown it away a long time ago.

I knew this feeling of waking, hot and damp and uncomfortable, from before Pater came home, before he was there to protect me. Living in the woods, I always woke to cool, sweet breezes in the summer, chickadees and bushtits twittering, or rain pattering on the wood roof and the smell of Pater's strong coffee drifting up, the sound of his whistling.

But one night, when I lived with Crystal, I woke in the dark to sweaty hands inside my nightgown, down my underpants, hot, foul breath covering my face. I struggled and turned my head away, trying to close my legs, to get away from the hands. Just touching, Crystal said to the man, or I'm calling the police. Then she said to me: Hold still, please, kitten. It'll be over soon. She had a desperate sound to her voice. Whoever it was touching me had something she wanted. Something she needed. That's what methamphetamine can do to a person.

At the library, I didn't just read about Nature.

I lay awake thinking of everything bad that had happened in my life, something I never let myself do. Whenever I felt this way, I would pray like Pater taught me to, like Reverend Rosetta said, and I would feel better. But this time I couldn't pray it away. I'd thought I was safe forever from bad things, and then I went and messed it up by being selfish. I should have paid attention. I should have watched where I was going. Where were Pater and I going to live now? We couldn't live at the reverend's house forever. There was no place for us in the city, with no money, and if we tried to go back to the woods, they'd just come find us again.

I lay awake until I heard sparrow song and it was almost light. Then I must have fallen asleep again, because the next thing I knew, it was bright and even hotter in the room, and crows were cawing, and Pater was sitting next to me on the bed.

"Wake up, Lindy," he said. "Get your things together. We have to go."

IN THE KITCHEN, REVEREND ROSETTA was cooking again.

"Come get yourself a plate, honey," the reverend said. "Eat up. It's going to be a big day."

"What's going on?" I said. I heard a television in the other room, a news voice talking, but who was watching it? Everyone was in the kitchen.

The reverend and Pater looked at each other, then he turned to me. "People are looking for us, Lindy. The police aren't happy that Officer Villareal disobeyed orders and they want to find us and bring us both back to the station." He looked angry and tired. Had he gotten any sleep? I wondered. "And now the TV and newspaper reporters want to find us, too, because they're bloodsucking—"

"Oh, no, is Officer Villareal in trouble?"

"Lindy, sweetheart," Reverend Rosetta said, "the first thing you're going to do is eat, and we will discuss everything that's happening, and how to keep you safe, okay? We have a place for you to go where no one will find you; we're good at this sort of thing. Here, take your breakfast back to the table. There's a good girl. Ray, honey, you want more bacon? There's plenty."

We all sat again at the table: a man, a woman, and a girl. If everything weren't so awful, it would have been nice to pretend we were a family.

"We have a wonderful couple who live out in the country," Reverend Rosetta said. "They've agreed to have you two come stay with them. There are lots of animals, Lindy—chickens and a couple of horses. Some goats, I think. They have a real nice dog, too. You like animals, right, sugar? They even have peacocks!"

"Are we breaking the law?" I asked. "What's going to happen to Officer Villareal? Can we call her?"

"Michael's working on that now, sweet pea," the reverend said. "Have another pancake, why don't you?"

"Are they going to find us?" I could hear the TV voices in the other room, all fast talking and official sounding. Too close, too insistent.

"Not if we can help it." She picked up a pancake with her long fingernails and laid it across my plate, even though I shook my head no. "They don't call us the Underground Northwest Passage for nothing."

"What are they saying?" I asked. There were familiar words: Joseph Woods, Columbia Police, something about birds and a girl running away. Were they talking about me?

Pater said, "Hurry up and finish, Lindy. Then go brush your teeth and get your things. We have to get going."

As I was packing away my towel and toothbrush and yesterday's clothes, Reverend Rosetta came in and walked to the closet. Inside were so many clothes it reminded me of her kitchen, with things filling every space. She hummed as she pulled hanger after hanger along the rack, like she was looking for something.

"Yes, I think it will do just fine," she said, finally pulling out a rose-colored dress, lace over silky material. Other than Crystal's silver one, I'd never owned a dress before. She held it up to me. "Want to try it on?"

"Do I get to keep it?" I asked, afraid to touch the material until I knew for sure.

She snorted like I sometimes do, and didn't even seem embarrassed. "Well, of course you do, Miss Lindy. Something tells me you didn't get to pack your Sunday clothes. We'll see if we can't find you some good shoes at the church clothing bank. Your daddy looks like he could use some Sunday clothes, too, don't you think?"

She winked at me, and I said, "Yes, ma'am," so anxious to try on that dress that I practically pushed her out the door. Pater would have told me to behave, not to dawdle trying on dresses, but she just laughed.

# 22

On Jess's bedroom TV, the pert young news anchor looked serious in a gray suit and pearls. Jess pulled her wet hair back into an elastic band and sat on the bed to put on her hiking sandals. She'd wear sensible shoes today, by god.

"In breaking news this morning . . ."

The picture changed to the exterior of the North Station House, Officer Madison walking through the employee entrance in her civvies. She didn't even realize she was being filmed. Jess gasped as a clean-shaven, short-haired Ray appeared next on screen, a driver's license photo from before he'd gone feral. He'd been handsome. Jess supposed he still was, beneath the hair.

The TV image changed to file footage of the wildlife sanctuary, the forest surrounding it. "The transient Iraq war vet and his daughter have been living . . ."

*They know everything,* Jess thought. *Stupid goddamn David Greiner.*

". . . custody of human services, but late last night . . ."

The cell phone rang where she'd left it in the kitchen. Jess ignored it. It was probably her mother.

And there it was: her ID photo from work, the frumpiest picture of her ever taken. The newscaster sounded suspicious when she said, "The girl was last seen in the custody of this woman, who has also disappeared, Columbia police officer Jessica Villareal, a fourteen-year veteran of the force. . . ."

"Fifteen," Jess said. "And I'm right here."

The picture changed to the front of her house, with the word LIVE stamped in red in the upper-right corner. A small crowd of her neighbors stood in a clutch to the side.

"Shit," she said, and clicked off the TV. She stood and holstered her weapon under her shirt, then walked to the kitchen, grabbed her cell phone, and checked her purse for her badge.

She heard a light rapping at the back door and checked again to make sure she had her keys, then opened the door slowly.

"Officer Villareal?" One of the tallest, meanest-looking bikers she'd ever seen stood at the bottom of three steps, yet still towered over her.

"You're . . . you're Michael?" she said. From his voice she'd expected a mild bookkeeper type, a pale, nerdy church guy. The behemoth before her was bald and tattooed and pierced, and well . . . intimidating. How had he not been seen?

He nodded, then motioned for her to follow him along the line of birches that rimmed her side fence. For a large man, he was quick and nimble. They cut through the neighbor's backyard and onto the greenbelt, then wound their way along a footpath until they reached a street two blocks from Jess's house.

He strode quickly toward a parked Harley and handed her a helmet.

"You got any ID or anything?" she asked. "How am I supposed to know you're legit? You could be some weirdo who saw me on TV this morning." He looked like the guys she busted for drunk and disorderly outside Patsy's Tavern at closing time.

He reached inside his leather vest, pulled out a business card. "We really should get going before someone sees us," he said as she read: *Michael Rogers, Assistant to Rosetta Norton Albert, City of Refuge Church.* "I already had to scare a couple of reporters away. Luckily they assumed I was a garden-variety badass."

Jess could understand the assumption. "Are we going to the church?" she asked, slipping the card inside her purse.

"We're on our way to a farm out in wine country, right past Seven Hills."

"Wine country? I don't know abou—"

"Don't worry," he said. "I've been sober for eighteen years." He swung his leg over the bike, settled into the seat. "We're going to see the reverend and the Wiggses."

"Oh," she said, wondering why she trusted him, but the thought of seeing Lindy again clutched at her, compelled her to pull on the helmet and climb onto the back of the bike.

Michael let out the throttle and settled his boots onto foot pegs as they rumbled away from the curb.

They made their way out of her neighborhood, then along back roads until they reached Highway 20. The wind stung her arms as they gained speed. She tried to peek at the speedometer, but he was too large for her to see around.

"I'm doing the speed limit, Officer," he yelled above the roar.

Jess sat back, her mind racing as quickly as the pavement beneath the tires, so close to her feet, her bare toes. She tried not to let in images of what it would look like, feel like, to crash and scrape along the road.

It was still only seven a.m. Depending how far away this place was, she could be back in town before her noon deadline with the chief, but she knew she wouldn't be bringing anyone in.

Could the church really help her? Should they? What she had done was technically wrong—she was still cop enough to believe in consequences. *No matter what,* she decided, *I will go to the station house, take my licks.* She'd never feel worthy of being a police officer again, should that be an option, if she didn't.

As they left the city, Jess tried to relax, to take in the rolling green hills, a few blanketed with juvenile Christmas trees, giving way to fruit orchards and rows of trussed grape vines. Inside the purse on her lap, her cell phone trilled every few minutes, but it wasn't safe to answer it, so she closed her eyes and held tighter to Michael's jacket. The sun felt warm on her back; the air smelled of peat and motorcycle fumes. Who could be calling so often? Maybe she should have called Z back and apologized for her rudeness. He was just being nice, and she was no doubt quickly losing friends on the force. She wondered what Ellis and the others were making of all this. What would she think if she woke to one of them on the news, disobeying orders, hiding two people who weren't suspects in anything, exactly, other than extreme hard luck, but who'd been ordered turned in? She felt the heat in her chest again, drew a deep breath to expel it.

After another twenty minutes, Michael downshifted, slowed, and turned onto a small, barely paved road. After twisting up and over hills of nut orchards and vineyards, they finally pulled in at a dirt driveway, through old stone gateposts and a wall of towering poplars, then downhill to a large white farmhouse. A white dog ran out to greet them, followed by two middle-aged men, the shorter man carrying an orange striped cat.

Michael found a flat spot to park the bike and Jess climbed off, removing the helmet. The dog loped toward her and let her pat it on the head.

"Welcome," the taller man said, now close enough to shake hands. "I'm Mark. You're much prettier than your picture on TV."

Jess cringed; the others laughed. She shook hands with the other man, John, who was short and compact but looked strong and had a grip like a pro wrestler. The men were a couple, she realized, and this was where Ray and Lindy were going to live.

Inside her purse, her cell phone rang again.

"I'm sorry," she said, reaching for it. She looked at the display but didn't recognize the number. *Reporters,* she thought. That was probably it. At least it wasn't the chief or Everett. She switched the phone to vibrate and swung her purse back on her shoulder. "I seem to be very popular this morning," she said.

"Oh, you're notorious," John said. "But you did the right thing, you know."

She pasted on a tight smile. She could only hope. "Where are Ray and Lindy?" She saw no sign of them.

"On their way," Mark said. "Rosetta just called from the highway. She always gets lost trying to figure out which turnoff to take."

Jess took a deep breath and looked around. Lindy would love it here. There were trees everywhere, graceful limbs undulating in the breeze above them. Twenty or so yards behind the house sat an elegant old barn, a few orderly chicken coops. White fences delineated pasture area for the two horses that grazed the emerald grass at the far end and a small band of goats by the coops.

"Who wants coffee while we wait for them?" Mark asked.

"Michael and I have to talk, actually," she said. As much as she'd kill for a cup of coffee, she'd waited long enough for an explanation.

"Come on, I'll show you around," Michael said. "These guys built a great apartment down in the barn."

The two men walked back to the house, and Jess and Michael picked their way down a gravel path surrounded by tall flowers. She quickly checked her messages as they walked along. Sure enough, there were calls from all the local network affiliates and *The Oregonian*. How on earth had they gotten her cell phone number? She shook her head. Everyone wanted to know what was going on with the "forest people," to know where she was hiding them, to interview them. Knowing Ray, that was the last thing he wanted.

They bypassed large barn doors and walked along a concrete sidewalk, entering the building at the back, and climbed a flight of steps. At the end of a short hall was a door and, through it, an apartment.

The smell of Pine-Sol and freshly laundered linens greeted them. Though sparsely furnished, the apartment was full of light from wide windows and, in the small kitchen, a skylight. Michael walked in and took a teakettle from the stove, filled it with tap water, turned on the burner.

"This is pretty nice," she said. "How many bedrooms?" She tried to see it through Lindy's eyes, and wondered when the girl had last slept indoors.

"Just one, but the couch folds out." He fished in the cupboard above the stove for a box of tea bags. "But as many as eight people have slept here, when they really needed to."

"Don't tell me," Jess said. "I shouldn't even know this place exists." But now she did. Heat crept into her throat. She was accumulating secrets at a troublesome rate.

Michael leaned against the counter, dwarfing the refrigerator. His head gleamed in the sunshine from the skylight.

"So," she said, "who are you people and what exactly is this plan?"

The kettle whistled on the stove. He turned to the cupboard, his thick fingers daintily plucking out two delicate cups.

"Want some tea?" he asked.

"Is it caffeinated?" she asked, and he nodded. "Thank god," she said, and they sat at the small table to talk.

The plan was not complex, or even out of the realm of possibility, but Michael had been correct in saying that it would require faith—and a lot of it—on Jess's part. And if she agreed to it and it went awry, she would further alienate herself from the police department, the city, and the world as she knew it.

According to Michael, the City of Refuge Church had many supporters in the city of Columbia, the vast majority of whom regularly championed social causes and human-rights organizations. Some were individuals, and some of them were among the wealthiest and most powerful in Oregon. Others were corporations that funded everything from spaying and neutering feral cats to funding attorneys for illegal immigrants. This powerful social network had historically rallied around Reverend Rosetta's causes.

"Where do you think we get the funds to do all the work we do?" Michael asked, sitting across the small kitchen table from Jess, cradling his teacup. "I know it's a lot to ask," he said, "but if you continue to go to bat for Ray and Lindy, keep their whereabouts and the church's involvement unknown, then we will encourage our extended family to do all they can to support you in a very public way." He took a sip of tea, contemplating his next statement. "Now, I wouldn't want to promise you that, say, some state senator would be able to pull any strings with the police chief, or that one of the city's leading defense attorneys would fight this case to the Supreme Court. There are no guarantees. But you will have a lot of people on your side. A lot of important and grateful people who will want to support the courageous thing you've done."

Jess frowned. "Courageous? That's how you see it?"

"How do you see it?"

She looked down into her cup, the tea barely touched. "Emotional. Risky. Insubordinate." She looked back up at him. "All the things a cop's not supposed to be."

"To each his own," he said, draining his cup.

"So, what? You want my protection or something?" She'd never been one to accept favors for anything. Like her dad, she'd always kept it clean.

"We don't do this to protect ourselves, Officer. We do it to protect people like the Wiggses who need someone on their side, and people like you who do God's work even when it breaks all the rules."

Tears filled her lower lids and she blinked to try to get rid of them before they fell. "Whew," she said, sniffing. "I so did not see that coming."

# 23

As we drove out of the city, I pushed open the window in the back of Reverend Rosetta's minivan, the breeze warm and sweeter smelling the farther away we got. She and Pater sat up front, talking quietly about important things probably, but I didn't mind not hearing. There was too much going on. All I wanted was to be where it was quiet again, with not too many people around, and it sounded like that was where we were going. If only I could be back at home, reading a book on my favorite flat rock by the creek, or helping Pater collect firewood. I missed Sweetie-pie. She'd be sitting on her peg right about now, eyes closed, but she'd ease one open if I told her hello, then go back to sleep. I wondered if she was missing us.

We started to drive through trees and more trees, then big green meadows and pastures. A flock of starlings whirled and careened in front of the car just as we turned off the main road, and I watched them as long as I could out the side and then back windows. How do they know to turn and swoop together like that? It's like God is painting across the sky, big black swirls and strokes disappearing as quickly as they appear.

Finally, we turned through a wall of trees and down a bumpy driveway, and a big white house came into view. An even bigger white barn behind it was surrounded by velvet green fields. As we got closer, I saw a white dog waving its tail. I knew I was tired and woozy from all that had happened, but it made me wonder if somewhere during the night I'd died and now I was arriving in some kind of heaven. I shook my head to check. I definitely felt alive.

Two men came from the house, and then Michael and Officer Villareal walked up from the barn. I pulled open the van's sliding door and rushed toward her, into her arms.

"I didn't know if I'd see you again," I said, trying to explain myself, but it didn't matter. She wanted to hug me as much as I wanted to hug her. "Did they fire you from your job?" I asked. I hadn't only messed up my life and Pater's when I made my mistake.

"Don't you worry about that," she said.

"*Aaah OW!*" cried a loud voice, then again, "*Aaah OW!*" It sounded like a baby wailing, and then more babies joined in, and I looked around in horror.

The two men laughed. "There they go," the taller one said. "They know someone special is here to see them."

Officer Villareal looked as scared as I did, but Reverend Rosetta and Michael were smiling.

"That's the peacocks, sugar," the reverend said. "They're just telling you hello."

"And trying to attract females," the shorter man said. His name was John and his eyes looked like he was laughing even when he wasn't. He offered to show me around the farm while the others went inside and talked. I was glad to stay outside. There were horses at the other end of the pasture, goats with babies, and I was more than curious about the peacocks. I'd read about them but never seen a live one, and I'd never heard such an awful cry. It was worse than a barn owl's.

We walked down a narrow dirt path to the chicken coops. Inside, the hens sat in rows of boxes along the walls. A few clucked around and scratched in the dirt, and a tall rooster strutted around pecking at things. I tried to pet him and he fluffed up and squawked at me.

"The hens are friendlier," John said, picking one up off the ground and making kissy noises at her. "This is Lucy."

"Hi, Lucy," I said, combing my fingers through her feathers. She made a *nulp nulp* noise and softly tapped my hand with her beak.

"Do they all have names?"

John sighed. "Yes, which is why we will never have chicken for dinner at our house again, but we do get some nice omelets out of the deal. Want to help me collect eggs tomorrow morning?"

I nodded as fast as I could.

"I hear you like birds," he said, settling Lucy gently on the ground. "Me, too."

We smiled, like we'd each found a new friend.

"Where are the peacocks?" I asked.

"Let's go find them." He pushed open the screened gate for me to walk through. "They roam around the place, but they mostly like to get into the scrubby areas, and the trees. They fly up into them at night or onto the roof sometimes. It's the craziest thing you ever saw."

"It's where it's safest, up high like that."

"Ah, that's it." He looked thoughtful, and smiled at me. "Anyway, they're molting right now, so there's a ton of feathers around the place. You can collect some if you'd like."

I'd left my feather collection behind. To think I could start one again—with peacock feathers!

I had met so many nice people during all this bad stuff that I was starting to wonder if maybe I had followed that heron for a reason. Maybe he was an enchanted creature after all, and he'd been leading me somewhere I might not have gone otherwise, out into the world that I'd always thought I wasn't a part of. Maybe I was more normal than I'd thought.

# 24

In spite of their obvious wealth, Mark and John's farmhouse was unpretentious, comfortable and homey. Mark had invented some nano-something or other several years prior that the communication industry adopted with zealous fervor, and he'd clearly made a bundle. Jess had often witnessed the guilt that drove certain rich people to donate huge sums of money to help those in need, to generally prove that they weren't the heartless bastards they worried the "have-nots" assumed they were. But rarely did the "haves" offer their homes to people they'd never met, essentially changing their own lives and putting themselves at risk to accommodate them. Poor folks did it all the time, but Mark and John were a first for Jess. How did she not know about Rosetta's underground? She was willing to bet that no one on the force did.

"We try to spread the load," the reverend explained as they sat around an oak table with coffee cups. "We have several families with the space, the means, and the privacy to take people in, but Mark and John are the best for deep hiding."

"Yeah, who'd suspect two faggots in wine country?" Mark stood to walk into the kitchen. "More coffee anyone?"

Jess nodded. Ray looked away, embarrassed, she thought. Mark grabbed the pot and brought it back to pour refills.

"So, what about a long-term solution?" Jess asked, turning to Ray. "Do you know where you'll go from here?"

"Well," Mark interjected, "they're welcome to stay. We need help around here, keeping the grounds up and the animals cared for. We could work out a small salary plus the apartment, enough to provide everything you two would need."

Ray was quiet as Mark studied him. "And not to say your look isn't perfect in its own right, Mr. Wiggs, but while everybody's looking for you, you might want to let John cut your hair, shave your beard. You'd be harder to recognize."

Jess remembered the driver's license photo on TV. "Better dye your hair dark, too, for a while, anyway." Now she was thinking like a criminal. Great. Ray squirmed under the scrutiny.

A sudden noise startled everyone. It was Jess's purse, buzzing against the wood floor. "I'm sorry," she said, reaching down to grab it and look at the phone's screen: a New York number. *Shit,* she thought, and turned the phone off. The national media, no doubt. This was getting out of control.

"What's wrong?" Rosetta asked. "Was that the department?"

Jess shook her head and leaned forward on the table, clasping her hands in front of her. "We're going to have to deal with the media. There's no ignoring it. We need a spokesperson."

"Indeed, we do, Officer," the reverend said, reaching to place her hand on top of Jess's. "One who is capable of keeping Ray and Lindy safe, first and foremost, but we also need to know our underground won't be compromised. It can't be anyone from the church. Do you know all of the good we're able to do in our community because we fly beneath the radar?"

"Please, don't tell me any more details. I get it. I want to help."

Rosetta squeezed her hand, then let go and sat back. "Bless you, Officer Villareal. Now, the hard part for you is that it needs to appear as if you're acting alone. As if you're a free spirit, which I'm guessing isn't that far from the truth. Is that something you're willing to do?"

Outside, the peacocks started to wail again. Their cries were so human it was distressing. Jess wondered how Nina would see her if she sacrificed her job, her reputation for these people. How would she see her if she didn't? She tried to imagine what her dad would have done and hated that she didn't know. She'd been too young to know his true character before he died, even though she'd always imagined him a hero.

Maybe she was meant to be part of something larger than herself, something more human than the police force, more effective than DHS. Even though it would be easier to do what her superiors expected—especially now that she knew Ray and Lindy's whereabouts—she couldn't. Her path lay in front of her as clearly as the path out of the forest had the night before.

"What if I say I reunited Lindy with her father last night, and that they intended to buy bus tickets to an undisclosed location and are now probably long gone?" She looked at Ray. "Okay by you?"

"You're taking the fall for all of this?" Ray's eyes flitted from her to the reverend, back again. "You'll lose your job."

"I promised you last night I'd do all I could, and, well . . . that's what I'm doing." She shrugged.

"You could face charges," Michael said quietly.

Jess nodded, and the group sat silently for a moment. "A lot could happen," she said, "but that doesn't mean I can do the wrong thing to avoid it."

Ray blinked his eyes a few times, thin fingers endlessly worrying a knot in the oak table. "I don't know how I'm supposed to thank you," he said.

"There's no need," Jess said. That was what she told the people she helped every day, followed by: It's my job. Instead she said, "It's my choice, Ray. Really."

He nodded, but didn't meet her eye.

Jess stood. "I guess my next step is to go back to the station, tell them I'm not bringing anyone in."

"God bless you," Rosetta said, splaying her manicured hand to wipe her eyes with the pads of her fingers.

"Somebody'd better." Jess felt better than she had since they'd first set out on this mission the afternoon before. "Can you run me up there?" she asked Michael, and he nodded.

There was no going back; she could only move forward. The caffeine was starting to kick in.

"Ready?" Michael asked.

"It doesn't matter," she said. "Let's go."

## 25

We couldn't find the peacocks, even though we looked in every bushy area, in the trees at the back of the property, and along the sides of the house and buildings. John said they were clever at finding secret places to roost when they weren't feeling social.

We gave up after a while and I collected feathers on the way to go see the goats. As we hand-fed them fresh hay, we heard those mournful crying sounds again: *aaah OW!* From right where we'd been looking in a tangle of wild roses and blackberry brambles out strolled the most amazing blue creature I'd ever seen, even more dazzling than in pictures. The great blue heron is majestic and beautiful in its own way, but it's certainly not a peacock, all glistening blues and greens, exotic silk tapestry patterns in its plumage, an elegant little doodle bobbing on its head as it struts through clipped and perfectly green grass. This peacock seemed a civilized bird, not a wild one, not one content to live among muddy marshes and tall reeds. He seemed to be king of the bird world, his home a palace, with humans as servants and everything neat and in its place.

It was a new kind of beauty I'd never experienced before. I could have watched him all day, but he kept strutting until he found the insects he was looking for in the dirt beneath a Douglas fir. He followed their trail back into the bushes, his tail sparkling in the sunlight, then dulling down in the shadows before it disappeared.

I tried to imagine myself living inside a big fancy house, like Mark and John's. They'd put our backpacks near the barn when we arrived, though, so I'd already guessed that would be where we'd stay.

"Where are Pater and I going to sleep?" I asked, picturing corrals and bales of the same hay I was holding.

"Come on, I'll show you," John said, scattering the last of his hay on the ground.

One baby goat hadn't gotten much to eat because the others kept crowding it out, so I bent down in front of it, shooing the others away as I watched the smallest kid chomp its weird flat teeth, one strange sideways eye watching me.

"That's Vanna . . . like Vanna White?" John looked at me, smiling, but I didn't know what he was talking about.

"You name them after friends?" I guessed.

"No, no, that's a TV star." He blushed. "I don't guess you . . . no. Anyway, she lost her mom. We had to bottle-feed her for the first few months, so she's pretty sweet. Looks like she likes you."

I patted her bony head and stood. "I'll be back later to feed you more," I told her, brushing my hands on my jeans. Her coat was nearly all white, with a few patches of gray on her left side. They looked like continents on a map.

"Oh, I know," I said, as we walked across the pasture. "You named her White because she's white."

He chuckled. "Something like that."

Inside the barn, we went up a long flight of stairs toward a door at the top, me carrying my pack and my feathers, and John carrying Pater's backpack. Inside the door, I couldn't believe my eyes; we were in a real apartment inside the barn! It wasn't just a room with a bed on one side and a couch on the other, like the apartments I remembered. It was more like a real house, with separate rooms, only smaller.

"This is it," John said.

"It's very nice," I said, and it was. There was a green couch and a chair and a table with a lamp, and a small television on a stand against the wall. Over the couch hung a big photograph that looked just like my forest.

"Do you recognize where that is?" he asked softly. "I took that at the Woodburn Trailhead, near the Joseph Woods Visitor Center. You ever go there?"

I shook my head. Too many people, Pater always said. We stuck to the back ways in and out of the forest.

"I used to have a beach scene there from the coast, but I thought this one might make you feel more at home, so I swapped it out."

I nodded, swallowing hard. My legs trembled. I wanted to run into the picture so badly I could feel the twitch in my feet. "It's a good picture," I said, because I could hear Pater saying, *Mind your manners*. I cleared my throat. "Thank you very much."

"So, the bedroom's back here," he said, carrying Pater's pack down the hall, past a kitchen and a bathroom.

*A real kitchen!* I was thinking. *A bathroom!* I hoped the towels and sheets weren't white. I hadn't lived in a place with a bathroom since the motel when we first got to Oregon. The last time we'd had a kitchen was back in Colorado when Pater was gone, before we started getting kicked out of every place we tried to live.

I followed John and settled my backpack on the floor next to Pater's. There was only one big bed.

"The couch in the living room folds out into a bed, too," he said, but I didn't want to spend another night without Pater nearby. I pressed my lips tight together so I wouldn't say anything rude. Maybe we could put the mattress from the couch on the floor in this room.

We stood looking at everything for a while; then he said, "Well, why don't I let you settle in, Lindy? You can unpack if you want. There's the closet, and there's a dresser with enough drawers for each of you."

"Thank you." All of a sudden I felt shy. These people were so nice, almost too nice in a way. How could you say "thank you" enough to pay for all this?

"We're really looking forward to having you here," he said. "Both you and your dad, but I have to admit it'll be nice to have a young person around the place again."

"Have other kids stayed here?" I asked and he nodded. "Who?" Were there other people like us, people who couldn't live at home anymore because the police wouldn't let them?

"We've had quite a few families. Mostly people who are from other countries and trying to get their citizenship before the government makes them leave."

"Oh, I've read about that," I said. "But I didn't know they did it to children, too."

"I'm afraid they do."

"Do you have children?" I asked.

He shook his head.

"You should," I said. "You'd make a good father."

He got a funny look on his face, then smiled. "Well, thank you, Lindy. Maybe someday."

After he'd gone, I walked into the kitchen and opened the refrigerator. It wasn't as full as Reverend Rosetta's, but there was an unopened carton of milk, a jug of orange juice, a full loaf of bread, and new jars of peanut butter and strawberry jelly. In one of the drawers at the bottom, there were four apples. Were these things for us? I wondered.

In the cabinet next to the sink were glasses and coffee cups. In the next one there were plates and bowls, and in the next, cereal, rice, and crackers. Bags of flour and sugar, cans of pinto beans and tomato soup. Pater would be happy. We'd left all our canned goods behind.

The stove was shiny white. I opened the oven door, closed it, turned the far right knob to "high," then jumped back when a ring of flames leapt up. The stove at Reverend Rosetta's had a flat coil that got hot, not fire. I couldn't remember anymore what other stoves were like. I turned it off and tried the others, then turned on the faucet in the big sink and played with the sprayer for a while. I dried my hands on a flowered towel hanging on the handle of the oven door, but I couldn't make it hang as prettily as it had before.

The best thing about the kitchen was the small round table and two chairs. Pater and I would have meals there, like real families do. I would do my homework there. I would write in my new blue notebook there, and daydream and draw.

I wandered into the bathroom. The towels there were a beautiful shade of green, like the peacock feathers. I was so happy they weren't white. On the ledge of the tub sat bottles of shampoo and conditioner, a fresh bar of soap. I looked up, and sure enough, we had a shower. Sometimes, Pater and I hiked into the Joseph Woods campground with our towels and soap, but the showers there had only cold water. I closed my eyes and imagined how it would feel to take a warm shower. I'd probably just stand there forever, never wanting to get out, until Pater said I had to.

Out in the living room I sat on the couch and sank deep into it. Calm washed over me as I looked out the window. I could see trees across the pasture, leaves glittering like coins in the breeze. I could see blue sky and a wedge of cottony cloud. I got up and sat in the chair and looked out the other window. From there I saw the back corner of the main house, two tall windows side by side with open curtains, and a veil of giant maple leaves at the edge. All was quiet except for the occasional *aaah-OW* of a peacock, the bleat of a goat, the cooing of a pigeon.

It was almost as peaceful as the woods.

I felt I might fall asleep, so I stood up, walked to the television, and turned it on. Two people sat in a fancy restaurant. The woman wore too much makeup and talked weird, all fake and loud, and the man was almost prettier than she was. I carried the channel changer back to the couch, sat, and pushed buttons until the picture changed. I wondered if there were any cartoons on. You never knew—I might still like them.

Every channel had a commercial for something: car crashes, dishwashing liquid, technical colleges. I kept pushing the button.

When a picture of Pater filled the screen, I dropped the channel changer to the floor. "Uhn!" I said, like somebody had punched me in the stomach, and my heart started to beat hard. It was the picture on his driver's license, from when we first got to Oregon, but how did they get it? It was in his back right pocket with his VA card, his library card, his money.

"The two were last seen in police custody late last night," a man's voice said. "In a bizarre twist, police officer Jessica Villareal disappeared along with the man and girl, and hasn't been seen since."

The picture changed to a man and woman at a desk. The woman said, "Do police suspect foul play, Dan, or do they think the police officer disappeared on purpose?"

Now a smaller picture floated to the left of the man's head. It was Officer Villareal. Jessica, a name much prettier than Jess. I could barely breathe.

"At this time, there's been no activity at her home, and neighbors say they're concerned. We'll have those interviews in the next hour, and a press conference with Police Chief Gleason is scheduled for noon today. We've got it all right here for you, so stay with us on KEAN News Seven."

Someone knocked on the door. I reached down to pick up the channel changer, trying to figure out how to turn off the television with fingers that no longer worked, using eyes that no longer saw clearly.

"Hello?" Officer Villareal said from the other side of the door. "Are you in there, Lindy? I came to say goodbye."

She knocked again. I couldn't find the right button, and now another woman was standing in front of the wildlife sanctuary, talking about Pater and me, saying we were "transient," which is just another word for "homeless"—I'm not stupid—and then the door was opening, and I was crying, and Officer Villareal was walking in, her smile changing when she saw what I was watching.

"Oh, honey," she said, walking toward me, taking the thing from my hand and turning off the television, then pulling me against her, her arms around my back, her cheek on the top of my head. *"Shh shh shh,"* she whispered in a rhythm like a heart-beat. Her body was soft where I wrapped my arms around her, where I laid my head.

Outside the window, a flash of white flew by. Too big for a seagull, maybe an ibis, but I was tired of thinking about birds. I was tired of thinking about everything. All I wanted to do was go to sleep in my own bed back home.

# 26

It was nearly ten thirty when Michael dropped Jess off several blocks from the North Station House at her request. She needed a few minutes to walk, to clear her head, to form words and arguments.

The morning was brilliant, bleached by sunlight, breezy. A train moaned in the distance; a homeless woman dressed in too many coats shuffled by. It was just another day for those driving along busy North Point Boulevard, for the baggy hooded boys on skateboards in the park across the street, the moms pushing strollers, holding toddlers' cherubic hands. There'd been a shooting in east Columbia the night before, according to the front page of *The Oregonian* in the corner box. Fifty-two Iraqis had been blown to bits as they gathered for a wedding. What would be the headline on tomorrow's paper? Jess wondered.

It would have been nice to grab a muffin or a cookie at the old snack bar on the next block, but the chatty owner would have the TV on. She probably already knew Jess was a fugitive. Jess walked slowly, head down, listening to the nineteen messages that had accumulated on her phone over the past ten hours.

She listened to Sergeant Everett's calls from the previous evening in full, her stomach tensing at the sound of him realizing she wasn't just dawdling on her way to Wood Dock. Each message was more stern than the last, and then there'd been his nasty call that morning.

It was starting to make sense—right after she spoke with Everett that morning, he'd made her cell number available. Curse words were not his only intimidation tactic.

The first media calls had been from assistant producers at local network affiliates. Now she listened to the next round, from the big-gun investigative reporters at all of the local channels. *The Oregonian* had called several times, as had various talk radio shows.

And then the call from New York. A producer from *Good Morning America* asking if Jess would tell Mr. Wiggs and his daughter that they'd love to have them on the show as soon as possible. They could offer travel expenses, hotel expenses, and a generous gift toward the girl's college fund, if they'd agree to come on and talk about what their lives had been like, what it was like to live in the forest, what had driven them away from civilization, and how it felt to be "captured."

Her breath caught at the word. They weren't interested in Ray and Lindy as human beings. These people only wanted to portray their story as entertainment, as reality TV rather than real life. *The Swiss Family Robinson* meets *Survivor* meets *Law & Order*. They had no qualms about the ramifications of that kind of media attention on someone like Ray, and how that might affect Lindy's future. Jess didn't even know how what she was doing would affect them, but she believed it was better than the alternative. Lindy was a good kid, smart and scrappy. She hadn't been given the best of circumstances in life, but Jess sensed in her the soul of someone who could do anything she felt determined to.

The last message was from Z. "Hey, sorry I'm such an insensitive oaf. I only meant to tell you that I hope you're okay, and I wish I wouldn't have been such a boot licker last night. I feel pretty crappy about caving like that. So, whatever's happening with you, with those folks, if you need a friendly voice or help, or anything, I'm . . . Well, I'm here." She listened twice to his message, thinking, *Who uses the word "oaf"?*

She paused before hitting SAVE, letting it sink in. He believed in her. So did Michael, and Rosetta, and the couple on the farm. These were all sensible, reasonable people, she thought. Yes, her decision to help Ray and Lindy stay together and in a safe place was going to have dire consequences on her career, on her life, but she'd also gained something in making the decision. Maybe it was courage, as Michael had said, but it just felt like stubbornness, the need to do the right thing. She'd always thought these qualities came from doing what the law demanded. But in the past nineteen hours, she'd listened to her own voice, and even though it scared the hell out of her, it felt more genuine, and more important, than anything she'd done in a long time.

At the next street she turned and the station house came into view, flanked by three television satellite trucks and a small platoon of media vehicles. She combed her fingers through her hair, fished in her purse for lipstick. *I'm an idiot,* she thought, *caring what I look like on TV,* but she couldn't help herself. The damn ID photo had been bad enough.

Before crossing the street to the station, she stopped, turned her back to the building. Everett's cell number was on her phone; she pulled it out and hit SEND.

"Everett," he growled.

"Sarge, it's me. Villareal." She pronounced it "Villa-reel," rolling her eyes. Like she could kiss up now. "Are you at the station?"

"Never mind where I am. Where are you?"

"On my way in." She looked over her shoulder. Would he be looking out his office window?

"You got 'em?"

She paused, and he knew.

"Goddamn it, Villareal. Don't even bother coming in unless you've got the girl with you."

"I was hoping we could talk, Sarge. I'm two minutes away."

"What do we have to talk about? You lied to me, Officer. You said you were on board, so I trusted you. You fucked up a perfectly good career, Jess. Goddamn it."

"I wasn't planning anything when I said that, Sarge. I swear. It's not like this is a big conspiracy or anything. I'm just doing what I feel I have to do." She paused so he wouldn't hear the emotion in her voice. "I'm looking at the building. I'm almost there." She turned and started to walk toward the eerily still scene—equipment everywhere but few people milling about.

She saw him now, watching from his second-floor office, and met his gaze.

"Just hear me out."

"Do not cause a scene out there, Villareal."

"I won't," she said, then snapped the phone shut when he turned away. It buzzed in her hand. Another New York number. She wondered how long it would be before all the morning shows and the cable news channels started calling. She'd have to get her number changed. There was no way this wouldn't be a long, drawn-out drama the media would salivate over, with hearings and trials and god knew what. She might be helping Ray and Lindy hide away, but she was becoming more and more exposed.

She would apologize to the neighbors about the satellite trucks, the intrusive reporters. Maybe she'd take them brownies; everyone loved her brownies. She hoped she wouldn't have to move. She'd been pregnant with Nina when they'd first rented the house, and after the divorce she'd signed a rent-to-own agreement with the owner. It wasn't the best house in the world—it was small and suffered far too much neglect on her part—but it had been her home long enough that she didn't want to imagine another.

She kept walking, avoiding eye contact with the camera operators and sound techs, the reporters filing live updates of nothing much happening. They didn't notice her; out of uniform she could be anyone. It was hot already for midmorning. How did their makeup not melt off? she wondered. How did they not sweat through their suit jackets and silk blouses?

Out of habit she walked to the employee entrance, passed

her keycard over the plate. No green light, no beep, no lock clicking open. They'd taken her out of the system.

"Officer Villareal?" A female voice, right behind her. "You are, aren't you? May I ask you a few questions over by my van?"

*Shit,* Jess thought. So much for slipping in unnoticed. She turned toward the main entrance, head down at first, the way suspects always did on camera. She lifted her head and kept walking.

"Hey," another voice called, male, excited, "it's her."

Car doors slammed, people scurried, grouping around her, hastily pulling on headphones and raising booms and mounting cameras on shoulders, arranging hairdos and grabbing microphones.

"Officer Villareal! Officer Villareal! How about an exclusive?"

"Where are they? Where are Ray and Melinda?"

"Has the girl been abused? Is the father mentally competent?"

Jess strode quickly, not looking at anyone, just trying to make it to the end of the sidewalk, then up the steps, then through the door—

"Where are they, Officer? Come on. Why are you hiding them?"

"Can you confirm or deny rumors of white suprema—"

"Jessica! Were you the kidnapper or the kidnappee?"

The door was in reach. She grabbed the handle, then turned to face them. "I'm a police officer, for god's sake, not Heidi Fleiss. Back off."

They went silent, seemed about to retreat, then surged forward again as she slipped inside. Their clamoring faded behind the glass doors. They'd no doubt been ordered to stay outside.

Behind the glass at the front desk, two newbie officers

looked up, freshly post-academy, here for as long as it took them to get a better posting. They were both blond, and Jess could hardly tell what gender they each were until she got close enough to see breasts on the one on the left.

"Officer Villareal here for Everett," she said. "He's expecting me."

They knew why she didn't just buzz herself back. Everyone knew everything, of course. They'd probably been glued to the television in the conference room all morning. The officers looked at her differently from the way they would have the day before, like she was either Norma Rae or Norman Bates—she couldn't tell which. She wished someone from her shift was on, but they wouldn't be in until three.

The female officer picked up the phone, murmured, then set it down. "The sergeant says to go straight to his office."

What was she going to do, run naked through the crime lab? Steal marijuana from the evidence room? Influence others to turn actual criminals loose on the streets?

"Fine," she muttered.

The door buzzed. Jess stepped through, wondering if the cameras outside were getting all this, wondering, in spite of everything, how big her butt looked. Even when everything had changed, some things never did. Thank god she wasn't in uniform pants.

Everett looked tired. He, too, was in civvies, a golf shirt and chinos. His day off.

"What are you trying to do, kill me?" he said. "Get me fired? Your ass is already grass. At noon, the chief's going to announce you're under investigation. Is it worth it, Villareal? One kid?"

"What if it were your kid, Sarge?"

He slammed his open hand on the armrest of his chair. "Don't pull that shit with me. Just tell me what the fuck is going on. We're going to find them, you know. It's only a matter of time. Help us now so we don't look like complete morons, and you'll get your old job back in two months."

"May I sit?"

"I don't care if you goddamn spin on your head. Spill it."

Jess sat in the chair she'd used the night before, dropped her vibrating purse between her feet, and pulled out the doctor's report.

"Here," she said, sliding it across his desk. "No sexual abuse. Healthy, normal."

He scanned it, then looked up. "What does this prove? They're still homeless. She's still going to be truant come fall, living in unacceptable conditions. Or have you managed to fix that, too?"

Jess chewed her bottom lip. She'd planned on telling him they'd taken a bus to who knows where. She'd be in more trouble with the department if she told the truth, but the truth was so much better.

"Actually, they've found a place to live where Ray can work for room and board and a little money. Lindy can go to school there."

He cocked his head. "What? Where?"

She shook her head. *Add obstruction to the list,* she thought, realizing she should have called an attorney before coming in. Things were moving so quickly. She was reacting from instinct, whether or not that was a good thing.

He sighed and picked up his phone, punched in numbers, then sat back in his chair, staring at her.

"Everett here," he said after a moment. "Villareal's in my office."

He closed his eyes, pinched the bridge of his nose. "Nope. Just her." He nodded. "Mm-hmm, yup. Well, she has a doctor's report for the girl. No sex abuse. And she's got them hiding out somewhere, won't tell me where."

"Hiding out?" Jess felt her jaw unhinge. She scooted forward in her chair, looked the sergeant in the eye until he looked away. "Tell him Ray will be working, they'll have a home. They'll have a normal life."

"Mm-hmm, mm-hmm," he said into the phone. "Okeydokey." He hung up and looked at her. "Until you either A: tell us where they are, or B: bring them in, you're on administrative leave. And if you do neither by noon, he's pushing forward with an investigation. He's pissed, and he's not going to let you add yet another black mark against the department, not on his watch. They'll haul you in to question you on the Wiggses' whereabouts, Jess, under oath, and I wouldn't be surprised if this turns into a criminal investigation. They'll throw it all at you: kidnapping, endangerment. Trying to smooth things over this late in the game isn't going to help a thing. It doesn't matter where they're living now. None of it matters because the game we're playing here is political. I suggest you calm down, think straight, and consider this your last chance. Do the right thing."

"That's what I am doing," she said. She wanted to argue how stupid it all was, to storm out at the very least, but she knew Everett had a soft spot; she'd just been wrong about how to find it.

She lowered her voice. "You were there last night, Sarge. You saw how they are together; you know they're all each other has. They're doing pretty good, don't you think, under the circumstances? Don't you see we could put a positive spin on this, finally get some good PR? 'Columbia Police keep family together.' Bringing Ray and Lindy in now, under all this public scrutiny, isn't going to be the best thing, not for anyone."

"Do I have to remind you who brought the goddamn public scrutiny on? The media is having a fucking field day."

"What?" she said. "Come on, that's not fair. You know it wasn't me. It was that little prick Greiner and his huge ego. And I'm the one being skewered by the press. You think I'm enjoying it?"

Everett folded his arms across his chest. He was too far gone; there was no way to reach whatever humanity was left inside him.

"So, tell me this," she snapped. "Who gave out my private cell phone number?"

He shrugged. "Could've been anyone. It's on the roster." He was the calm one now, believing he had her, believing he was the victor.

"Fine," Jess said. "You know what? I welcome an investigation. Fucking subpoena me. And the chief isn't the only one who can have a press conference." She looked at her watch. It was a few minutes after eleven.

"Ah, Jesus, Villareal." He looked weary. "Fine. If you don't need anything from your locker, I'll walk you to the exit."

"And then get back to your golf game?"

"And I'll need your badge and your weapon."

"I don't have them on me," she lied.

"Officer."

She drew a breath, then reached inside her purse for her badge, unholstered her weapon, and laid both on his desk.

Everett came around the desk and took her arm, cordially almost. They walked out into the hall, both silent, then down the stairs. Jess could feel eyes peering from doorways and cubicles, whispers shushing. They passed the female newbie as they exited the secured area; the young cop looked away.

*Why won't you just help me?* she wanted to ask the sergeant, surprised at the surge of sadness it brought on. What did she expect from him? He was doing his job, but he seemed a different person from who he'd been in the woods the night before. He'd tried to make sure their decision was fair; he'd treated Ray with respect when he could have just hauled him in like a common lowlife. He'd had fleeting moments of humanness that seemed to suggest he wasn't all badge, but he was buckling under, caving to the chief's bluster, his vanity. The last thing Gleason wanted was bad press, and both he and Everett were willing to sacrifice a kid to avoid it.

Jess blinked back tears, hoping the sergeant wouldn't notice. *I want one man in my life to not let me down,* she thought, then groaned at herself, at the cliché all this was. Why did it always come back to her dad, to wanting a man to be on her side? The sergeant looked at her and she turned her head, swallowing against the raw saltiness in her throat. It was worse than that: she wanted a man to protect her, to tell the world: *She's right, goddamn it, so leave her alone.*

At the front door, Everett let go of her arm. "You've got an hour to think this over, Jess. You're a good cop. We need you."

"Yeah," she said, "you've got that right." She pulled the door open and walked into the blare of sun, ignoring the bustle of reporters and cameras around her. She rounded the side of the building, feeling like a beekeeper in the middle of a swarm, and headed toward the lone female reporter who leaned against the KORB satellite truck talking on her cell phone. She looked up, saw Jess approaching, and snapped her phone shut, called to her crew. The sidewalk became a hive, buzzing, regrouping, the drones all tightening the circle around the two women.

"Do you want to do this privately?" the woman asked.

*You wish,* Jess thought, and shook her head. She'd just wanted a female face, a female presence to talk to. Her mouth went dry. Her vision blurred. Her purse vibrated against her side.

"Okay, listen up," she said in her cop voice, surprising herself. "I'm only going to do this once, so you all better get it right." She looked up; Everett watched from his window. She turned her attention back to the crowd, took a deep breath, and began.

# 27

I sat alone in the apartment for a long time, staring at the dark television set and the reflection of me in it. The peacocks had gone silent. The breeze had stilled. It was bright outside, brittle with sun, and inside it was starting to get hot. I watched my head and shoulders and arms in the TV-set glass, moving my head one way, then the other, one shoulder up, then the other. I looked like a child in the big chair. I'd never known my head was so small, my hair so flat against it. I tried running my fingers through it to comb it and fluff it up, but it fell limp against my cheeks. I had sweat beneath my arms, down my back, and behind my knees. I never perspired this much in the forest, with its cool breezes and dark patches of shade.

I wasn't sure what to do. Should I unpack as John said, or would we even be staying for very long? I wanted to hang up my new dress and look at it in the closet. I wished Pater would come tell me what was going on. I considered walking up to the big house to find him, but I didn't know if I was supposed to. Was it okay if I went back outside? I didn't know, so I just kept sitting there. I was getting tired of looking at myself.

My stomach gurgled; I was hungry. It seemed like the food was for us, but without Pater saying so, I couldn't be sure, so I tried to think about something else.

I tried not to think about what they said on the television. I put my hand in my front pocket, felt Officer Villareal's card safe in there. She'd written her home number on it, and her cell phone number, and her address at home, and told me to call her anytime, for whatever reason, even if it was only to say hello. She said she didn't think we'd be seeing each other again, but if I ever needed anything . . . She didn't say the rest, but I knew what she meant. Reverend Rosetta had told me the same thing, and I guessed they both meant if something ever happened to Pater.

I'd never thought before about what would happen if he weren't with me anymore. What if he'd been arrested? What if he disappeared one day, or (and I knew it was burn-in-hell bad to think this) what if he died? I'd never believed anything bad could happen to him, or to me when I was with him. He wore Uncle Robbie's war medal on a chain inside his shirt, and it kept us safe from bad things. But just like with the svastika, I was starting to realize you couldn't count on such things to keep you safe. Seemed to me you had to do that for yourself, somehow.

I got up and looked out the window toward the house. Reverend Rosetta's minivan was gone now, and the big motorcycle. Where was Pater? Surely he wasn't in that big house alone with the two men. He would never be comfortable having to talk to

them alone. I guessed that he was walking the property, checking the boundaries, like he did every day up in the forest, trying
to make sure we were safe.

I went into the kitchen to look at the clock on the stove. It
wasn't even eleven. Lunch wouldn't be for an hour yet. I opened
the refrigerator door and looked at all the food. I was so hungry. I looked behind me, then reached inside for the bag of
bread. If I took a piece from the middle, maybe no one would
notice. I untwisted the tie, reached down inside to pull out a
piece. It was soft and spongy, not like the dry, rough bread we
always got from behind the natural food co-op, the stuff that
was too old to sell. I pressed the sweet softness to my face, in-
haled. It was such a heavenly smell, I almost ate the whole thing
standing right there, but I wanted to make it last, so I took it
with me back to the living room and sat down again.

I picked up the television channel changer. This time I really
would try to find cartoons. I would avoid any news, just keep
changing the channel until I found *SpongeBob SquarePants* or
*Pinky and the Brain*, if they were even on anymore. It had been
five years since I'd last watched a cartoon. The moment I clicked
on the TV, though, I knew I was lying to myself. Something
bad lurked inside me, wanting to see the pictures they were
showing of us, wanting to hear the things they were saying.

The picture was of an old brick building surrounded by
trees—the police station where they had taken us last night. I
gasped as I realized it was the back of Officer Villareal they
were showing, at first from far away, then up close, as she tried
to open the door, then turned to walk away when all the people crowded around her. The pictured bumped around, then
focused on the side of her face. She looked straight ahead

and didn't say anything, even though people were asking her all kinds of questions, yelling them and repeating them but I couldn't understand the words; it was too chaotic. The camera stayed on her until she came to another door and acted like she was going inside, then turned around. She looked mad. "I'm a police officer, for god's sake," she said, "not hiding flies. Back off." I didn't know what she meant about hiding flies—did that mean us?

When she disappeared inside the building, I remembered to breathe again. She was safe; she'd gotten away. But then they showed the exact same thing, this time with a man's voice talking over the top of it, saying, "And that was the scene just thirty minutes ago, when Officer Jessica Villareal arrived at the Columbia Police Department's North Station House, whether to turn herself in or report for duty, we don't know yet, but we hope to learn more at the press conference, coming up very soon. Bill? Back to you."

Then it was the man from before, the one at the desk, nodding, looking grim. "Thanks, Dan. We'll cover that press conference live at noon. Stay tuned for your ten-day Accu-Point forecast, and all today's news, right here on KEAN News Seven."

A commercial came on for cars, and the scenery was a lot like our forest, so I watched it, and then some others about diamond rings, which were pretty; a casino where people have lots of fun; and then one about how to stop your legs from being restless by calling your doctor. I was waiting to see if cartoons actually might come on, but then the picture changed back to the newsman, who looked excited now. "We're taking you back live to the North Station House, where Officer Jessica

Villareal has just emerged from behind closed doors, and is about to make a statement. Dan?"

"Yeah, Bill, we're live now, with this surprise appearance by the woman everyone in Columbia is talking about today, Officer Jess— Wait, she's started to speak, Bill. Let's go directly to her."

And then they showed her, standing on the sidewalk with people crowded all around her again, but this time they left space in front of her, empty enough that they could reach their arms forward with microphones and little tape recorders.

She looked tired, like she might have been crying. But she looked strong, and in charge, the way she had last night in her uniform, before I got to know her and found out she was also a nice person.

"My name is Officer Jess Villareal," she said, loud and kind of bossy, "and I was on the search team yesterday for a juvenile girl spotted in Joseph Woods. After a difficult four-hour search, we did indeed find said juvenile and her father living in a clean, well-stocked encampment, both healthy, in no distress other than that there were a lot of police officers trying to track them down."

"Can you verify their—"

"My terms," she said. "Shall I continue?"

She waited, then started again. "The girl has received a complete physical, which found her to be in excellent health and with no evidence of any kind of abuse whatsoever. Her father homeschools her and she appears quite bright and articulate—"

I felt myself blush.

"—and if I had to take a guess, I'd say she probably reads and writes at a far higher level than most thirteen-year-olds.

She and her father attend church regularly and lead simple, quiet lives. The only crime here is that they don't live inside four walls, due to the father's injuries acquired while serving as a United States Marine in Iraq. They can't afford housing, which is the story you should be chasing, and thank god her father didn't choose to raise her on the streets."

The view of Officer Villareal kept getting closer, her face now filling the screen, catching every blink of her eyes. Dots of moisture beaded on her top lip; her eyes looked as shiny as dark marbles.

"It was the decision of the responding officers last night that the girl be placed in protective custody." Now she looked directly into the camera, right at me, right at everyone who was watching. "But I didn't agree with that assessment, and it was my sole decision to redirect the girl not to the foster care system, as were my orders, but back to her father instead. They have now been reunited and relocated and wish to continue on with their lives in private. It's my hope that by standing here and telling you the truth, well, that you will leave these people alone and move on."

"Are you speaking on behalf of the Columbia Police?" a woman's voice asked. The camera backed up finally, out of Officer Villareal's face, and now I could see that everyone was clustered even more tightly around her. No wonder she was sweating.

"No," she said, in the tone people use with small children. "I'm speaking for myself, and on behalf of the man and his daughter. The police department has chosen to place me on administrative leave for taking these actions, so I'm not speaking to you in any official capacity. Just . . ." She paused and wrapped her arms around herself. "Just as a human being, and, well, as a parent myself. I wouldn't have done this if I'd thought the girl was in any jeopardy, any possible danger. Ask my daughter. I barely even let her go to sleepovers when she was younger."

The people around her laughed.

"Will you be disciplined further, Jessica, or fired?" the woman asked.

Officer Villareal said something I couldn't hear and turned away, and the spell was broken. People started yelling again and following her.

"Lindy!"

I turned and Pater stood in the doorway. His face was red; he was practically yelling, too.

"What are you doing? Turn that off!"

"I got bored, and, um . . ." I fumbled with the channel changer, first turning the volume so loud Pater put his hands over his ears. I finally got it turned off. My hands shook.

"You shouldn't be watching that. And what are you eating? Where did you get that?"

My bread still lay on the table, three-quarters eaten, surrounded by crumbs.

"I got hungry, and it was in the refrigerator, and I—"

He walked past me, angry, but I didn't know why. I didn't think it was that bad to watch the television. He'd never minded before, whenever we had one. I knew I shouldn't have eaten the bread, but it was only one piece.

He went into the kitchen, pulled open the refrigerator door, then closed it. He stood with his back to me, fingers still gripping the handle. "Where are our things?"

"In the bedroom, down the hall," I said. "There's only one bed."

He was silent.

"Pater?"

"I'm going to lie down for a few minutes."

He walked to the bedroom and closed the door. I had never known him to take a nap.

I sat holding the channel changer, wishing I could turn the television back on, wishing I'd never turned it on. Wishing I could see Officer Villareal again, hear her tell the whole world how smart I was, and what a good father Pater was. If only he'd seen that part, he wouldn't have been so angry.

I hoped he'd be done with his nap by lunchtime. I hoped we wouldn't have to leave this place. Not before I got to take a shower, and feed the baby goat again. Not before I figured out where the peacocks liked to hide.

The wind picked up again in the treetops outside, making that sound like something was coming from far, far away. It was one of my favorite sounds in the forest, but here, now, it made my skin prickle, my chest close in. I wanted to run from the sound, but all I could do was sit there, and wait.

And then I remembered the blue notebook that Officer Villareal gave me. I could keep myself busy by writing all of this down, everything that was happening.

Pater hadn't quite closed the door all the way. He lay flat on his back, his arm over his eyes. I tried to slip in quietly, but he heard me unzip my backpack. He didn't say anything. I could just tell.

"I'm getting my notebook to write in."

He cleared his throat. "I know none of this is your fault, Lindy. I just need some rest."

"It's okay," I said, feeling awkward, but the funny thing was, I was starting to believe that. All of this was too big for it to be something I could have started.

"I'll be out in a while," he said. "Close the door, please."

I did as he asked and then tiptoed back out to the living room, notebook and pen in my hands. I clicked the pen once or twice, turned to a new page, and let thoughts fill my head.

Usually I only liked to write about Nature, about birds and plants and geography, but once Officer Villareal started asking me questions about my life, I'd started thinking more about me. What was I if I wasn't Nature? I was as much beating heart as a hummingbird, as much instinct as a bobcat. I could be timid like a deer mouse and stealthy like a mink. I could run as fast downhill as the creek and forage as well as a raccoon. I was a part of everything in this world, of all that was happening, all around me. Wasn't I worth writing about, too?

# 28

She should have worked out a better exit strategy, Jess realized when she'd finished. She had no car to walk to, no building to escape inside. She turned toward the street, thinking she might catch a bus, hail a cab, but cabs only came this far out when you called them. She didn't know the bus schedule. There were stops along North Point, she knew, but had no idea what routes would take her all the way across town, and where the hell was she going to go, anyway? She couldn't go home.

Almost all of the reporters and camera crews had peeled off to file their reports on air. A couple of stragglers continued to film her. Anything she did now they'd use against her, or against Ray and Lindy.

She headed toward the parking lot, as if she were going to pick up her cruiser. *Right,* she thought, *who am I fooling?* She pulled out her cell phone, trying to think: who could she call to come get her?

"Jess, over here," a familiar voice said. Darryl polished the hood of one of the unmarked cars the detectives used. "Come here," he said, then spoke loudly to the cameramen following her: "Leave the officer alone. Go on, get the hell out of here."

They stood filming him now.

Darryl walked toward Jess and took her hand with his thick, callused one, pulling her toward his maintenance shed. His "garage," he liked to call it, but it was just a Tuff Shed, tricked out with a space heater and shelves filled with tools and supplies, a portable hydraulic jack in the middle of the asphalt floor. Inside, it was dark with no windows, a sliver of light coming from the top and bottom of the door after Darryl closed it. Jess breathed in the smell of motor oil, gas fumes, that weird-smelling hand cleaner for getting grease off. She heard a click and a rectangular fluorescent fixture blinked on.

"Thank you," she said, taking a seat on a low stool. She hadn't realized how badly she was shaking. "But you're going to get yourself in trouble. I'm not one of the good guys anymore."

He took a seat on a taller stool opposite her, folded his beefy arms over his stomach. "The hell you're not," he said.

They listened. All was quiet.

"I can't believe all this," she said. "How am I going to get out of here?"

"One step at a time. I was about to have lunch. Want a ham sandwich? Wife always makes me two, even though she says I need to lose weight." He reached behind him to pull a small blue cooler off the shelf. "And if we're lucky, there might be some cole slaw left over from last night."

"Your wife's the lucky one," Jess said. "I'm glad she feeds you well."

He shrugged and handed her a sandwich. She was starving. She hadn't eaten since lunch the day before. She took a bite of soft bread and too much mayonnaise and good smoky ham, then pulled out her phone.

"You know the number for Metro Taxi?" she asked.

Darryl pulled out his own phone and hit SPEED DIAL, then ordered her a cab. "VIP treatment," he said to the dispatcher, winking at Jess.

Soon it would be twelve o'clock. The chief would give his press conference. Her deadline would be up. Her ass would officially be grass, and even if the press now left Ray and Lindy alone (which they wouldn't, who was she trying to kid?), they'd no doubt show up at her court dates. Would they treat her like friend or foe, victim or perpetrator? Only time and the whims of a ratings-hungry media would tell.

She took another bite, tried to concentrate on only the food in her mouth. She wished Darryl's wife would have thought of mustard.

"You're on early, Darryl. You really like your job, huh?"

He nodded.

"You ever do anything else for a living?"

"Oh, hell, yeah." He finished chewing his bite before continuing. "This is just my semiretirement career. I ran my dad's hardware store in Klamath Falls for twenty-seven years. I always liked tinkering with cars, though. Washing them, waxing them. I don't know. Weird, I guess."

She shook her head. "Not really. It's good to be doing what you love."

He chuckled. "You've never been anything but a cop, huh?"

"Never wanted to be anything else." Her chin trembled and she clenched her jaw against it, the way she had her entire life against anything too sad or unfathomable.

At five past twelve, Darryl cracked open the shed door. All but one straggler had moved on to the press conference. He was probably a freelancer for those stupid tabloid shows, trying to get footage of Jess emerging like a celebrity from rehab. Darryl strode over to him, motioning for Jess to stay inside. She watched as he argued with him at first, then slipped him some bills. A cab idled at the curb.

"Keep track of the bribes, there, big fella," Jess whispered as she reached to hug him. "I'll pay you back."

"When you're back on the payroll."

"Thank you," she said, then trotted to the taxi and ducked inside.

"What's going on? Was there a shooting or something?" The driver, an older woman in a Sierra Club cap, looked in the rearview mirror at Jess.

"It wasn't a shooting. Just a good old-fashioned lynching."

"Doesn't surprise me," the woman said.

"I take it you don't watch TV."

The driver shook her head. "Only the political stuff on Sunday morning. *Meet the Press, Face the Nation.* I miss that Tim Russert. Only honest guy on TV." She turned to look at Jess. "So, where to?"

*Home,* Jess thought. "8774 Southwest Formosa. Just take the South Columbia exit off 319, then—"

"Yep," the driver said, turning forward, putting the car in drive. "You got it."

Jess sat back, taking a long last look at the station house, turning in her seat to watch it fade. She loved that building, its old brick exterior, the green tile roof and arched leaded windows, almost like church windows. Would she ever walk inside again as an employee? Would she get back her badge and weapon? She didn't care about the gun so much, but she felt naked without the badge in her purse, without the credentials that certified who she was, who she'd always wanted to be.

She turned around, pulled out her cell phone, and dialed her mother.

"Ma, hi," she said, bracing herself. She should have called her hours ago.

"Oh, Jessica, I just saw you on TV and you were just so . . ." Clara sniffled, blew her nose. She'd been crying. "What you said was so good. How on earth can you be in trouble for that?"

"I . . . I don't know. That's the way the world works, I guess. I just couldn't follow orders this time." Her eyebrows drew together; she swallowed back emotion. "I think it'll be okay, though. The worst that can happen is I get fired." She wouldn't yet mention being investigated or prosecuted, possible jail time if they wanted to make an example of her.

"Are you still in that shed?"

Jess snorted. "Wha—? No, Ma. Don't believe everything you see on TV." That would probably be the image that marked her for life: the disgraced police officer hiding out in a Tuff Shed. "Are they still showing my house on TV?"

"Not in a while. And they quit using that awful police photo of you, once they filmed you at the police station. What happened to your hair, Jessica? Maybe I should send them some better photos of you."

"Yeah." Jess closed her eyes. "You do that."

"You know I'm proud of you, don't you, honey?" her mother asked, and suddenly Clara was the adult again, and Jess the child, needing this praise more than anything. The transformation was so quick, so absolute, even if temporary, that Jess felt needy enough to ask the question that had been lurking in the back of her mind.

"Mom, what do you think Dad would have done, if it were him instead of me?" She glanced up at the rearview mirror, self-conscious that the driver could hear, but the woman stared only at the road.

"Well," Clara said slowly, "he would have done what he thought was right."

Jess nodded and looked out the window. "He would have taken her to foster care."

Her mother was quiet for a moment, then said, "Your father was a good man, Jessica, but you're different than he was. Everything's different now. The important thing is you did what you thought was right."

Jess nodded, wiping beneath her eyes. "I did."

They were both silent for a moment; then Jess said, "Thanks, Ma. I love you, you know."

"I know. I love you, too. I'm sure everything will be all right, once this all calms down."

Jess marveled at Clara's newfound optimism, but agreed and hung up before she could ruin the nicest moment she'd had with her mother in years.

At the South Columbia exit, Jess sat forward. "Left here, then about a mile to the second right. Turn in at the Arbor Acres neighborhood."

The familiar houses, the elementary school on the left, the front yards passing by in full summer flower, all seemed to shimmer. She wanted to be in her neighborhood, on her block, in her home, at her kitchen table, having a cup of freshly brewed coffee.

As they turned at the second right, Jess could already see the towers on the satellite trucks on the next block. Her block.

"Can you just pull over for a minute?" she asked, and the driver pulled up in front of a yellow two-story, where Nina's friend Blaine had lived before they moved to California.

"I'm sorry. This isn't going to work," Jess said, noticing that another car had stopped a few hundred yards behind them, a white sedan, ordinary enough, but it was odd. No one got out. It just sat, as if waiting.

*Shit,* she thought. *It's like I'm in a movie or something.*

"God. I . . . um, I don't know where to go."

"No problem," the driver said, as if she drove media outlaws around all the time. "Take your time." She took an emery board from the console and whistled softly as she filed her fingernails.

Jess tried to think of places she could go. A public place maybe, the mall, a park, but then what? She couldn't go to her mother's. Even if Clara could put up with the drama, Jess couldn't put her through it. A silver car turned into her neighborhood, slowed, then pulled a U-turn and parked.

"How about . . . ?" Jess said. "I don't know. Could you take me to the South Columbia Mall?"

"Sure thing," the driver said.

"I'll . . . I'll pay you extra, for the trouble."

The driver waved her hand. "Don't you worry. Darryl put this ride on the city tab," she said. "They're good for it."

Under other circumstances, Jess might have said she'd pay for it herself, but now she thought, *Let them pay.* She settled back, trying to see inside the other cars as they passed them. They didn't immediately follow. Maybe she was just being paranoid. She tried deep breathing to calm herself, counting backward, but nothing helped. If only she'd gotten more sleep the night before.

At the mall, the driver pulled up to the entrance of Macy's. "This okay?" she asked, and Jess nodded, fishing in her wallet for a tip.

"No, really," the cabbie said. "It's okay. Darryl takes good care of me."

"Thank you," Jess said, "thank you so much," and pushed open the door into the afternoon heat. As she walked across the white concrete toward the glass doors, the driver sat and watched, then pulled away once Jess was inside.

Jess stood and waited for a few moments, watching for the cars she'd seen earlier, but the parking lot was swarming with white cars, silver cars. Nothing had changed since she'd been there the day before, shopping for Teo—it was a teeming mass of back-to-school shoppers.

Where could she go? Whom could she call? She pulled her phone from her purse and scrolled through her address book to Ellis's cell number. She shook her head. She couldn't involve him, not unless he offered to help, and even then maybe not. He had too much at stake.

And then she remembered. Someone *had* offered to help. She scrolled through her recent incoming calls until she got to "Zusmanovich, Christ." Apparently, there wasn't enough room on the display for Christopher. She hit DIAL, and when he answered, she said, "How would you feel about being a savior?"

"Excuse me?"

"Christ," she said. "That's who it says you are on my caller ID."

"Wow," he said. "That's kind of tough to live up to, but I'll try. How can I save you today?"

She sighed. "I could use a friend."

"Location?"

"South Columbia Mall. Macy's entrance."

"Give me twenty," Z said, "no, eighteen. I can do it in eighteen minutes."

Fifteen minutes later, a small Toyota pickup pulled up in front of the store, Larry's distinctive hamlike tongue hanging out the window. Jess walked from the store into the sunshine, over to the truck, and leaned down to look in. Z, Zoo, dog man pulled Larry back by the collar to make room for her.

"What am I supposed to call you again?"

He shrugged. "Chris?"

"Right. Okay, then. Thank you, Chris," she said, sliding in and sinking her hand into Larry's soft fur. He licked her arm, then laid his chin on her shoulder.

"Wow, and it's only our second date," she said, reaching to pet his smooth forehead. He smelled like dog. Clean dog, but dog nonetheless.

"Where to?" Chris asked.

"I don't know. I tried to go home, but . . ." She had to stop.

He nodded. "Yeah, not a good idea, not right now. You show up and you're going to be tried by media."

She turned to look at him. "You've been watching?"

"Oh, yeah. They're in such a frenzy right now they're inter-viewing your neighbors, the mailman, the squirrels. Pretty much everything that moves."

"Shit," she said. "I gave them a statement. What more do they want?"

Chris put the truck into gear. "How about this," he said. "I've got a futon in the living room. I'm a fine, upstanding citizen. You may not know this, but I'm actually a police offi-cer." He smiled the charming smile he had when she first met him the day before. He had a nice face, a wide jaw, a mole on his neck. Hazel eyes too much like Rick's.

"Thanks, but I don't think that's such a good—"

"Listen, I just want to help," he said, shrugging. "Really. No weirdness. I'm sorry about the J-Lo comment yesterday. I mean, I meant it, but not as anything more than, you know. Whatever. A description. Eyes. Your eyes. That's all."

Jess was silent. He knew as well as she did that he'd be plac-ing himself at risk. He barely knew her; why was he being so nice?

"And I'm on duty at three," he continued, "so you'll have the place to yourself. You can stay as long as you want and have some space to figure out what to do next."

"And you won't tell anyone?"

"That would be lame."

A futon. She hated futons, had slept on one all through college. A flat place to lie, though. She was so tired. She hoped he wouldn't look at her when he came home in the middle of the night. Her mouth would probably be hanging open, and god knew what she'd wear to sleep in. She wished she'd brought at least a couple of T-shirts, a change of underwear. Her toothbrush.

"I'm not quite sure how to say thank you in a meaningful enough way, but—"

"Just doing my part." He looked over at her and nodded, then pulled away from the curb. They headed north again until they were back in the city proper, then to a strip of freshly minted condo buildings along the south side of City Park.

Inside Chris's condo, Larry headed straight for his crate, circled twice, and settled in to chew on a rubber duck that squeaked as though being killed, over and over again. Chris gave her a quick tour: open kitchen, living-slash-dining room, tiny bathroom (with a supply of unopened toothbrushes she could choose from—no doubt for the lady friends), and the door to his bedroom.

"I think that's the biggest TV I ever saw," she said, turning back toward the living room.

"You're not really a grandmother, are you?" he asked. "What are you, like thirty-five?"

She shrugged, trying to hide the annoying pleasure she felt at this. "Some of us start younger than others." There was no need to tell him she'd be thirty-nine on her next birthday.

"Wow." He fidgeted, then said, "Well, I'd better go get ready for work. I need a quick shower."

Jess felt her face redden. *For god's sake,* she thought. How was she going to handle the morning? The bathroom sharing, the peeing sounds, the smells?

"Yup, you go. I'm fine here. I'll see if I can figure out how to work the freakishly large TV."

"It's easy, really," he said, grabbing a remote control from the glass coffee table.

"Got it," she said. "Really, I'm technically adept. Go. Shower."

He handed her the remote. "If you're hungry, or need a Coke or something, help yourself."

She nodded. "Will do."

"Okay."

"Okay."

"Right," he said, and backed away.

When she finally heard the shower, she relaxed. This was not good. She'd need to find another place, or buck up and go home. But then she'd be a prisoner, under watch at all times. She'd look guilty of something. Chris was right: trial by media.

If only she could go stay with Ellis and Maggie. They were probably her best friends. Would they still be? Their kids called her Aunt Jess. God, their kids. No matter how Ellis might feel about what she'd done, there was no way he could risk associating with her now. She wouldn't do that to him, to his family.

Who else? Not Nina, of course. Even if she'd allow it, which she wouldn't, Jess knew it was just a matter of time before she'd be required to stay within state lines. She tried to think of what her other options were, rejecting casual friends, other officers, and coworkers. It was disconcerting to realize that she had no one to turn to under these circumstances.

"Okay, dog man, I guess it's you," she said. In a way, he was the perfect choice. She had just met him; no one would think to look for her here. Turning on the television, she leaned back against the upright futon. As soon as he was gone, she'd fold it out, lie down, and catch a nap.

After only a moment, or what felt like a moment, Jess was being pulled from thick, downy sleep by the sound of drilling, or an electric screwdriver, like the one Rick had given her for Christmas early in their marriage. She sat up and looked around, wondering where she was, wondering what the sound was, and then it stopped. A huge Pat Sajak smiled idiotically from the television screen in front of her. The sun slanted through the blinds at a low angle.

"Great," she said, wiping something crusted on her cheek. She'd drooled in her sleep, or . . . wait. No. Something had licked her. She remembered now. Larry, hopefully.

It was almost evening. They'd been gone for almost two hours; Chris had seen her passed out before he left.

She heard the noise again, and realized she'd been hearing it in her dreams for some time. It was her phone in her purse on the coffee table, vibrating against the glass. Jess leaned forward, dug through the bag until she felt the plastic rectangle and pulled it out. Without thinking, she answered.

"Hello?"

"Is this Officer Jessica Villareal?" It was a woman's voice, harsh, beat-up, opinioned in some way already. She didn't sound like media. She sounded like the women Jess busted for petty theft, the ones who had black eyes and bruises but never reported domestic abuse, the ones who had kids to support and couldn't find work, who turned to the streets sometimes, who medicated their pain with anything they could afford.

"Who's this?" Jess asked, internal alarm sounding.

"Faith Wiggs."

"Melinda Faith Wiggs? Lindy?" Jess said, but of course it wasn't. "Who is this?" she said again. Was it an aunt? The grandmother?

"You know damn well who this is. I'm calling to get my daughter back, and I know you have her. You have no right to her. She's mine."

Jess shuddered. Why hadn't she tried harder to find the mother? What if this woman was who she said she was, had cleaned up, been looking for Lindy all along? There'd been no missing-person report but maybe she'd given up after a couple of years, or maybe they'd just missed it. "I don't have Lindy," she tried to explain.

"Don't give me that shit. You're the only one who knows where she is, you pig dyke."

"Excuse me?" Jess snorted. "You sure you want to be calling an officer of the peace that? You know what kind of penalty that carries?"

"You tell me where Lindy is and I won't make your life miserable."

Jess rolled her eyes, but held her tongue. At least she no longer felt guilty about not looking for this woman, but she had to figure out how much of a threat she might be. "Where are you?" Jess asked.

"Phoenix, not that it's any of your business."

"I'm on TV in Phoenix?"

"You sure are, and I called the TV station here and they got your number for me. They say they'll get me a plane ticket to come out there if they can come along and film me and her, our reunion. But first they say I have to know where Lindy is. Are you going to tell me or not?"

"If you're really her mom, why didn't you call the police?"

"'Cause I don't trust you pigs, not a one of you."

Jess shook her head. "Let's slow down, Ms. Wiggs. A: you have to quit insulting me, and B: I thought your name was Crystal."

"Oh, that's perfect! Don't you believe a word that goddamn Ray Wiggs tells you. He doesn't know a thing about me, and he's one to talk, Mr. I'm-so-fucked-up-by-the-war chickenshit loser. What kind of man is that, anyway? He can't even provide for her, let alone both her and me, and then he stole her and the car. And I made the payments on that damn thing the whole time he was in Iraq."

Jess closed her eyes. "Did you ever file charges, Ms. Wiggs? A missing-person report? Did you do anything about it?"

"I—I was sick."

"And are you still . . . sick?"

"What are you saying? That I don't deserve my daughter because I have a few personal problems? Everybody has problems."

"Maybe," Jess said, "but you know what? You can't be a drug addict and raise a child. That's one of those little rules it's my job to enforce. Are you still using?"

"What the . . . ? Fuck you! Just . . . just fuck you. You're going to be sorry you spoke to me that way. The man at the station thinks I can get on the *Today* show, and maybe *Inside Edition*, and I'll tell everyone what you said to me. He said they'll probably even fly me out to New York, if I have Lindy with me. They're talking about giving her a college fund, too. You think you're in trouble now? You better watch out. When I'm through with you—"

Jess hit the OFF button, trembling. The woman might be Lindy's mother, but she'd never gone looking for her before, not until someone mentioned money. Jess would be damned if she let her get even a glimpse of the daughter she'd given up on so easily. And she was definitely still using. Whatever kind of mother she'd been early on, she was too far gone now. Some effects of long-term drug use were irreversible, like brain damage.

Her phone rang again, with the same number. Jess ignored it, wondering how many times she'd call before she'd finally give up.

Crystal. Had it been Ray's name for his wife, or Lindy's? How much did the girl know about her mother? Jess wished she could go back over their reports from the day before, the statements Ellis had taken from Ray, to see what he'd called her.

Ellis was on duty now. Her pulse revved as she found him in her address book and hit SEND.

"Jenkins," he said. From the background noise, she guessed he was in his cruiser.

"Villareal." She bit her lip.

"V!" The concern in his voice brought tears to her eyes. "Where the hell are you? I tried your cell phone, but you never picked up."

"I know. The press is calling constantly so I'm not answering," she said.

"Are you okay?"

She blinked rapidly. "Mm-hmm."

"Where are you? You're not at home, I hope. You know, if you need, uh . . ." His voice faltered, and Jess knew to take it as a kind gesture. It would be too difficult for him if she said yes.

"I'm good. Staying with a friend."

"Listen, you know our friendship is solid, right? It's not that. I just can't be taking chances with my career right now. With my family."

"I know."

"Troy's going to need braces next year, and Alison—"

"It's okay, Ellis. I wouldn't do that to you."

They were quiet for a moment. His police radio crackled in the background.

Jess cleared her throat. "So, Officer Jenkins, I have a question for you. What name did Ray use for his wife? What did he call her when you were questioning him yesterday?"

"Uh, let's see. Fay? Faith? Yeah, Faith. He was actually pretty respectful, considering. Why? Is he calling her something more appropriate now, Meth-head Momma?" He chuckled at himself.

"Read my notes from questioning Lindy," Jess said. "When you get back to the office. Just in case this blows up into a custody battle. I think the kid's got more street smarts than we suspected."

"Yeah? What makes you think so?"

"You'll see." She paused. "I, um, haven't had the courage to watch the chief's news conference. Without being too graphic, exactly how deep is the shit I'm in?"

"You didn't watch? You're telling me your job's at stake and you didn't watch?"

"I just said I didn't watch, butt head, so tell me."

"Oh, no. I'm not telling you. Turn on the damn TV. It's playing over and over. And over. You can't miss it."

Ellis wasn't a sadist. How bad could it be?

*Bad,* she thought.

"Fine. Be that way. You gotta go, anyway. You're on duty, and you're driving. Haven't you heard that driving a car and talking on the phone don't mix?" She paused. "Thank you, Ellis. Say hi to Maggie and the kids."

"You gonna be all right?"

"I don't know yet," she said. "I'll let you know."

# 29

Pater keeps looking out the windows, walking from one to the other, hitching up his pants. He reminds me of a finch, all nervous and fidgety, eyes darting this way and that. He woke from his nap when a plane flew over, just one of the normal kind that flies up in the clouds, a big sound from far away, but he asked me to move away from the window.

Now we are sitting here, him staring into space, me writing. I don't know what will happen. When he gets like this, it usually passes quickly, but we've been sitting here for a long time. When he first got up from his nap, I asked him if he wanted something to eat for lunch, and he shook his head no. I asked him if it was okay if I ate, and he looked like himself for a moment.

"Yes, of course. Go fix yourself something."

I went to hug him, and laid my head against his chest. His heart was beating too fast.

"Don't be scared," I said. "I'm not scared, so don't you be."

It was what he used to say to me when we first got to the forest and I was afraid of everything, of every twig snapping and insect buzzing. Back then I thought that every bug that flew was a bee that would sting me, but Pater showed me the differences between all of the flying insects, the shapes of their wings, the articulation of their bodies, the sounds they made. And like all of Nature's creatures, bees don't want to hurt you. They just don't want to be hurt.

Mark and John have invited us for supper, but Pater said no, thank you. We've imposed enough as it is, he told them, and we just want to be left to ourselves.

I don't want to be left to myself. I would like to eat dinner in that big house, sitting and talking and laughing at a table with other people. John told me Mark is a very good cook, even now that they don't eat meat. I want to go collect eggs in the morning and find out what an omelet is. I told John I knew where to find mushrooms in his woods, and we're supposed to do that, too. If I never get to go outside, I don't think I'm going to like living here very much. I have to be outside to breathe, to move, to feel like myself, and I can't even go near a window.

For now, all I can do is write.

# 30

Jess wandered the confines of Chris's apartment. While well stocked in dog chow, there was very little for humans to eat. He'd left her a pair of police-issue sweats and a T-shirt on the dining table with a note: "I'll pick up more food on the way home. Sorry. All I have is cereal and hot dogs." He signed off with a smiley face. Jess rolled her eyes, but, yes, it was nice. He was nice.

She grabbed a Coke, poured a bowl of Cheerios—smelling the milk before using it—then sat back down. The five o'clock news would be on in a few minutes. She was glad she'd waited to watch; by now it might all be old news. Maybe some politician had been caught having a sex life. Maybe peace had broken out in the Middle East.

At the sound of the station's fanfare, the roll of red and blue graphics, Jess's throat constricted against the food she was eating. As the last graphic fell away, a sign appeared on-screen: "North Station House" in governmental white on brown.

"Great," Jess said, mouth full, but as the camera zoomed out, it revealed a group of people standing on the steps in front of the building. Women mostly, but a few men. Twenty, thirty people maybe. She couldn't be sure.

The female voiceover said, "Our top story tonight: public outcry in the case of the missing forest people and the police officer trying to protect them."

*Protect them?* Jess held her breath.

A few people held signs: "Support Our Troops—Even At Home," "Leave Them Alone." She reached for the remote and turned the volume higher, as though that might help her see more clearly, to examine the faces and expressions, to discern the words the people chanted in the background, behind the self-important voice of the anchor, who said, ". . . in what has become a movement by citizens to protest recent decisions made by the Columbia Police Department . . ."

Jess set down her bowl. Her stomach fluttered with nervousness and excitement. What was happening?

The anchorwoman sat at her blue Plexiglas desk now, her face as rapt as someone reporting a cure for cancer. "And now to our reporter on the scene in north Columbia. Paula?"

The image switched to the female reporter Jess had spoken with earlier, disheveled and tired, standing in front of the small crowd of mostly white people singing "We Shall Overcome," like it was the 1960s or something.

Jess laughed, hand to her mouth. *Oh, Oregon,* she thought. *Oh, Columbia, city by, for, and of the people.* They were goofy—

they would be viewed by the rest of the country as hopeless bleeding hearts—but damn if they weren't a beautiful sight.

Toward the back she saw a towering presence with a shiny bald head, and next to him a regal silver-haired black woman in a clerical collar and robe. The Lord worked in mysterious ways, all right, she thought, wondering how she'd ever thank them. If this was all they could do, it would be enough, she realized, just this show of support, this voice against the empire.

"That's right, Ann. The people of Columbia have a new cause tonight. And these people who've been gathering here all afternoon say they just want their voices to be heard."

The image switched to an earlier taped interview of an older woman with frizzy gray hair and wearing a loose-fitting sundress. *Oh, god,* Jess thought. *Not a hippie.* But the woman was articulate and sounded sensible.

"We'd like to know why this family must be separated," she said. "Too few of the children living in poverty in our country get the parental care they need, the education they need. So why do we allow that to happen, but persecute the struggling parent who is actually doing a pretty good job? Are we really helping that little girl by taking her away from her father?"

"Exactly," Jess said. She wished someone were here to watch this with her. She hoped Everett was watching. She hoped everyone was watching. Not that it would change anything; she'd still be investigated—she had obstructed the department's idea of justice, and yes, she'd been insubordinate. There was no doubt about it. Worse, they'd still try to hunt down Ray and Lindy. The wheels were rolling, and governmental wheels were hard to stop once in motion, even if people involved wanted them to stop. Rules were rules. It was all about perception— the perception of weakness if an organization admitted mistakes, when really, wouldn't they look stronger by appearing to be run by humans?

A short clip of Chief Gleason came on next, and what had apparently become his sound bite: "We are not opposed to helping people. That's our job. But we believe the girl is in jeopardy."

The anchorwoman reappeared on screen. "A spokesman for the police department says this protest won't change anything. The father and daughter involved will be located, and Officer Jessica Villareal, the policewoman who went against orders to keep them together, will face an investigation and remain on paid leave until further notice."

Maybe Jess should have been watching all day, like those O.J. addicts and car-chase weirdos. She changed to channel seven, which had much the same scene of picketers, only from a different angle. A small black girl in a pink tutu held a sign. Not just any girl. It was Alison Jenkins, her little hand in Maggie's. The sign read:

### FREE JESS VILLAREAL

· · ·

AFTER A SHOWER, JESS PULLED on the sweats and T-shirt, then settled in to check all the phone calls she'd let go to voice mail. Faith Wiggs had called exactly ten times, then given up, and

Jess hoped forever. The media calls had not slowed, even after her impromptu press conference.

Jess sat cross-legged on the futon, trying to figure out how to call the farm to get a message to Ray about his wife. Jess's cell phone records would be investigated, and subpoenaed if they pressed charges. It didn't feel safe to call the church, either. They had so much at stake. And she couldn't use Chris's phone to disguise herself. He'd be investigated, as well, if they thought he was helping her. She had to make sure she didn't implicate him in any way.

Jess stared at the phone in her hand, the small oblong of hard plastic, running her thumb in small circles over the face, then flipped it open. She dialed the only number she didn't need speed dial for.

"Hello?" Nina sounded distracted, but happy. She hadn't looked at her caller ID, Jess guessed, and she was probably getting Teo ready for bed.

"Hi, honey. Am I interrupting?"

"Oh, hi. Actually, yeah, I'm reading Teo a story right now."

Nina never offered to call her back when she couldn't talk, which was most of the time.

"Okay. Your grandma said you two were coming down, so I just—"

"Well, maybe," Nina said. "I still haven't decided for sure."

"Oh, okay. Um, I'll let you go then, but . . . Well, could you just put Teo on for a second?" Jess felt emotion rising, heard the nasal quality in her voice.

"Are you okay?" her daughter asked, and Jess knew she would always remember the concern in Nina's voice at that moment. She closed her eyes, breathed in, out, fingers along the top of her collarbone. She could feel her heart thud into the heel of her hand.

"No, actually. I've been suspended, Neen. I didn't take a kid to foster care because she had a perfectly capable parent, but it's become a big deal around here. It's on the news."

"What? Mom!"

"I know. I know I always say that you have to play by the rules, that laws may not always make sense but they're for the greater good, blah blah blah." She paused. "I couldn't do it this time. I snapped."

"It's on the news?"

Jess could hear fumbling, Teo being shushed. She guessed Nina was walking through her apartment to the TV in the living room.

"What channel are you on?"

"I don't know. All of them." Jess sighed. If it was on in Phoenix, it was on in Tacoma. "Don't watch. It's just so stupid."

"Of course I'm going to watch. Where are you? Are you at home?"

"No, our house is staked out with reporters. It's just insane. I'm staying with a friend."

"Damn it, I can't find any news on," Nina said. "But, Mom, if someone like you snapped, well. I don't know. You must have had a pretty good reason."

Jess paused in surprise, then said, "Well, thank you. But I think it might be a good idea to postpone your trip down here, with all that's going on. As much as I want to see you both . . ."

"No, we're going to come," Nina said.

Again, Jess was surprised, but happily so. And they could stay with Clara, she realized. Once Nina had something in mind, that was it. This time, it was in Jess's favor, and she knew a miracle when she saw one. She didn't argue.

As THE SUN WORKED ITS way up the blinds the next morning, Jess woke to the sound of metallic banging. She turned her head toward the noise to see Larry lying in his crate, watching her, whacking his tail against the side of the enclosure. The crate door was wide-open; apparently he just really loved lying in the thing.

"Good morning," she whispered, and his tail thumped faster. She patted the futon beside her. "Come here."

His ears perked.

"Come on, Larry," she whispered. "I haven't had anyone to spoon with in ages."

He pulled himself gingerly from the crate, tail still wagging, making a small whining sound.

"Shh," Jess said. "You'll wake your dad. Come here."

He walked over and sniffed the futon, sniffed the hand Jess extended, then licked it. She scratched behind his ears and patted the bed again. "This is my final offer."

Larry lumbered his large body onto the futon beside Jess, grinning down at her with his tongue hanging directly over her head.

"No drooling, buddy," she said. "Lie down, okay?"

He circled twice, nearly fell off the edge on his final rotation, then settled next to her, his head on her hip. Jess stroked him until she grew sleepy again, and he shifted and pawed his way over the blanket so that he was lying against her.

"Good boy," she said, hand on his side. His ribs rose and fell, and he was warm and soft. Her thoughts jumbled into snatches of imagery: downed trees and sticker bushes, white sneakers with hearts, dark alleyways, church choirs. And then the comfort of nothing.

Her next conscious thought was a panicky "I'm late." She reached over the dog for her watch on the coffee table, opening her eyes to a bright morning. Behind her, in the kitchen, someone coughed. Larry jumped off the futon and trotted away.

Jess pulled the blanket over her head.

"Good morning," Chris said.

"Mm-hmm." The blanket trapped her voice. She lowered it. "How long have you been up?" She looked at the watch in her hand. Nine thirty.

"Just long enough to feel seriously inferior to my dog. He always gets the ladies."

"Funny," Jess said, arranging the T-shirt and sweat pants into a presentable position beneath the blankets before she crawled out. "You better have coffee or I'm not sleeping here ever again."

"Nice outfit," he said, turning to pull a mug from the cupboard. His own sat on the counter. He was already dressed in long cargo shorts and another police-issue T-shirt.

"Thanks. It's the police department's. Someone seems to have a thing for contraband casual wear." She crossed her arms over her chest, walked barefoot into the kitchen. "Actually, I do want to thank you, for, well, everything. I don't know wha—"

"Hey," he said, handing her the filled mug. "It's not everyone who gets to have a local hero living under the same roof. Sleeping with their dog."

"It was Larry's idea," she said, face turning warm as she took a sip. "And I wouldn't exactly say I'm a hero. I've disgraced the department."

Chris leaned back against the counter, studying her. She wished he'd stop. She knew how she looked in the morning. Why did men always look like themselves when they first woke up?

"You know," he said, "I bet they'll find a way to spin it so that it sounds like it was actually their idea, just to get in on some of the good juju. The department hasn't had much in the way of positive PR in a long time."

Jess didn't buy it. Reality was sinking in, and she felt numb at the thought that she could no longer go to her job or her house, or drive her car. If she could go back in time, two mornings ago . . . She sighed. Would she still muscle her way in on the search for Lindy?

Of course she would.

"You're the hottest thing going in this town at the moment," Chris said. "Have you actually watched the coverage?"

She shrugged. "I made myself watch the beginning of the five o'clock news yesterday. I saw the people standing on the steps." Saying this, she felt shy. "It was nice."

He did that thing again where he leaned his head sideways, smiled that smile. It was starting to piss her off. She didn't want to have to worry that she had bed hair or sleep wrinkles or crud in her eyes; she didn't want to contemplate whether he liked her *that* way. She had no appeal, anyway, to a guy this good-looking, this young, who kept extra toothbrushes for overnight guests, who couldn't fathom what it meant to be a parent. Anyway, Jess preferred the easy comfort of Larry to snuggle up to.

"What?" she asked. "Why are you looking at me like that?"

"Not telling," he said. "You'll see. I want to take you somewhere, okay? Humor me."

She rolled her eyes, but drained her coffee cup and went to get ready for the day.

ONCE IN THE SMALL PICKUP, Larry again lodged between them, Chris drove north.

"We're going to the station house," Jess guessed.

"Yup." Chris flipped on his turn signal at the interstate entrance.

"Okay, yeah, there are supporters there. I get it. I saw it on TV. I know you're probably trying to make me feel better, but it's not actually going to be a pleasant experience for me. I've been suspended, remember? My future with the department is . . ." What was it? "Bleak," she decided.

"Ah, come on, it'll be fun," he said. "Here." He removed the OSU Beavers cap he'd tugged on as they left his apartment, tossed it to her. "Put that on so you won't be recognized."

Jess fingered the black-and-orange cap, studied the bucktoothed—and apparently rabid—rodent adorning it. "I can't. No way I can wear a Beavers cap."

"Why? Did you go to U of O? Tell me you're not a Duck."

"No, I just refuse to put something on my head that says 'beaver.' Call me quaint."

"Hey," he said, "my mom was a Beaver mom, and a proud

one. She had the bumper sticker and everything. Don't go saying anything creepy."

"But this picture is ridiculous. Since when is a beaver fierce? They build dams and stuff. They're nature's engineers, not warriors."

He looked at her, shook his head. "Man, you think too much."

She looked out the window, tall trees zipping by, interspersed with office buildings and hotels. "No kidding," she said, drumming her fingers on the armrest.

They pulled off at the North Point Boulevard exit and headed west. As they neared the station, Chris slowed down. "Oh, wow," he said.

Hundreds of people filled the lawns and sidewalks, the steps: men and women, children and teenagers, grandparents. Babies in strollers and backpacks and slings. Dogs on leashes. There was a festive air to the crowd, signs and banners.

"It's a street fair," Jess said, heart pounding. "It's the neighborhood block party."

"Right," Chris said, slowing to a crawl. "Better put that hat on."

Jess twisted her hair and pulled it through the cap's back opening, snugging the bill low on her forehead. Where yesterday there had been three news satellite trucks, there were now six or seven, dwarfing the old building. "Great," she muttered, slinking lower in her seat. Some of the signs even had her photo on them, that damn police ID photo. Where was her mother when she needed her?

Chris whistled softly between his teeth. "This is amazing."

"It's freaking me out."

"In a good way, though, right?"

Jess closed her eyes and nodded. What would happen if she got out of the car, ran into the crowd? She shuddered, imagining enthusiastic trampling. It should have been dying down by now; she'd hoped that people would forget Ray and Lindy existed as soon as the next big story broke.

"I don't know," she said. "I'm not so sure the department will feel warm and fuzzy about this. I think it just might inflame everyone, including the media."

Today she felt further removed from the Columbia Police Department than she ever had; the force had always been her surrogate family, but now it had deserted her. The public display in front of her was both frightening and moving, seeing this many people assert that her actions were correct and honorable.

Being a cop had always seemed the way to achieve those things, but too often she'd had to choose the least bad alternative when trying to help others. Leave the kid with the negligent but loving mother or drag him away from all he knew to be raised by competent strangers? Or sometimes incompetent or downright evil strangers? Let the battering spouse off with a warning, or arrest him, knowing the violent reprisals he would visit upon his wife when he got out? Ignore the kids smoking pot in the park and hope it was a phase they'd grow out of, or bust them and cause untold repercussions in their families, their educations, their social lives? She'd always tried to find a balance, but—unlike now—within the law.

They'd driven the length of the entire block. Chris stopped at the intersection and looked at her. "I didn't think it would make you feel bad," he said. "I'm sorry."

She shrugged. "No, it's good. Really. I'm just . . . I don't know. Overwhelmed."

"What would feel better? What can I do for you?" he asked.

Jess wasn't sure if anyone had ever asked her that before. She had to think for a moment. "I want to go home," she said. "But I can't."

"Let's go check it out," he said, turning south then east to head back to the highway.


JUST AS THE DAY BEFORE, Jess saw satellite trucks on her block as soon as they turned into the development, towers spiking up through her neighbor's monkey-puzzle trees and her own half-dead cedar.

"Forget it," Jess said, tears springing to her eyes. "Damn it."

"Hang on," Chris said. "What if I sneak in and get some things for you?"

"They'll see you." Jess sniffed, embarrassed at her emotion.

"Do I have to keep reminding you that I am a trained law enforcement professional? I'm Batman, remember?" He flashed his tattooed knuckles at her. "I have stealth on my side. I'll go through the back."

Jess turned in her seat to study his profile. He was serious, and Michael had pulled it off the day before. "Well, then circle around this loop and make the next right," she said, directing him to where Michael had parked.

Once there, Jess handed him the house key and gave him directions from the greenbelt to the back of her house. "It's the only one without a screen door," she said. "Well, it's there, but it's leaning up against the house." It had always been too far down her to-do list to ever get fixed.

"And? What do you want me to grab?"

She tried to think. Nina's baby book? Photo albums? No. This wasn't a hurricane or a tsunami; it only felt like one.

"The back door goes into the kitchen. You can get a grocery bag from next to the fridge. Then go into the living room and turn left down the hall. My room's the last one. In the dresser, second drawer on the right, just grab a few T-shirts. I don't care which." She couldn't ask him for underwear, as much as she wanted to. "Then in the bottom drawer on that side there are two pairs of jeans. Grab the light-colored ones." The dark jeans had been purchased in an optimistic moment when she'd been going to the gym for two weeks.

"T-shirts, jeans. Check. What else?"

"I would love my face cream out of the bathroom. It's in the medicine cabinet."

"I'm a guy. You're gonna have to give me more to go on than that. Does it say 'face cream' in big bold letters or something?"

"Hope in a Jar. It's called Hope in a Jar." This was more than embarrassing. This was revealing her deepest insecurities to a complete stranger.

"Hope in a Jar. Check." He struggled not to smile.

She shook her head. "Back out in the living room, on the bookshelf, there's a photo of my daughter and grandson. Actually, there's a ton of photos of them, but I want the one in the small blue frame that says 'I Love Grandma' on the bottom. That's it. That'll do for now."

He nodded and started to get out of the car. Larry lifted on his haunches to follow, but Chris turned and said, "Hold. Protect the lady. Don't let the bad guys near her." He winked at Jess and closed the door.

Larry resettled and put his paw on her leg. She took it in her hand and watched Chris walk away. She scanned for reporters, for nosy neighbors, for boogeymen until he reappeared.

He strode toward the car carrying a paper bag more filled than she'd expected, grinning like he'd slain a dragon or won the lottery.

"Here you go," he said as he slid behind the wheel.

She took the bag and tucked it away at her feet without looking inside, embarrassed that he'd been through her personal things. But one thing was clear: he wasn't a jerk. He probably wasn't even a player. Maybe he just went to the dentist a lot and stocked up on the freebie toothbrushes.

Jess had a new idea.

Larry sat tall and serene between them; she had to lean around him to see Chris. "How would you feel about letting me borrow the truck to drive out into wine country?"

He squinted. "Isn't it a little early in the day to be drinking?"

"I need to go see Ray and Lindy." She worried that she shouldn't have revealed their general whereabouts, but she felt compelled to go. If she drove out there, she could tell Ray in person about the *Good Morning America* offer in case he wanted to take it, which she doubted, and about Faith's whiff of blood money. She was pretty sure he and Lindy were safe at the farm, but he should know what was happening outside of the news reports. He should be able to make decisions based on all of the facts. And, Jess had to admit, she wanted to see Lindy one more time, to make sure she was okay.

Chris turned the key in the ignition. "I'll take you," he said.

"Uh-uh." Jess shook her head. "You're already too involved."

He put the truck in first gear. "We could argue for the next ten minutes, or you could just tell me now how to get there."

He meant it; Jess shook her head again, but gave him directions.

As they drove, she listened to the new voice messages she'd accumulated. She'd gotten so used to her phone vibrating that she barely noticed it anymore.

As she listened, she lowered her window a few inches to let in air. Larry stood and stepped into her lap, pushing his nose out into the wind rushing by.

"Down," Chris said, trying to pull him back, but Jess waved him off.

"It's okay," she said. "Look how happy it makes him."

Chris shook his head. "All that training down the tubes," he said, but Jess had a feeling he was thinking the same thing: look how happy it makes her.

In addition to repeat calls from the local stations, she had three new calls from the *Good Morning America* person, one from the *Today* show, two from someone with Anderson Cooper's show, and several from FOX. Now Ray had even more options. Personally, she wouldn't be responding to the requests she was receiving for interviews. She'd said everything that needed to be said.

She wondered if Ray had watched any news coverage, if he was freaking out. If he and Lindy could just keep their heads down long enough, eventually it would all go away. That was what she'd tell him. She hoped he'd believe her and not make any decisions just yet.

In addition to media calls, she'd received nice messages from Maddy and one of the detectives who she'd always assumed didn't like her, but here he was telling her to stick to her guns on this one. Her mother had called again and then, oddly, Rick. They never spoke about anything unless it was related to Nina or Mateo, and that was rare now that Nina was on her own.

"Um, hi," his voice said on the message. All these years apart and they still didn't need to identify themselves to each other on the phone. After a long pause, he said, "I don't know what's going on exactly with you and these, these forest people, but, um, I hope you're doing okay. I mean, I'm sure you are. You're one tough lady."

Jess couldn't believe what she was hearing. Her ex, the man who'd stolen her daughter away, was making nice.

"So the deal is," he continued, and Jess rolled her eyes. Of course. There was a deal. "The deal is, I'm moving to Dallas with, with my, uh, my fiancée. I figure Nina's pretty much on her own now; she doesn't need me anymore. Never did, really." He laughed in an unfunny way, and Jess realized that maybe he hadn't had it so easy with their daughter, either. "So, uh, okay. Just wanted you to know. I'll talk to you later."

"Loser," Jess said. Nina would hate that he'd be living so far away, and what about Teo? Rick was the only father figure in his life.

"Media?" Chris asked.

She shook her head. "No, my ex-husband. He's moving to Dallas with his fiancée. I didn't even know he was dating."

"How long have you two been split up?"

She blushed. "Ten years."

"Well, then," Chris said, rubbing his chin, "I'd say it was time."

She started to throw a punch at his shoulder, but a flurry of growling fur blocked her, a snarling mouthful of teeth grazed her wrist.

"Larry, off! Off!" Chris pushed the dog's muzzle away from Jess's arm, and Larry backed his hindquarters down to the floor beside Jess's feet. He whined, then swung his head toward Jess, eyes like melted Hershey's.

"Jeez, sorry about that. He's trained to protect me."

"No, god, of course. I just wasn't thinking." Jess clasped her shaking hands between her legs.

"Are you all right? Did he hurt you?"

"No, I'm fine. He just surprised me," she said.

Larry looked up at her as if begging for an apology.

*Men,* Jess thought, shaking her head, the old push me–pull you of relationships evident even in this simple canine friendship. "Can I pet him?"

"Sure, yeah. No problem. Soon as I say 'off,' he's over it."

She gave the dog a good scratch and he licked her hand, then climbed back up on the seat to look out the windshield, a sentry, a fierce but fair protector. Jess liked him better all the time.

Chris stopped for gas soon after they got off the highway. He got out of the truck and walked toward the mini-mart, and she quickly pawed through the paper bag he'd brought her, finding three T-shirts and the pair of jeans she requested, along with a random handful of underwear. At least she hoped that it was random, that he hadn't stood there deciding which ones to choose. The heat crept back into her face. He'd remembered her face cream and added her deodorant, toothbrush, and a small vial of perfume she never wore. At the very bottom, another T-shirt wrapped around the photo she'd asked for. Jess rearranged everything neatly and put the bag back on the floor.

When Chris opened the door and slid back into the driver's seat, she said, "Did I mention how much I appreciate all you're doing for me?"

"Several times," he said. "I think you're good now."

"Thank god," she said, and he started the truck.

They both heard the helicopter at the same time, and craned their necks to look up at it through the windshield.

"What is it?" Jess asked. "It's not military. Not flight-for-life. Shit."

"It's not a news copter," Chris said. "Let's wait and see what it does." He shut off the engine.

It was true. There were no logos emblazoned on its sides, no long camera arm extending from it. It proceeded slowly from east to west, roughly the direction they'd been traveling in. They watched until it was out of sight.

"Must be a private owner. Or maybe it's agricultural, tourism—who knows?" Chris started the truck again.

"Crop dusting?" Jess had a bad feeling. "The aerial winery tour? Kinda tough to take advantage of free wine tastings from up there."

"It's out of here now, anyway," Chris said. "Right? You okay to keep going?"

She looked out the window again, then got out of the truck

and stood on the hot asphalt, listening, turning to look in every direction, hand shielding her eyes. The skies were clear except for a commercial jet thirty thousand feet overhead, leaving a slim white stripe across the sea of crystal blue.

She got back in. "God, I hate being paranoid," she said. "Yeah, let's go."

# 3 1

When Pater told me to work on my algebra problems, I hoped it meant he was all right again. He knows I would rather write all day or read than do math, even though I'm good at it. He says I'll be doing calculus before you know it, and then I will have surpassed his own math skills. I will have to learn the rest from books, but that's fine. I learned geography from books and even taught Pater about it some, and when I wanted to know about what was wrong with my mother, I figured that out, too, even though I didn't share those details with him. He'd never mentioned the drugs to me, so I never brought it up either. Maybe he didn't know.

I finished my equations but he said he would check them later. He always checked my schoolwork right away, but things were changing so fast I didn't know what to expect anymore.

I asked, "May I please go outside now? I've been inside practically all day."

He turned to the window. I thought he might not let me, but then he relented. "Stay close," he said. "And keep out of their way."

I almost ran to the door, and he called after me, "And don't bring in any more feathers. They're dirty."

I closed the door without answering. He'd never cared how many feathers I had before, or how messy they were. I wondered if maybe I could find my own way back to our camp in the forest, without him, and then realized what a horrible thought that was. What would he do without me? He wasn't his right self, and I was the only one who knew how to be with him when he was this way. And besides, he'd saved me when I needed saving. How could I be so ungrateful?

Outside it was like a dream. The air was hazy and wavered in the heat rising from the earth. It had been too warm and still in the apartment, but the sun outside scorched the top of my head and my shoulders. Sweat trickled down my ribs, leaving a trail of wet dots on either side of my shirt. My jeans felt heavy and thick, like canvas.

The white dog stood from her nap beneath the porch of the big house and loped toward me. I don't much like dogs, especially after having that mean-looking one almost attack Pater and me, but this one was friendly. She came right up and stopped and looked at me, a question in her eyes.

*What shall we do?* she seemed to be saying. She hopped up, then bent down on her front legs, waggling her bottom in the air, then suddenly turned and ran, and just like when I saw my heron, I followed. She kept looking back at me, slowing a little, then bolting ahead. I chased after her, laughing.

We were nearly at the top of the pasture, near the horses, when I heard something coming from far away, something big and loud like a train. The noise was overhead, behind the tall pines across the road. As it got louder and louder, I started to run back toward the house. The white dog ran with me, barking at the sky.

"Lindy!" Pater called from the door of the barn, waving his arm frantically. "Get over here! Hurry!"

I'd just made it to the barn and Pater had pulled me inside when a huge metal insect appeared from behind the trees, chopping the air with steel blades, my chest and head vibrating with its roar, the chill of its shadow passing directly over us and continuing on, past the woods at the back of the property, and then farther and farther away, the terrible sound dying out like an echo.

"Why was it so low?" I asked, both of us staring after it from just inside the open door.

"Looking for something," he said, rubbing his forehead like it hurt.

"For us?" My heart was pounding. I took his hand.

He stared and stared at the place it had disappeared, but it didn't come back. The world was silent again. Even the pigeons had stopped cooing. His fingers were tight around my hand. It hurt, and I wanted him to let go, but I was quiet.

"Stay inside, now," he finally said. "We haven't done our Bible study yet this week."

"Okay," I said, because I always say okay to him, but I didn't want to. If we had to do it, I wanted to do our Bible study beside a creek, or up in our tree. The stories sound better when accompanied by birdsong, the breeze riffling through the trees. It was too quiet inside the apartment, too dead sounding, but I followed him back up the stairs.

We sat on the couch together and took turns reading aloud in the stifling, still heat, our voices bouncing back from the walls and ceiling. Pater read his parts feverishly, like he thought he himself was Moses following the pillar of light by night and the clouds by day. We'd read this part before, but I've never understood how you can follow clouds. They're not like stars, which are constant. Clouds swirl and break apart, re-form and drift. There's nothing to follow, but I didn't say so to Pater. His hands were shaking on the page, and when we finished, he got on his knees in front of the couch and prayed for a long, long time, lips forming silent words meant only for God, and when he was through, he opened his eyes and slammed his fist down hard against the Bible.

"What?" I asked, scared, but mad now, too. I didn't like him this way. I wanted the real Pater back. I wanted my dad. "Why are you doing that?"

"They can't take you, too. Goddamn it, they just can't." He shielded his eyes with his hand, and I realized he was crying, something I'd never seen before. I'd rarely heard him curse, either, but the crying was more frightening, and I regretted speaking sharply. He was thinking about his brother, he had to be. Who else had been taken? We'd left Crystal; we'd left his parents. We'd left everything behind when we left Colorado, and we thought no one would ever find us.

"We're safe here, Pater," I said, reaching out to touch his arm. "That big old thing wasn't looking for us. It went right over us and didn't care, just kept going. I bet it never comes back. You don't have to worry, okay? Everything's going to be fine."

I wished there was someone else there to talk to him this way, like a parent to a scared child, but there wasn't. I was the only one, and he'd have hated it even more if I'd run up to the house and told Mark and John that something was wrong with him. He began to cry harder, his body wrenching forward, his mouth open but silent, beaded strings of saliva stretching from his top teeth to his bottom lip. His eyes were squeezed shut. I put my arms around him, saying *"Shhh"* and trying to rock him, but he was rigid and far away, gone from me, gone from this place.

I heard something coming down the driveway and ran to the window. I hoped it was Reverend Rosetta or Michael on his motorcycle. I hoped it was Officer Villareal in her messy car. I hoped it was Moses to lead us away, or Jesus to save us, save us from the dark thing that Pater had become, because I was frightened and I didn't know how to help him.

Outside, a small dark truck had pulled into the driveway, and then like a miracle, I saw Officer Villareal opening the passenger door.

"Hurry, please!" I yelled, but the window was closed, so I slid it open and yelled again, "Help, Officer Villareal! Help us, please!" like I was a hostage waiting to be freed.

Officer Villareal looked up, her face surprised. She started to run.

"No!" Pater screamed. "Get away from there! Goddamn it! Get away!"

I went back to him, if only to stop him from screaming, but he frightened me with his ranting and shaking. It felt like forever before I heard feet on the stairs, pounding, a bang on our door and shouting. Then Officer Villareal was pushing in, and my heart was filling with love and hope, but then there was a man behind her, the man and the dog, the ones who'd found us behind the tree, and Pater was grabbing me, pulling me to the bedroom, me pulling against him for the first time in my life. He slammed the door, shoved the dresser in front of it like it didn't weigh anything, even though I was crying and saying, "No, they're here to help us, Pater. Please let me out."

Officer Villareal banged on the door, yelling, "Ray, come on, open up! We're just here to help. Open the door!"

Pater pulled me across the room to the window. From that high we could see the whole pasture, the horses, the goats, and the chicken coop, the peacocks now all standing in the middle of the field, the cocks with tails fanned and brilliant in the sun, the hens gathered together, pecking at the ground but watching the males, waiting to see what they'd do next. I watched Pater, his fingers white against the window frame, trying to pull it open but it wouldn't budge, and then he was pounding both his palms against the glass, pounding so hard it broke into small pieces that glittered in the sun as they flew out and away, falling to the ground like diamond rain. There was no sound anymore, only the things that glittered: the glass lying in the gravel dirt far below, the peacocks' plumage in full display, Pater's eyes, wild, as he turned to me with bloody hands.

I froze, remembering the tree house and how afraid I was before we jumped, Pater first in his camouflage jacket, and then me, and how it was like flying. It wasn't hard at all, as long as you remembered to tuck and roll at the bottom.

I looked down at the ground again. I looked at Pater. I knew he didn't want to hurt me, but this thing was happening, and he wouldn't stop until he thought he had saved me, the way he couldn't save his brother, the thing that would haunt him the rest of his life, no matter what I did.

"No!" I screamed. "Don't make me jump! It's too high!"

"Stick to the plan, goddamn it," he said. "We have to get out of here!"

His eyes weren't right; his voice was all wrong and his profanity stung. This was not the Emergency Plan anymore.

"You go first," I said, crying and choking on my words. "I'll be right behind you." I looked him straight in those crazy eyes and lied, even though it was terrible and I'd probably go to hell for it, but it was all I could do. I was too young to fly out that window. I wanted to survive.

# 32

Jess rammed her right shoulder against the bedroom door as hard as she could, budging whatever was behind it only a few millimeters.

"Ray," she yelled, "come on, I'm here to help!" She hit the door again, realizing it was her bad shoulder, and felt something tearing and giving way inside of it. Chris pulled her back.

"Let me," he said, and managed to shove the door open just enough that they could see Lindy and Ray with his mangled hands at the window.

"No!" Jess yelled. "Lindy, get away from the window! Ray, no!"

She and Chris frantically shoved and pushed at the door, the gap widening but not enough, watching helplessly as Ray tugged at Lindy's hand. She pulled away from him, falling back as he let go. He turned then, seeing Jess and Chris at the door, and hoisted himself through the jagged edges of glass, crying out in agony as it cut him more. He scrambled until he was squatting on the window ledge, then leapt, arms extended like a paratrooper, and disappeared. A nauseating thud was followed by silence.

Lindy lay on the floor, staring at where he'd been, her mouth open, her eyes unbelieving. She scrambled up and Jess pushed one last time and squeezed through the opening, past the heavy dresser barricading the door. She ran to grab the girl and pull her away from the window. Chris raced to the sill, Larry on his heels, and looked down. "No, don't get up! Stay down. We'll get you help!" he yelled, then turned back to Jess. "Son of a bitch is still alive. That must be a twenty-five-foot drop."

Lindy screamed, "Pater!" then leapt from Jess's arms and squeezed out through the narrow doorway.

"No, Lindy!" Jess pulled herself back through, tensing at the pain it caused her injured shoulder. "Lindy, wait!"

Chris and Larry pushed past her, and they all charged down the steps, out into the open. Ray was already halfway across the pasture, dragging a leg, holding his thigh with bloodied hands, and Lindy had nearly caught up to him. The peacocks scattered as if a bomb had detonated in their midst, flying up in a spectacular explosion of green and blue. The white dog ran into the fray, barking.

Chris ran after them, Larry like a bullet once in motion. Pain forced Jess to stop at the edge of the pasture, yelling, "Lindy! Ray! Stop!"

Larry caught up to the pair in a flash, grabbing at Ray's pant leg with his snarling sharp teeth. Lindy screamed and turned to look at Jess. "Make him stop! Please!"

Chris slowed, and turned to Jess.

"Call him off," Jess said, crying now. "Please. Stop him."

"Larry, off!" Chris yelled. The dog pulled up, twitchy and anxious, and Ray and Lindy began to run again. Chris turned to Jess, arms raised in question. Jess held her shoulder. Fire burned inside it, a pain unlike anything she'd felt before. Her legs and feet throbbed, her back hurt, and her chest felt ripped apart.

Chris looked from her to Ray and Lindy. Larry whined, watching the two figures in the distance. Mark and John came running from the house.

Jess started to tremble, her blood pressure dropping from pain, from shock, from all of it. She fell to her knees so she wouldn't hit the ground face-first. Tuck and roll, she remembered from police training, but she couldn't quite figure out how to tuck.

At the edge of the woods now, Lindy had her arm wrapped around Ray's waist, supporting him. She turned to look at Jess one last time as they moved into shade, then disappeared into the trees. Straight above them, a thunderous noise and mighty wind swayed the boughs and branches. The helicopter that Jess and Chris had seen at the gas station flew directly over where Ray and Lindy were now hidden among trees, but kept advancing toward the farm. Those on board hadn't seen the escape, only its aftermath: three men and two dogs in the middle of a pasture, a woman slowly sinking to the earth.

THE MAN IN THE OPEN bay door of the chopper filmed the fainting police officer, thinking it was probably a waste of

videotape—although a tabloid might want it. His orders
from the network had been to track her and the other police
officer without their knowing it, but they only wanted footage of a man with a blond ponytail and beard and an adolescent
girl with long dark hair. Problem was, they weren't here; they
weren't anywhere. No one had seen them, and a lot of people
were trying.

When the men below had the woman inside the house, the
man asked the pilot to turn around and head back to the city.

"Giving it up?" the pilot asked in his headphones.

"Yeah, we're never going to find them," he said. "I don't
think they even exist. They're phantoms."

# 33

Jess came to on Mark and John's leather sofa, roused by three worried-looking men and the sensation of fire in her right shoulder. Her eyes filled without her knowing why exactly: the caring faces? The pain? Or the shock of watching Lindy run away, knowing she was out there somewhere with a father who was not in his right mind, and Jess had let it happen?

"I'm taking you to the ER," Chris said. "Can you stand up yet?"

"Of course I can stand." She pushed up with her good arm and an ocean wave plowed through her. "Uh," she said, lying back down.

"Not so fast there, Speedy," Chris said. "Slowly. Here, roll to your side and get your feet on the floor first."

Nothing she did was without sharp, jarring pain in her shoulder, without dull nausea and the sense that something was grossly off-kilter in the universe that was her body. In stages, she let Chris and the others help her to her feet, walk her slowly to the truck, and tuck her inside. Even Larry knew to be careful, settling immediately between her and Chris and not moving, just looking at Jess with his melting brown eyes.

No matter how valiantly she tried not to, Jess cried off and on during the drive back to town, and through the long wait in the emergency room. She asked Chris to dial Nina on her phone; every move she made with her right arm overwhelmed her senses. As Nina's voice-mail message kicked in, Jess sobbed too hard to form comprehensible words. Chris took the phone and spoke quietly into it, then snapped it shut.

"We'll keep trying," he said. "Who else should you call?"

She couldn't bear to call Clara, but she had to. "My mother," she said, and again, Chris made the call and spoke softly to her mother, downplaying the injury. He handed the closed phone back to Jess, smiling triumphantly. "I'm very good with moms," he said.

Chris called Sergeant Everett to tell him that Ray and Lindy had disappeared, and when asked to give their last known location, he declined, making Jess cry even harder. She hadn't been this emotional since . . . since when? Since Nina had left? Since her divorce? Since her father had died? She couldn't even remember. Grief had been constant, perhaps, but crying had been a long time coming.

"I'm not like this," she tried to tell him. "I never cry, especially not in front of . . . well . . . anyone."

"Quit messing with my 'rescuing a damsel in distress' fantasy," Chris said. "It's okay, really. Larry cries all the time. I'm used to it."

"But now you're in as much trouble as I'm in."

"Hey, maybe I'll get on TV, too." He shrugged. "Why should you get all the glory?"

She snorted, pain shooting through her. "Ow. Don't make me laugh."

"Can do." He sat back, looking around the busy waiting room, then sighed. "Let's just hope Ray gets himself to a doctor."

They both knew it was unlikely. Ray Wiggs had clearly crossed the line between human coping and animal instinct when he jumped out of the window.

Jess wiped her eyes, then looked at Chris as directly as she ever had. She wanted him to understand what had happened to her out there, even though she didn't quite get it herself, not yet.

"I . . . I just couldn't betray her again," she said. "If those birders had never seen her . . ." She stopped, hoping Ray's craziness was as fleeting as Lindy had described when questioned the day before. For now, she had to believe that once away from the world again, Ray would quickly settle down. They could never know how Lindy's life would have turned out, whether found or not. It was never going to be easy for the girl. But one thing Jess felt sure of: Chris would have apprehended them in that pasture if she hadn't stopped him.

"At least she has my card. If she needs us . . ." She shook her head again. What? She'd find a phone in whatever wilderness Ray dragged her to next?

"She'll find a way," Chris said. "She's one tough girl."

Jess nodded, pulling her lips between her teeth. He was just trying to make her feel better.

Would she and Chris ever talk about this again? Would they let themselves speak openly enough to figure out what she guessed they were both wondering: had they done the wrong thing? Was there a right thing to do in this case? Jess sighed. Would they even see each other again after all this was over? She would miss him now that she knew him this way, this easy, funny, contented way.

The waiting room chairs were cushioned and more comfortable than the ones she remembered all those years ago with her mother and brothers, waiting for news of her father. The television mounted overhead showed images of soldiers in Iraq instead of hostages in Iran. Life had circled in on itself, touch points presented with such clarity that Jess knew she was still in shock. Lindy was Nina was Jess—all girls who'd lost too much along the way. Ray was Jess's father—two men whose souls were broken while doing their best to serve.

*You can't do good in this world without being hurt by it,* Jess thought, her mother's old lament. But you can't not try because that hurts worse—she knew that now. Or maybe she'd always known it. She'd shut herself down when Nina left. She hadn't gone running after her because . . . because what? Because it would hurt when Nina pulled away again? Or because it had become easier not to continually witness Nina's pain, and feel the weight of it every day? What a piss-poor excuse for a mother, Jess thought, closing her eyes and breathing deeply, trying to come back to her normal self, her practical self, but all she could see was Nina, and Lindy, then Nina again.

When a nurse finally called her name, Jess stood, wincing as she reached for her purse.

"I'll watch your stuff," Chris said, pulling her bag onto his lap and wrapping his arms around it.

"No way," she said. "You have to get to work." It was nearly two o'clock already.

"Go on." He nodded his head toward the nurse waiting in the doorway. "I'll be here, unless I'm out checking on Larry."

After a painful exam and a series of X-rays, a surgical consultant was called. It took another thirty minutes for him to arrive in the exam room, and Jess wondered if Chris would still be in the waiting room when she was finally done, or if he'd be smart and turn her purse over to the receptionist and get his butt to work.

"The good news is, you didn't break any bones," the surgeon said, studying the films. "The bad news is, we need to get in there and see what's going on with your rotator cuff, and see here? Those are bone fragments that need to be cleaned up or you're going to continue to be in a lot of pain. I'd like to get you into surgery as soon as possible. What are you doing tomorrow morning?"

"I just happen to have the day off," Jess said, hoping her medical benefits still applied.

Back out in the waiting room, Chris dozed, a magazine open on top of her purse in his lap. A gossip magazine, she noticed, wondering if she should tease him about it. She stood looking at him for a moment, studying the black lines of lashes against his tanned face, the dark stubble on his head and cheeks.

"Okay, sleepyhead." She nudged his foot with hers.

His eyes opened. "I was just meditating."

"Sure thing, Deepak." The doctor had injected her shoulder with something, packed it in ice, and put her arm in a sling. It only ached now, but she felt altered, drugged, less in control of her feelings than ever.

"So? It's broken?" He stood.

"Nope," she said. "Just a little torn up, like the rest of me. They're going to clean me up and sew me back together to-morrow morning. I'll be as good as new."

"Okay, then," he said, shouldering her purse. "Let's go."

She felt her chin wobble, but fought it. He was taking her back to his place. "Really? You're going to wear that all the way out of here?"

"What?" he asked. "It matches my outfit."

This time when she laughed, it didn't hurt.

AFTER DROPPING HER OFF AT the condo, Chris left to go see if he still had a job. The throbbing in Jess's shoulder intensified again, so she broke down and took another of the pain pills they'd given her to get through the night, slugging the huge thing down with a few swigs of Coke, her eyes watering and nose running at the hit of carbonation.

Jess sat on the futon, but she didn't feel like watching TV. She wished Larry were there, head in her lap, feet twitching in dreams. She sighed and pulled out her phone. She wanted to call Nina, but first she dialed Ellis's wife, Maggie, to thank her and Alison for their show of support at the station house.

Jess felt weepy again as Maggie said that they were proud and happy to support her, that they should have done more, that Ellis had wanted to but didn't know how.

"No, it's okay. I know," Jess said, feeling the medicine start to take hold of her. "You guys are my best friends in the whole world." She'd never said that aloud before, and it sounded sappy, but Maggie was crying, too, saying she was like a sister.

When they hung up, Jess knew she had only a small window of time before she was completely high. She called her next-door neighbors to apologize for the trucks in front of her house. Apparently, a wildfire had broken out near Yakima and the trucks were gone. Three thousand acres were ablaze and dozens of homes were at risk, making for much better footage than one empty suburban house.

And because she knew she had to, Jess called Clara. To her surprise, her mother didn't break down in hysterics. The first thing she said was, "So, who exactly is this Chris Zoozawhatever that called me?"

Jess laughed. Her mother was so funny. How had she not known that before? "Oh, Ma, he's just another cop," she said, then convinced Clara to wait for her call after the "procedure," as she'd decided to call it. It was handy, saying a man was taking care of her—her mother could finally let go. With fewer mind-altering substances on board, this would have just made Jess angry, but it certainly made life easier.

As she clicked off, the phone beeped.

"What?" Jess asked it. The sound was familiar, but . . . Oh, yes. It meant a message had come in. Jess fumbled with the keypad, hitting END, SEND, trying to call the caller back, but she couldn't remember the sequence or focus on the buttons. *Maybe it's Nina,* she thought, trying to stay upright under the influence of the pain pill, just long enough to call her daughter, but then the phone was slipping from her hand, and then nothing.

When Chris roused her, Jess's mind felt thick with gray cotton. It was morning. It was a different day, but which day? What time was it?

"Up and at 'em," he said, standing over her, Larry next to him, smiling. "We gotta sign you in by six fifteen."

"Wha . . . ?" She tried to roll over, but the sharp pain in her shoulder stopped her. "Stupid pain pills," she said. "I passed out."

"Come on, dope fiend. Let's go get that thing fixed. Need help getting ready?"

She moaned and rolled onto her good side to sit up. "No, I'm fine," she said, trying to smooth her hair with her good hand. "Go away, please."

"Nice," he said, and walked toward his bedroom. "Come," he said to Larry. The dog gave Jess a mournful look.

"It's okay," she said. "Larry can see me naked."

"Right." Chris laughed. "I forgot. My dog gets the perks."

In spite of her bravado, Jess couldn't move her arm enough to remove any clothing, so she decided to wear yesterday's to the hospital. Slowly, she stood and went to the bathroom to try to do something to her hair, and brush her teeth, and relieve herself, all left-handed. She looked in the mirror only once, then decided that wasn't a good idea. It didn't matter what she looked like; they were just going to knock her out again.

Before she'd gone to the hospital in labor at nineteen years old, she'd been so careful to put on makeup, to style her hair. There would be pictures; there would be people there. Nurses and doctors of course, but her mother, and Rick, her newly beloved, who chickened out of staying in the delivery room during most of Jess's long, agonizing labor. In the end, he forgot to take photos, and the next time Jess saw herself in the mirror, many hours after Nina's arrival, she had raccoon eyes, ringed in black. Perhaps Rick hadn't forgotten, she realized now. Maybe he'd been being kind, and she'd resented it all those years for nothing.

Baby Nina hadn't cared what she looked like. Once Nina was out of the womb, it seemed all she wanted was to be as close to Jess as possible, burbling and nuzzling into the nook of Jess's neck, all soft and warm, filling Jess's hands like a six-and-a-half-pound bean bag.

Jess closed her eyes, cupping her good hand as if around Nina's tiny bottom, remembering her hormonal ecstasy at the smell of her daughter, the heat of her, but most especially, the weight of Nina in her palms. She had a child who was born loving her, trusting her. She hadn't realized the call to motherhood would be so immediate and absolute.

She hadn't realized so many things.

# 34

"Jessica? Ms. Villareal?"

Shades of murky, deep water gave way to pale gray; Jess tried to swim up, to reach out to the voice, but a pain deep and primal stopped her. She opened her eyes and swallowed against a raw throat, a mouth as dry as chalk.

A stocky blond man in blue scrubs injected a syringe into a tube that appeared to be attached to Jess's left arm. "How're you doing, sweetheart?" he said, his accent smoothly Southern and comforting. "Having some pain?"

Jess's right shoulder felt as big as a ham, a ham that had been chewed on by a pit bull, and then melted into nothingness a few moments later. What day was it?

"You're in the day-surgery recovery room," he said loudly, as if talking to someone hard of hearing. "The surgery went well. The doctor stopped by earlier but you were still out like a big old drunk on Saturday night." He smiled and withdrew the syringe. "He got your shoulder all fixed up, but you're going to have to take it easy for a while."

Jess tried to nod, but couldn't tell if she'd been successful. Above the nurse's head, she became aware of square acoustic ceiling tiles, a brown water spot in the shape of Africa. A hum in the background, other voices. A phone trilling, no one answering. She turned her head slightly to the left, to the right. Curtains surrounded her bed.

"Think you can sit up?" Without waiting for a reply, he pushed a button on the side of the bed, and a whirring sound escorted Jess into a sitting position.

"Hi, Mom." Nina sat in a chair at the foot of the bed, holding both her own purse and Jess's. With no makeup and her hair pulled into a ponytail, she looked as young as Lindy. "The doctor said you did great."

Tears filled Jess's eyes. She tried to speak but her lips would not move. Only air would pass from her throat through her mouth, like heavy breathing. Her emotions loomed large and buoyant inside her, but she had no voice. No way to say, "I love you, I love you, and I am more sorry for everything than I can ever forgive myself for."

"The surgery took longer than expected," the nurse explained to Nina, "so they had to intubate her. That's why she's having trouble talking, but it'll pass."

Nina stood and walked over, leaned down to kiss Jess's cheek. She left behind fruity girl smell, a smear of lip gloss on Jess's cheek. "Does it hurt?" she asked, sounding worried.

Jess tried to shake her head no as tears ran down her cheeks. Nina's eyes filled, and she looked at the nurse. "Is she okay? Is she in pain?"

Oh, how Jess wanted to reach up to hug her daughter, to take her small dark hand in her own, but her arms remained as still as her voice was quiet. Waves of murkiness kept trying to pull her back under.

"Don't worry," the nurse said. "It's just the anesthesia. She's still coming out of it. Sometimes people get kind of emotional when they're under. She's fine. Aren't you, Jessica?"

"Uhn," Jess heard herself moan.

"Are you sure?" Nina asked. "She just looks so . . ." Tears escaped, ran down one pretty cheek.

"Honey, why don't you take a break and go get a Coke or something? It's going to be a while before she really comes to. She'll never even know you were gone."

"Stay with me," Jess tried again, her eyes closing.

"I'm staying here," Nina said, her slim, soft fingers wrapping around Jess's, tethering her as she slipped back underwater.

AT TWO THIRTY THAT AFTERNOON in the recovery room, Jess finally felt alert enough to sit on her own, legs hanging over the side of the hospital bed. The IV had been removed; her shoulder felt simply like a bag of air next to her head. She couldn't even feel her forearm or hand.

Nina had driven down early that morning and sat with her the entire time she'd been sleeping off the anesthesia. Nina hadn't wanted to take the time to drop Teo off with Clara, so he was being well cared for in the waiting room by Chris, who was clearly going to be late for work, again.

Nina helped Jess dress, improvising with two hospital gowns around her upper body and the huge dressing on her shoulder and arm. The skill with which she figured out how to make it all work surprised Jess, but it shouldn't have, she realized. Nina was a mother, used to taking charge. She stuffed Jess's bra and blouse inside a backpack with Teo's toys and snacks. When they were ready, the nurse wheeled in a chair, saying, "Here's your ride, darlin'."

Even though she still felt nauseated from the anesthesia, Jess claimed she was fine so they would let her go. Out in the waiting room, she grew warm and queasy, wondering if perhaps she should have waited a little longer. She just wanted so badly to be home, on her sofa, with Teo toddling round, busy with blocks and toys, Nina doing . . .what? She closed her eyes, remembering closed doors, bodies brushing against each other in the hall, the years of silent standoff.

"Are you all right?" Chris asked. He had Teo on one hip, slung there as naturally as he wore his sidearm. Nina carried both their purses and the backpack. Jess took several deep breaths and tried to smile, but it was an awkward moment made worse by the feeling that she might throw up, and she had turned down the little puke dish the nurse had offered.

"So, you all have . . . met?" she asked.

"Oh, yeah," Chris said. "We've been talking crap about you the whole time, believe me."

Nina looked at him with her familiar old scowl, then back at Jess. "Who knew cops could be such comedians?"

Jess started to say something, to explain, to defend, then realized Nina was kidding. Her daughter could use that dour face in jest now.

Teo struggled to get down, saying, "Grammy go for ride?"

"No, baby," Nina said. "You can't ride in Grammy's wheel-chair. She's hurt."

"It's okay," Jess said. "Just put him on my good side." She patted her left thigh, and Chris let the boy slip down his leg. Teo walked carefully toward her, then stood with big eyes in front of the wheelchair, taking it all in.

"Grammy hurt?"

"Never too hurt for you," she said. "Come here."

"Careful, buddy," Nina said, lifting him to sit in Jess's lap. He laid his chubby hand carefully on the layers of dressing protecting her shoulder.

"Owie?" He looked at her, the same worry in his eyes as Nina's. As her own, Jess knew.

She bent down to kiss his forehead. "Everything's okay, sweetie."

Nina went to fetch her car from the parking lot. It seemed to have been decided already without Jess's input that Nina would drive her home, but it was for the best. It was amazing that Chris had been with her all this time, had stayed through the whole ordeal, but now it was time for Jess to be with her family.

As they waited for Nina's return, Teo sang a reasonable ren-dition of "The Itsy-Bitsy Spider," and Chris stood a few feet away, hands in his pockets. He'd probably heard it hundreds of time already that day. Jess looked up at him. "I guess I'll just get my things tomorrow, or . . . whenever."

He shrugged. "That's okay. I'll bring them by later."

She breathed deeply for a moment, quelling nausea and try-ing to figure out how not to feel so awkward with him now that there was no reason for them to see each other. "Aren't you on this afternoon?"

"Day off," he said, and she couldn't tell if he was telling the truth or if he'd been suspended. She hadn't even asked him early that morning. She'd been so groggy from the pills, so caught up in her own drama.

"Don't worry," he said, as if reading her thoughts.

"They suspended you," she said, and he shrugged.

When her eyes filled again, he cocked his head at her. "Enough with the waterworks already, okay? I did what I felt I had to do. Just like you."

Jess nodded. Of course he did.

Nina pulled up out front, and Chris rolled Jess's chair through the automatic doors into the afternoon heat.

As Nina loaded Teo into his car seat, Chris took Jess's good arm and helped her navigate from the wheelchair to the front passenger seat.

She would have tried to thank him again for all he'd done, looking up at him through the open door, but she knew he'd be more comfortable if she didn't. "See you later?" she asked.

He nodded, closed the door, then waved as they pulled away from the curb.

"He's nice." Nina sounded like she might actually mean it. "Dad's girlfriend is such a flake."

"Really?" Jess said. "Well, as long as they make each other happy."

Nina looked at her suspiciously, then said, "I guess."

Jess had thought they'd be beyond their old hit-and-miss style of conversation, but it didn't seem to be so. She knew she should be patient, but she was so tired of waiting.

"So," Nina said, "what do we do about the reporters at our house?"

*Our house.* Jess felt her sinuses fill, but it was just a turn of phrase. "Actually, they've left," she said, trying to sound casual. "Thank god."

"Bummer. I wanted to be on TV. I wanted to say 'No comment' or something." Nina looked genuinely perturbed. "'Leave my mom the hell alone.'"

*My mom.* Jess closed her eyes, swallowing, and turned her face to the window. She waited until she thought her voice would be steady, then turned to face her daughter.

"Nina, do you know that I will never give you up? That I've never given up on you?" She wanted to reach across the console and touch her, but it might be too much. "From the moment I first felt you fluttering around inside me until the moment I die, I'm going to be here for you."

Was it the drugs talking? Maybe, but she felt clearheaded, almost unnaturally so. Why had she never said this before?

Nina's face turned dark pink. Her jaw quivered. Her nostrils flared.

"Then how could you have wanted me to give up *my* child?" Her voice was quiet but wounded. Still. She glanced in the rearview at Mateo. A fast line of tears escaped down her cheek; she wiped it away.

"Oh, god, Neen. I just wanted you to make the decision that was best for you so you could have the life you wanted."

"All I wanted was somebody to love me," Nina said, her voice shaky. "And he does."

Jess flinched at the remark, but she remembered the feeling of holding Nina for the first time. That was why so many teenage girls had babies, Jess knew now, after so many years of police work: so that they could have someone in their life who they knew loved them. Maybe that was why she'd had Nina.

"There isn't a day that goes by that I'm not thankful we have Mateo," Jess said. "I was just so freaked out back then, and scared. It's really, really hard, Nina, this mom stuff. We don't get everything right."

Nina nodded, wiping away more tears.

Jess paused. "Especially when you're all by yourself."

Nina nodded again, but stayed quiet.

Teo had fallen asleep in his car seat. Jess studied the small colorful Virgin of Guadalupe on Nina's dash, which, like Jess's, had been given to her by Clara.

"You know," Jess finally said, "if you'd like, I could help you more."

Nina sniffled, wiped her nose, but did not assent. She said nothing, just signaled to make a left, then a right, driving with impeccable attention to the road.

Jess wasn't surprised that her daughter made her wait; it was ingrained in Nina: *prove you love me*, over and over. Jess had helped make her that way, always putting job and safety and security before love, and now she had to deal with it.

"What I mean is, I'd really like that," Jess said when the silence had grown too long.

Nina finally sighed. "Yeah," she said, "I guess I could use some help."

The clear moment of ecstasy that had accompanied Nina into the world filled Jess now. The weight of having a daughter, the heft of the responsibility, was equal to the sweet warmth of closeness, no matter how fleeting or how occasional.

Nina stopped at a red light and reached into the backseat to squeeze Teo's bare foot, looking at him in the rearview mirror with a longing Jess felt in her own chest.

"So, anyway," Nina said, "I'll take you home and get you settled in, then go get your prescription and something to make for dinner. And I need to get Teo yogurt and grapes for breakfast. That's all he eats these days."

So, they were staying with her. Jess breathed in, perched at the edge of something lovely but not yet familiar.

As the light went green, Nina put her foot on the gas.

Teo roused at the forward motion. He looked around, instantly awake as only children can be, and began to sing in his husky little monotone: "Out came da sun . . ."

Jess exhaled, a smile easing across her face, and began to sing along.

# 35

White afternoon light spilled through the living room windows onto the couch, where Nina had settled Jess with magazines, her phone, ginger ale, pain pills, and a fresh ice pack. Nina and Teo were on the road back to Tacoma for the workweek ahead. It was a quiet Sunday, the way Sundays had always been in Jess's neighborhood. Four days had passed since she last reported for her shift the Wednesday before, the day a bird-watcher reported seeing a young girl alone in the Joseph Woods.

Jess had thought she'd relish sleeping in her own bed after two nights on the futon, but it just meant she was alone with her thoughts in the dark. Sleep was tenuous, fragmented by pain the medication couldn't reach whenever she tried to roll onto her right side, the side she'd always slept on. Lindy appeared in jangled dreams, and Jess missed her in a way that seemed ridiculous after spending an entire weekend with her own daughter—without fighting, no less.

Had Ray calmed down again, gone back to being the loving dad Jess had initially trusted him to be? After she'd witnessed his plunge from the window, it was tough to imagine, but post-traumatic flashbacks were generally temporary, if recurring. Should she have let Chris and Larry pursue him? Ray wouldn't have stayed on the farm, or accepted medical or psychiatric help. Jess knew it in a way that she'd always known her father could never have been able to go on living as only part of a man, had he survived his injuries. She'd never admitted to Clara that she'd prayed for him to join his parents in heaven that night in the hospital, rather than help her mother keep him alive. She'd long ago given up praying, but she hoped now that Ray could pull himself together for his daughter. His focus for the past five years had been to be a good dad, and he'd done a pretty great job until cornered. And Lindy loved Ray in a way Jess felt viscerally from her own childhood. The desire to be parented was absolute, regardless of the parent or circumstances.

When she couldn't sleep, Jess let her imagination run. They'd found a safe haven, another farm deep in rural Oregon where folks didn't ask too many questions. Lindy would go to school and make friends, attend 4-H fairs and sleepovers, and giggle with other girls about their crushes on boys. She would learn that she had options as she matured and became a young woman, and that it was normal to leave your parents when the right time came.

Jess could only hope all those things would happen for Lindy, and accept the fact that she'd never know for sure. Thank god the girl was made of steel, inside and out. Just like Nina, only Jess hadn't trusted her daughter enough to realize she would come back to her when she was ready. Now Jess had to trust that Lindy would find her if she ever needed help. If she didn't believe that, she'd never sleep again.

As Sunday afternoon became Sunday evening, shadows lengthened and the air cooled, a harbinger of fall. Jess pushed herself into a sitting position on the couch, mind thick with the semiconscious cycling of grief, worry, love—pieces of memory and dream and intuition. She no longer had the ability to do something physical to chase it all away, to work, or clean, or take care of others.

Without Nina, she wondered if she could even fend for herself, heat up the meals her daughter had left in containers, change out of the musty T-shirt and pajama bottoms she'd been wearing all weekend. Clara wanted to come over and help, but so far Jess had been successful in holding her off. Even if she starved and they found her dead in a smelly heap of unchanged garments and bed linens, that would be easier than having to care for her mother emotionally as her mother tried to figure out how to take care of her. Besides, Chris had also offered to help, a prospect that stirred Jess as much as it scared her. Maybe when she figured out how to change her shirt, she'd give him a call.

Outside, a dark red Chrysler pulled up to the curb. Jess watched with disinterest, running her good hand through her pillow-matted hair. Someone was visiting a neighbor. A man stepped from the car. Before she could see his face, Jess knew who it was from his erect posture and damn-the-torpedoes gait.

"Oh, great," she moaned, planting her feet on the carpet and struggling to stand. She moaned at the dizziness and disorientation, drawing deep breaths through her nose before proceeding toward the door. He'd only come to her house with bad news, but what could be worse than everything they'd already thrown at her? Could they fire her before they'd investigated the case? She didn't think so. Had they caught up with Ray and Lindy?

At Sergeant Everett's knock, she steadied herself and opened the door. He wore khaki shorts and a Seahawks polo shirt. She'd never seen his legs before, and kept her eyes averted now. *He'd be in uniform if it was official,* she thought, *and driving a city car. Wouldn't he?*

"Jesus Christ, Villareal," he said. He held a baking dish covered with foil. "You look like hell."

"Thanks," she said. "I try."

"My daughter, Megan, insisted I bring you dinner. She makes a good manicotti. Takes after her mom."

Jess held tight to the doorknob. She had to be strong, even in pajamas, even injured and sleep deprived and looking repulsive.

"Well," he said, "I'm guessing you can't carry this thing, so how about I put it in the fridge for you?"

She stepped aside, letting him in.

"I'll be out of your way in a minute," he said, heading for the kitchen.

The dizziness returned, and no matter how much she wanted to stand, she would have to sit. Everett walked into the living room and watched her return to the couch and carefully lower herself onto it. She couldn't read the expression on his face.

"That looks pretty serious," he said, nodding at the football pad–sized bandage that was her shoulder. "You did all that in the woods the other night?"

"They think the initial injury happened when I took that fall on my shotgun," she said, offering nothing more. Was he fishing for worker's comp fraud? "So, anyway—" she prodded.

"Yeah, anyway, I, uh, I have some updated information for you." He nodded at the chair by the window. "Mind if I sit?"

"Might as well be comfortable."

He took a seat, crossed his legs, then uncrossed them. Was he nervous?

"Seems the chief got a phone call this morning from someone . . . well . . . let's just say someone pretty high up on the city's food chain. This person was able to convince the chief to drop the investigation against you."

Jess drew a breath, held it.

"For the record, Jess, I was never on board with that, with the investigation stuff. I tried to tell him the same damn thing, but hell, I don't carry any weight around there." He sighed. "That doesn't mean I think what you did was right. But you're stubborn, like me, when you get your mind wrapped around something."

She nodded. This was Everett's idea of an apology, and it didn't feel half bad.

"What about Ray and Lindy?" she asked. "Still after them?"

"Nah." He leaned back. "We called off the search, too. That

was also one of my little ideas the chief ignored. Maybe I'm not as much of an asshole as you think."

"You know, Sergeant Everett, I really don't think you're that much of an asshole."

His eyebrows rose. She rattled her prescription bottle at him. "Teasing, Sarge. I'm kidding. I'm on drugs. I can't be held responsible for anything I say."

He shook his head but chuckled.

"It's not all rosy," he said. "Your suspension stands."

Of course it did; she'd gone against orders. "What about Z?"

"Dog man? Two weeks, paid."

It could have been worse.

"Your suspension and medical leave will run concurrently, however, and after that, you're on desk duty until you're back in fighting shape. Okay?"

Jess gave a crisp nod but smiled. She would cry and laugh and call everyone she knew after he left. "Thank you, Sergeant," she said.

"Yup." He stood. "Don't get up. I'll let myself out."

At the door, he stopped, turned toward her. "I never knew you had friends in such high places, Villareal. Who do you know in the mayor's office, anyway?"

"It's a mystery to me, Sarge," she said. "Maybe I just have a guardian angel."

"Huh." He looked at her for a long moment, like maybe she'd crack and spill something, then shrugged. "Take care of that shoulder," he said. "We need you back."

She watched through the window as he strode to his car, wishing she could call Michael or the reverend to say thank you, but she knew it would be best for them if she never made contact with anyone at the City of Refuge Church again.

Unless, of course, she came across someone who needed their help.

Jess reached for her cell phone. Whom should she call first to share the good news? Ellis? Nina? Her mother? She bit her lip, then dialed Chris. Maybe he liked manicotti.

# 36

Oregon is a state of many forests. Even though we couldn't go back to our home in the Joseph Woods, we found a nice spot after hitching a ride south with a logging truck. The driver knew the woods where he let us off, and told us where the nearest town was. He said if we stayed too near the river, we'd be bothered by hikers and boaters, so he pointed the way to a less-traveled area. He was sympathetic to our plight, having a nephew who had served in the war and came back missing the lower half of his body, not to mention any prospects for a job, or marriage, or a family. I don't think he'd seen us on TV, or if he had, he was too polite to mention it.

We found a flat, sheltered spot, already cleared by previous inhabitants. They'd built a wood structure on a platform, which gets us out of the rain now that it's the wet season. It's not exactly a cabin, Pater says, but it's a solid enough shelter. He thinks maybe we'll like it even more than the tree house, but I miss my nest. We'll work on enclosing it as soon as he is able to move around more and do physical work again. He can hardly walk more than a few yards at a time right now. I think he will always walk with a limp, and his back troubles him more than ever. His hands are still a problem, and they look just awful because he wouldn't go to the hospital or a doctor after he jumped out the window. He insisted he could clean and tend the wounds as well as any doctor, which he did in a service station bathroom, using the sleeves of his shirt for bandages. They are healing slowly, and he is frustrated that he has to have me do most of the chores. Pater is not one to sit idle, no matter how much pain he is in.

We are different now than we used to be. He acts less like the adult, and I act less like the child. We've had to start from scratch again. We will never replace everything we left behind; some things are gone forever, like my stories buried beneath the foliage up in the Joseph Woods, and the new one I was writing in Officer Villareal's notebook.

The twenty-dollar bill I used to keep in my shoe went for groceries when we first got here, before Pater could tell the VA where to find us. There's a little store a few miles down the highway, and I like walking there by myself, even though it makes Pater nervous, but he's not up for making that long of a walk. Before all this happened, I'd never gone anywhere alone. Not until I first followed the heron, that is, which led to all kinds of things, good and bad.

Bad is that we had to leave our home, and that the police wanted to take me away from Pater, and that all those TV people were lying about us, making us seem peculiar and scary.

Bad is that Pater went crazy from it for a while and nearly destroyed the both of us.

Good is that I didn't let him, and that we got away from all of it so he could be himself again. He survived his demons. That's what he says. He apologizes almost every day, and at night I hear him whispering, asking God not to ever let him get that way again. I pray for the same thing most nights, and I wonder what will become of me when I am older. For now, though, Pater needs taking care of, and I'm the only one he has. When I needed rescuing, he came and swooped me out of the arms of evil and brought me to a place of beauty. And now I can try to do the same for him.

The store in town is called Dixie's Thrifty Mart, and in addition to food and firewood and fishing gear, it sells *The Oregonian*. When we first got here, I asked if I could buy a used newspaper for a discount, and the man at the cash register just laughed, but in a nice way. He reached under the counter and pulled out a few old papers, let me look through them and take what I wanted, and now it's become a habit. The first thing I found out was that they weren't looking for us anymore. When I told Pater, he just shrugged, but I know that helped him settle down some. I've read everything printed about Officer Villareal and us in the past two months. I try to neatly tear the articles out, then fold them and put them in my pocket. At home I hide them in a dry space between two boards near my bed, where I keep her card along with Reverend Rosetta's phone number and my birth certificate.

There hadn't been anything in the news in weeks, but yesterday, on the front page of *The Oregonian*, it said that Officer Villareal was awarded a commendation for "heroism and humanitarianism." There was a picture of her in uniform with her arm in a sling, but she was smiling and looked happy. Next to her were the mayor and the chief of police and the older policeman who was in the group that found us. Sergeant William Everett, it said his name was. He was nice right up until he tried to trick us that night in the police station. I certainly hope he didn't get an award, too.

The other place I like to go in town is the church. It's small with no steeple, nothing like Reverend Rosetta's church, and the singing on Sundays is almost painful to listen to, but the people are mostly nice. They have a used-clothing box out front, which I went through when we first got here so Pater and I could have some decent clothes and coats for the winter.

On Sundays, I lie about who I am, say my name is Jessica and that I just moved to the area and live with my invalid father, and then I ask the Lord to forgive me. I don't think He minds too much. If I don't lie, I can't go to church. If I don't go to church, I can't meet other people, and if I don't meet other people, I will never be able to find a way to live in the real world again. Pater may not want to, but I do, someday.

After church, I like to stay and talk with some of the kids about what their favorite movies are, who the best bands are. Once I said I liked Green Day and two of the boys nodded their heads, and one said, "Old-school. Solid." When they've all drifted away to their families or their groups of school friends, I walk back to our camp and tell Pater what the preacher had to say. Pastor Sorensen is not that powerful of a preacher, even though he is a devoted man of God, so I embellish a little to cheer Pater up.

I have found that I'm pretty good at it, at telling stories, at writing them down. I don't think I'd ever want to be a preacher, but maybe I could be someone who writes down stories for books. Or a person who studies birds—an ornithologist, Pater says. Or I could be a teacher. Maybe I could do all those things at once, like Miss Carol Frischmann. Maybe I could write a book about my new forest and all the things I'm learning about here: the towering sugar pines with their long cones, the incense cedars that smell like pencils. Black bears roam these woods looking for anything humans leave behind, and deer browse the manzanita, ripping leaves and berries from stems with more force than you'd think a deer would have in its dainty jaw and slender neck. The big oaks and maples are getting ready to shed their fall colors and turn to bone for winter; the flowers of bear grass and white ginger are already delicate skeletons, rattling in the cold wind that comes down from the mountains.

I still miss Sweetie-pie so much, and I hope and pray she's all right, but the birds here are plentiful, with far more waterfowl than I used to see in the Joseph Woods. On misty mornings, when I am out collecting kindling, or foraging for blackberries or mushrooms, I see osprey and egrets, pelicans, geese, and too many kinds of ducks to name. I try not to feel sad that most of these beautiful birds will be gone soon; I know they'll be back next spring.

The most magical bird of all, of course, the one that makes my heart fill at the sight of it, is the great blue heron. I see them all the time now, standing tall in ponds fishing for breakfast or flying low, skimming the edges of the tributaries that feed the river, long stick legs tucked beneath them, wings spread wide and feathery. I study and draw them, crouching and hiding behind rocks and shrubs, but no heron has ever let me get as close as my first.

Somehow, I think it's better that way.

PHOTO BY DAVID HILLER

**Jennie Shortridge** lives in Seattle, Washington, with her husband, and juggles her time between writing novels and working in the community to foster literacy. To invite Jennie Shortridge to participate in your book group meeting, contact her through her Web site: www.jennieshortridge.com.

# WHEN SHE FLEW

JENNIE SHORTRIDGE

This Conversation Guide is intended to enrich the
individual reading experience, as well as encourage us
to explore these topics together—because books,
and life, are meant for sharing.

# A CONVERSATION
# WITH JENNIE SHORTRIDGE

*Q. This book was inspired by true events. What about the original story made you want to write* When She Flew, *and why as fiction rather than nonfiction? How does* When She Flew *differ from the true-life story?*

A. In 2004, a Vietnam War veteran and his young daughter were found living in a large forested park abutting the city of Portland. I think everyone in Portland was mesmerized by the events: that they'd lived there so long, something like six years, and that the girl was so well-adjusted. The reaction of the Portland community to their poignant story was exceptional. I wanted to write about people living and dealing with such extraordinary circumstances, but at the same time I didn't want to simply write a journalistic report of this particular father and daughter. Their story certainly inspired my book, but I have used the medium of fiction to explore and imagine broader issues of human and social relationships. The freedom that I have as a novelist allowed me to take real events as merely the starting point to create something new and inventive that hopefully entertains the reader while, at the same time, encourages thought and reflection about who we are and how we live in our society.

*Q. Is the creative process different when writing fiction inspired by true events, versus writing something purely imagined?*

A. Yes, it was quite different, because I had a naturally occurring story outline to write to; I don't usually use outlines. That said, most fiction is written from some kind of personal experience that the writer reshapes and reimagines into a new fictive entity, and I enjoyed creating all of the different characters and situations that moved the emotional part of the story along.

*Q. What surprised you about the book as you wrote it? What was the most difficult part of writing this story?*

A. Lindy's strong voice surprised me at first. She just started talking about birds in her unique way, and the metaphor was born. The hard part was that I had to quickly do the research to catch up with her! I knew nothing about birds or police procedure. I was helped a great deal by a friend who is a bird expert, and by the actual police sergeant on the case, who endured all of my questions, from "What do you wear on your duty belt?" to "How did you feel when you found them?" He is a cop's cop, a guy's guy, and he was such a good sport about all of it.

Q. *How do you think* When She Flew *is a departure from your other novels? How is it the same?*

A. The obvious difference is that it's more action-oriented, more plot-driven in some ways, especially in the first half of the book. But it's still very much a story about the frailties and strengths of people, and what happens when they all bump into one another. It's still about family and relationships, love and loss and healing, all the things I usually find myself drawn to write about.

Q. *Each of your books represents a point of view about the human condition. What would you like readers to take away from reading* When She Flew?

A. There is a metaphor in *When She Flew* that is apt for what I aim to do in each book, and that is to turn over stones and tell the story of what lies beneath them. In our society, we don't see the homeless, or we see all homeless people as one teeming organism. In this story, we get to know two people who live outside of traditional means and see their humanness, their struggles and small victories and disappointments. I also think most of us don't have a clue what it's like to be a police officer. Again, we lump them into a type or subspecies of human. In this story I hope I've humanized what it's like to be a cop—a person who, just like us, has hopes, dreams, strong feelings, and doubts, as well as family and friends, homes and pets and bills.

*Q. You also have a disabled Iraq War vet in the story; was that another kind of stereotype you wanted to humanize?*

A. Absolutely. The father in *When She Flew* is a disabled Iraq War vet doing his best to raise his daughter on a small military pension. He also struggles with post-traumatic stress disorder, something we're hearing more and more about in the news regarding our returning soldiers. Perhaps Ray doesn't make the kind of decisions you or I would when it comes to the way he and Lindy live, but he does a lot of things really well that are good for her. What makes a home? What is safety? Is there such a thing as the "right" way to raise a kid, to educate her? Each family is different, and I think it's dangerous when our society doesn't take those differences into account.

*Q. How did you come to the title* When She Flew? *What does it mean to you?*

A. Literally, it came from a postcard of one of Brian Andreas's artworks that I've kept propped in front of my work space for many years (I used the quote from it as the epigraph for the book). Each of the female characters in this story tries out her wings—tries something different from usual—and each experiences a metamorphosis by doing so. Their interwoven flight paths are what propel the story.

6. Should Jess have been disciplined for her actions? To what extent?

7. How did Jess's past affect her actions in the story? In what ways did this event change her?

8. Was Lindy also changed by this experience? How so? Do you believe she'll ever come back to live in society?

9. How might have the outcome of the situation been different if the news about Ray and Lindy hadn't been leaked to the media? Was the press at fault for pursuing the story, or were they just doing their jobs? How do you feel about the role media plays in our society today?

# QUESTIONS
# FOR DISCUSSION

1. What is the significance of birds in *When She Flew*?

2. What are the central themes of the story, and do they apply to your life as well? How so?

3. Which daughter—Nina or Lindy—was raised in the best of circumstances? The safest environment? The most loving? Did one have it better than the other? Was one parented better than the other?

4. Why didn't Ray utilize the services available for homeless families and veterans? Do you think Lindy is better off in the woods with Ray than in a foster home? What is she missing and/or gaining in either situation?

5. Do you believe the responding officers made the appropriate decisions? Who should be responsible for determining what is in a child's best interest, the parent or the state?